WHEN SUMMER COMES

WHEN SUMMER COMES

WILLIAM MALTESE

BORGO PRESS

WHEN SUMMER COMES

This edition published in 2009 by Borgo Press.
A Division of Wildside Press, LLC.
www.wildsidebooks.com

CHAPTER ONE

Summer comes. Maybe just around the next corner. Talbot Crane, Marky Matthews, and Jeffrey Layins can tell, even this far south where even winters are mostly sunshine and warm breezes. This sunshine is more intense, this breeze is more noticeably warm than when the trio weekended here just a couple of months ago. This summer-on-its-way late-spring surf has an entirely different intensity than winter-in-full-swing. These sea-to-shore cascades aren't nearly as stirred to wildness and fury by mid-Pacific storms.

Their cock-in-ass, cock-up-ass, cock-wrapped-by-hand daisy-chain fuck, complete with their collective heaves for breath, is audible, even above the distant sounds of water crashing isolated Baja California coastline. Oak leaves tremble, within the large canopy of limbs that overhangs them, seemingly disturbed by the guttural sounds of these three rutting prime specimens in heat.

"Oh, Jesus, yes!" Talbot says. His hand is on a down-stroke along the powerfully uplifted length of his massive erection. By luck (or un-luck) of the draw, his boner is the only one of the three not occupied by tightly squeezing asshole. The heel of his descending hand mashes his red-haired testicles. His scrotum pleasure-compacts to the shape and size of a regulation basketball.

Marky's hard cock jabs full-length up Talbot's butthole. Simultaneously, Jeffrey's stiff dick commences a deeper jab of Marky's tight-to-virgin behind. The bulbous head of Jeffrey's hard rocket of engorged male meat expertly butts Marky's prostate, then glides on by. Jeffrey's corn-yellow pubic crotch hair entwine with the platinum-blond strands that line Marky's asscrack, just as Marky's crotch hair mingle with the red-hair strands that line Talbot's asscrack.

"Ungghh!" Marky groans.

"Tight, tight ass!" Jeffrey whispers in Marky's ear. Jeffrey's face is in close. The attractive bang of his corn-blond hair, and his full and sexy lips, butterfly-tickle Marky's left cheek.

"I'm getting close," Talbot says.

"Me, too," Marky says.

"One for all, all for one," Jeffrey says.

It's not as if their three-way just starts. They've been at it for quite some time. They have so perfected their fucking skills, one with the other, these classmates, friends and sex-buddies, that they've just about milked this latest group effort for all it's worth.

"I'm soon . . . soon . . . soon . . . going to cream . . . cream . . . cream!" Jeffrey says.

"Me first!" Talbot says.

"My nuts get first rumble!" Marky says.

Marky's fingertips clamp all the tighter around Talbot's prominent hip-bones. The rest of Marky's hands firmly talon Talbot's naked hips from behind.

Jeffrey and Marky wear lubricated rubbers. Talbot's cock is a natural leaker. So, there are lots of wet sounds as Jeffrey's cock and Marky's cock go into higher gear up assholes, and as Talbot's cock begins its even faster fuck of its owner's juicy pre-cum sopped fingers.

The trio makes so many increasingly loud foot-in-mud noises that previously undisturbed birds, roosting in seaside treetops, take wing in a flurry of squawks. Dislodged feathers spiral-drift to the ground.

Talbot's masturbating fingers, combined with the inherent pleasure of Marky's cock up Talbot's butt, surprises Talbot in not having already coaxed his deluge of cum from his cum-bagged nuts.

"I am just . . . about . . . there!" he announces.

Marky can't deny the verge-of-burst pleasure he gets from frantically clinging to the on-the-brink Talbot, while Talbot's ass wrings Marky's dick, while Marky's asshole gives Jeffrey's hard prick the same strangle-a-fucking-dick workout.

"Ahhhhh, Marky," Talbot says. "That cock of yours . . . that cock of yours . . . that lovely, lovely cock of yours . . . shoved so deep up my . . . my . . . I'm fucking . . . going to come soon . . . ass!"

It's Jeffrey, though, who announces, "Now!", and explodes his dick up Marky's cock-clamping asshole.

Marky and Talbot's eruptions coincide with each other and lag too-slight-to-notice behind Jeffrey's first squirt of cum.

The three hold on for dear life, until the ecstatic orgasmic surf finally washes completely from their sweaty bodies. The surf of ocean, against shoreline, continues its backdrop.

"God, Marky, no one, except Jeffrey, fucks my ass as well as you do," Talbot says.

"Nothing like initiating a good camp-out by fucking and getting fucked," Marky says, finally able to talk.

Likely, novice campers would have set up camp closer to the sea, but these aren't novice campers. What's more, they've picked their spot for other than the obvious reason that it affords them a good deal of desired privacy. Even one additional tent would crowd their genuinely small bit of flat space among the hillside trees.

Although the late-spring day is downright balmy, any come-night exposure to the ocean, just on the other side of the hill, guarantees some very chilly hours. Large up-swellings of deeply frigid ocean occur all year around just off-shore. Nightly ocean-to-land breezes blow over that cold water and regularly chill the adjacent land. Cold breezes meeting up with warmer land causes year-round bone-chilling fogs. The fogs here in-come most every evening, just before nightfall and cover most of the area, with the usual pleasant exception of the small depression, this side of the hill, within which these knowing and been-here-before campers have pitched their tent.

Marky gives an audible grunt as Jeffrey removes cum-depleted erection from Marky's tight ass.

"As soon as Marky pulls his cock out of Talbot's ass," Talbot says, "I'm thinking a short nap."

"Better you nap now than during sex later in the evening," Jeffrey says.

"Right!" Talbot's tone insinuates the likelihood of his going to sleep during sex — any sex — is equivalent to the sun not coming up in the morning. Especially since the three don't have that many remaining chances for fun and games before their high-school graduation sees them go their separate ways at least for the summer (and probably for longer).

"I think I'll check the ocean view," Marky says. He has seen the panorama from the nearby hill-top countless times before, but he never tires of the ocean breaking on the rugged coastline that parenthesizes the beach below.

"I'll replenish our water," Jeffrey says. He comes off magnanimous, but it's his turn. There's a stream, downhill from where they camp. It veers south into an age-old gully that dumps the freshwater into the salty sea.

Once dressed, Marky leaves his two companions and takes the trail that meanders uphill through the trees. The slope strains to impressive high-relief the calves of his muscled legs. Marky, though, is in excellent physical condition and isn't even breathing hard when he comes out on top.

He's dead-center the cliff that rises at the leading end of the slight indent chewed by weather into this bit of Baja California coastline. The indent couches the prettiest of narrow white-sand beaches. The sand, and the frothy leading edge of the breakers that steadily whip the beach and the surrounding rugged outcroppings, are one and the same bleach-bone white. An untrained observer always thinks the beach is far more extensive than it is. In fact, it's an exceedingly thin crescent of sand whose westward edge, once disappeared beneath the shifting tides, descends rapidly toward a major subterranean drop-off less than a quarter mile off-shore.

During fall, winter, and early spring, the surf here regularly gets awesome. At such times, the spot attracts old-guard surfers willing to make the extra effort to hike in, surfboard in tow, to advantage the excellent but exceedingly dangerous water.

This verge-of-summer time of year, large waves are less predictable. Marky sees only one tent on the whole beach. Two surfboards, stuck upturned in the sand in front of the tent, resemble brightly colored gravestones.

A lone surfer appears from the rocks at the far north-end of the beach. He carries his surfboard hoisted over his head.

Marky doesn't head downhill, He heads south, then southwest, along the top of the cliff almost to its southwestern-most extremity. He stops a few yards short of the farthest edge of a rocky headland whose one side is deep gully. Within the gully runs the stream from which Jeffrey, out of sight, but not out of mind, presently draws their drinking water.

Marky steps around a lone, small, and wind-stunted tree. Only twelve feet of solid land now separate him from the sheer drop-off that punctuates the western-most spot of land for fifty miles in either north or south direction.

He sits, his back to the gnarled and twisted trunk. The tree is so sculptured by the elements, its branches and its trunk so nightmarishly configured, it gives the best hint that weather here can be far less ideal than it is at the moment.

Marky shuts his green eyes to a sun only a couple of hours from its final dip beneath the horizon. Already multi-colored clouds scroll the distant sky. Although, the faint and pleasant sea breeze is yet to be replaced by its soon-to-be-expected chillier cousin.

Marky doesn't mean to catnap, but he does.

It's a sudden decrease in daylight intensity, against his closed lids, that leads him to suspect fog rises between him and the distance.

When he opens his eyes, though, it's neither fog, nor cloud, nor official twilight. It's a human silhouette, on the very lip of the escarpment, between him and the sun, between him and the drop-off. Sunlight so hugs most of the silhouette and, by contrast, so intensifies the shadow, the person's facial features are hidden. However, it's the very same sunlight, caught within corn-blond hair, that's the dead give-away.

Likewise, anyone other than Jeffrey would send far less familiar vibes.

"You fetched that water faster than Jack and Jill ever went up their hill," Marky says.

"And, I returned to find Talbot not napping but busy beating his meat solo," Jeffrey says. His hand runs cascaded strands of corn-gold hair out of his blue-to-black eyes. "Granted, Talbot could be having a wet dream, inside the tent, what with all of his, 'Ungh . . . ungh . . . ungh!' But, I opt for it being pure self-abuse and fantasy. What do you think?"

"I think you and I pretty much always think the same," Marky says.

Jeffrey unfastens his pants. His trousers and underwear make a faint whoosh as they drop.

"What am I thinking now?" Jeffrey says and steps out of the pile of clothes around his feet.

CHAPTER TWO

There's a change in the wind. Jason Summer feels it, quite suddenly, as Steven Kalina, Jorge Westplain, and he literally stumble into the decidedly shabby interior of the way-off-the-beach Florida-state motel room.

It's the same change-in-the-wind sensation Jason felt when, over a year ago, he had arrived, all wide-eyed and bushy-tailed, for spring break, direct from Boulder's buried-in-the-snow University of Colorado. There had just been something about all of the bright sunshine. There had just been something about all of the half-naked bodies. There had just been something about the let's-party-down-'til-we-drop atmosphere, abounding with countless kegs of beer. Certainly, there had been something about the swiftness with which Jason had thrown away years of am-I-gay? wondering to jump headlong into the same-sex fucking and sucking that, while not as prevalent as the male-female stuff, was just as available.

No doubt about it, there had been something about that supposedly final night, in that Fort Lauderdale bar, when that attractive college student, all blond-hair and blue-eyes, on spring break from the University of Pennsylvania, turned to Jason to say, "What about you let me suck your dick, and I give you a hundred bucks?"

That spring-break change in the wind had resulted in Jason dropping out of college (never a rocket scientist, anyway), and opting for what he had assumed would be wondrous days of fucking and sucking other men in the forever-Florida-sunshine, making enough money doing so as to live happily-ever-after, or at least to live until he figured out just what he really wanted to do with his life.

"God!" Steven says, drops his pants and underpants, and jogs Jason back to the here and now.

Yes, a decided change in the wind," Jason thinks.

Without bothering to step out of dropped pants, dropped underpants, or shoes (no socks), Steven plops belly-down on the bed.

Steven's ass is milky white in comparison to the bronze tan of his back and to the bronze tan of his legs. His dimpled ass is so inviting that Jorge can't wait to stick big cock inside it. When Jorge's large fingers fail him in undressing, Jorge too drunk, too excited, too damned uncoordinated, or all of the above, he improvises a tug to his shirt that unceremoniously pops every damn button and makes the room suddenly seemed filled with ricocheting shrapnel.

Jorge is an Indian, or partly Indian. Anyway, he claims Seminole blood. Jason calls him "Seminal", but Jorge doesn't get the joke.

Before Jorge, Jason's experience with red men was what he saw in the movies, or on the television. Nor had he been all that impressed. All Indians seemed to have one body type that tended toward blah physiques that, more often than not, verged on outright fat.

Jorge, though, who dropped out of high school four years ago and joined his relatives in construction work, has muscle and muscle groups Jason can actually distinguish.

Jorge has square pectorals across a pectoral cleavage that's deep but not serrated. His belly is genuinely impressive washboard. His biceps and triceps are firm. His ass is neither too large nor too small, and it allows Jason the illusion that it keeps that way by Jorge regularly hopping a pony and riding bareback across the plains. Although, Jason has yet to see a horse in Florida, let alone see, anywhere in the state, where anyone could ride one without getting run over by one of the senile old farts in for Florida's balmy weather each and every fall/winter/spring. Maybe, somewhere in the Florida Everglades, there's a horse and someplace to ride it, but Jason is still looking.

Jorge's thighs are muscled. Jorge's callused hands and his feet are large. Jorge's body is almost completely hairless, except for the blue-black hair on his head, and the small vee of surprisingly straight black hair at his crotch. All of which — proof-positive there might, indeed, be some Seminole semen in the Westplain family woodpile — is revealed as he hurriedly wrestles open his trousers.

Somewhere close to genuine stud Indian brave, Jorge is exceptionally handsome. His almost delicate features (although, don't call them delicate, unless you want slapped alongside the head), are enhanced by his truly beautiful mane of unfashionably long blue-black hair.

His eyes, black as jet, have extra long eyelashes, black as jet. His lips are coral-color and sensuously bee-stung. When he smiles, he displays an even line of surprisingly white teeth.

Jason concentrates on Jorge's body, from neck to crotch.

Jorge's cock is close to ten inches long, if it's an inch. It seems awe-inspiring wishful thinking that Jorge even contemplates putting a cock the size of his up Steven's asshole. Once, Jason experimented with a cucumber from a grocery store that about matched the length and thickness of Jorge's cock. Jason greased the cucumber down with lard, and tried to shove it up his ass. He couldn't even get it in halfway. What he did get was a fourth of it lodged so tightly up his rectum that he thought he might have to go to a doctor to get it out.

The way Jason figures, the ease with which, before his very eyes, Jorge's hard cock does get fucked so successfully inside Steven's ass has to do with that ass having long ago been stretched far and wide by a whole line of dicks, Indian and otherwise, Jason's and otherwise, shoved inside it.

"Yessssss," says Jorge.

Likewise, what probably makes Steven so comfortable with Jorge's cock shoved deeply up his behind . . .

"Yesssssss," says Steven.

. . . is the truly awesome thick layer of loose foreskin that overcoats Jorge's steely inner cockcore.

The bulky wrap of loose skin worn by Jorge's dick is of the same genuinely gargantuan proportions as the nose of an elephant seal. Even when

Jorge's cock is hard, his cockhead is never visible unless a concentrated effort is made to roll back the always existing excess of snouted skin.

"I have to take a piss," Jason says. He's spotted the leading edge of the toilet bowl through the open bathroom doorway.

"Ungh!" says Jorge.

"Ungh!" says Steven.

Jason goes into the bathroom and pushes the door shut behind him. His left palm goes flat against the cool tile of the bathroom wall behind the toilet, his arm extended straight for drunken support. He unzips his pants and hauls out his cock.

His cockshaft is thickest at its base, with a distinct taper as far as the flare of bulbous cockhead; circumcised; its head big and fat, like the cap of a giant mushroom. His bush of black pubic hair is small, compact, and curly.

His cockmouth is a cockhead-cleaving aperture. Its moue releases a forceful and slightly unsteady stream of pale beer-yellow piss that hits the water of the toilet bowl with the same force Niagara's main cascade hits the pool below it.

"Ahhhh!" Jason moans appreciatively, doubtful Steven, Jorge's cock up Steven's butt, experiences as much pleasure as Jason does at that kidneys-relieving moment.

Jason is in no hurry to finish.

When finished, he doesn't push his cock back into his open trousers. Rather, his hand scoops to tumble out, by way of stellar accompaniment, his large and hairy balls. He's unsure he's capable of an erection. He can, sometimes, get too drunk to get it up. Not often, but . . .

"Ah, yes, rise and shine!" he says, complimenting his dick's lengthening toward stiffness within his cupping fingers.

He flushes the toilet with his free hand and turns to walk his still-hardening dick over to the mirror. He's confident now that his cock will for the twenty-five dollars promised him by Steven (of the fifty dollars promised Steven by Jorge for a three-way).

"Come on, Jason," Steven had cajoled earlier in the bar. "Jorge wants another guy. I pointed to you, and he said okay."

In the motel bathroom, Jason looks at himself long and hard in the bathroom mirror. He looks for wrinkles. He looks for any and all differences between what he sees reflected now and what he saw reflected by that first mirror after his stay began in Florida. From then, until now, not exactly the endless-summer (except for the cooperating sunshine), for which he'd hoped. After all, horny and obliging students leave after the conclusion of every spring break. Of the old people who stay on, more than a few need more than a little Viagra to get the old pecker up and keep it there.

Oh, Jason can't deny there are plenty of virile rich people in Florida, even plenty of virile rich gay people in Florida. He can't deny there are those among both groups ready, willing, and able to pay for hot and heavy sex. Nor can he deny how rich and horny gays are in Florida looking for the stereotypical blond and blue-eyed surfer. Jason's standout dark-complexioned good-looks only infrequently putting him at an advantage.

No doubt, he's good looking. His black hair is thick and looks it, even though it's cut short. His eyebrows are well-defined and don't meet across the bridge of his nose. His eyelashes are lush. His light-blue eyes have gold specks. His right cheek is dimpled. His chin is cleft.

Jason finds it ironic that the decidedly handsome and dark-complexioned Jorge (prime meat, if ever there was, in most watering holes of the world), pays, in Florida, to access the ass of the decidedly less-handsome but surfer-blond Steven. Jason is suddenly even more prepared to reward Jorge the man's good taste in having Jason along for the ride.

"Who says life is fair?" Jason says to the mirror.

He washes his hands. Doing so is pure reflex. It's something he always does, after pissing, after shitting. Although, why he bothers, considering what he'll likely soon be fondling in the next room, is anyone's guess.

He runs his damp fingers through his coal-black hair. He gives a shake of his head that jostles the damp strands into a more attractive arrangement.

His hard cock leads the way as he opens the door to the bedroom.

CHAPTER THREE

Jeffrey unbuttons his shirt and slips it off. His discarded shirt and pants become cushions for his knees. He kneels his ass atop Marky's thighs.

Jeffrey's corn-blond hair attractively leftward-bangs his forehead. His eyes are black-blue. His eyelashes are thick and dark and lush. His eyebrows are exquisite arches. His mouth is full-lipped. His teeth are white as white. His neck is muscular. His pectorals are well-chiseled and mirror-image one another across a narrow, deep, and serrated cleavage. His stomach is all scalloped muscles, some of which parenthesize his slightly indented navel. His cock is powerfully long and large. The flare of his cockcorona is like the flared neck crest of a triceratops. His blond-hair scrotum is a waterfall of gonad-weighed flesh that pools the crease of Marky's tightly closed thighs.

Attractiveness doesn't get much more attractive than Jeffrey.

Jeffrey and Marky have long-since explored each other's anatomy. Jeffrey's cock was the first, other than Marky's own, that Marky jacked off. And vice versa. Jeffrey's cock was the first, other than Marky's own, Marky sucked. And vice versa. Jeffrey's cum was the first, other than Marky's own, that Marky tasted. And vice versa. Jeffrey's asshole was the first Marky ever cock-fucked, the first Marky ever tongue-fucked and hungrily ate-out. And vice versa . . . and vice versa . . . and vice versa.

It's their last get-away-from-it-all holiday before Jeffrey heads off to Seattle to make a name for himself in modeling; before Marky heads off to make a name for himself on the popular TV series *SandBox,* shot in Hawaii; before Talbot (hopefully) heads off to make a name for himself within the ivy-covered walls of Princeton.

A friend of Marky's father opened the right doors for Marky to land the small recurring role in the TV series. A friend of Jeffrey's uncle got Jeffrey the modeling gig for the Creative Recreation Incorporated (CRI) clothes catalogue being shot in Seattle. Talbot's outstanding academic achievements, combined with his excellence in sports and community service, hopefully opens the doors of Princeton.

"You sure you wouldn't like me to get you a job in Hawaii with me, on the *SandBox* shoot, this summer?" Marky says.

"Nah!" Jeffrey says. He doesn't deny Marky can do it: he knows how persuasive Marky can be when he wants to be. Jeffrey just knows Jeffrey isn't cut out for acting. "How much practice did it take me never to get down even that one-liner in our last school play? I had Mr. Cunning and everyone else, including you, mad at hell that I couldn't get it. You thought I was pretending to flub up. No pretending, buddy."

"Beginner's nerves."

"Beginner's nerves, shit!" Jeffrey says. "Nothing more nor less than the glaring obviousness that I'm not an actor, nor do I have the stuff from which an actor can be made."

"You think there isn't acting involved in modeling?"

"Modeling is nothing more than looking great while preening for a camera," Jeffrey says. "Ask me to say something intelligent about the clothes I'm wearing, and I'd bomb out in modeling, too."

Marky's eyes are now fully accustomed to the backdrop lighting. Jeffrey's features are in full focus. Corn-yellow hair. Black-blue eyes. Sensuous lips. Cleft chin. Ridged abdominals. Indented navel. Well-developed legs. Veed pubic bush. Large cock. Bull-like balls.

Marky's hands parenthesize, ever so lightly, the smooth and tanned column of Jeffrey's neck. Marky's hands slide and splay fingers so his opened palms cover the tack-like centers of Jeffrey's dime-sized nipples.

Marky has a hard time imagining any summer without Jeffrey's hard body and cock always somewhere near.

Jeffrey begins unbuttoning Marky's shirt.

"Let's have you out this, yes?" Jeffrey says. "Then, I'll decide whether I let your big cock fuck my butt while your pants are still on or off."

It's difficult shedding the shirt, Marky's back so snug to the tree trunk, but it gets done.

"Talk about handsome!" Jeffrey says. "That platinum-blond hair of yours. Those cat-green eyes of yours. That snub little nose of yours. Those cupid's-bow lips of yours. That cute little dimple, right here." The tip of his index finger lightly touches down on the right corner of Marky's mouth. "What makes me think I'll spend my whole time in Seattle thinking of your golden good looks?"

"Compliments will get you anything," Marky says.

"What I hope it gets is your nine-and-a-half-inches of cock up my tight-as-a-virgin asshole," Jeffrey says.

He unbuttons the fly of Marky's trousers.

Marky's cock is hard and has been for quite some time. Sex with Jeffrey may be old hat, but there's never been a time the faintest prospect of a rerun hasn't quickly seen Marky's pecker stand tall.

Jeffrey has difficulty hauling Marky's hard dick through the opening provided by Marky's unbuttoned fly. Jeffrey makes more room for the recalcitrant cock by unfastening the waistband of Marky's pants and peeling back, one at a time, the resulting flaps.

Marky's hard cock springs upward. His cockhead is cushioned within the youth's indented navel.

"Love that blond cock of yours," Jeffrey says. His fingertip to Marky's cockhead draws a straight line down Marky's cockshaft to Marky's balls. "Love your cock's clean-cut lines. A twenty-first-century technological marvel, your boner machine-tooled by Almighty God, himself, to ultimate perfection. An exquisite flare of cockcorona from cockneck. A joyousness of seemingly veinless cockshaft that tapers from cocktip to cockroots. Do I wax poetical enough for you, or what?"

Jeffrey's right hand hooks the back of Marky's cock, his knuckles against Marky's belly. His fingers fold, one at a time, until his palm holds as much of

Marky's cock as possible. Marky's dick gets a little squeeze that makes its cockmouth pout all the more.

"Your cock is warm, like velvet," Jeffrey says. "It's hard, like steel."

He keeps Marky's dick aimed skyward and scoots his own upstanding dick in closer. His hand on Marky's dick extends its thumb to include Jeffrey's cock in the same fist-enfolding embrace. His cockbelly mashes Marky's cockbelly. His cockhead aligns almost, but not quite, with Marky's cockhead. Marky's cock is slightly longer, slightly thicker, so each cock is a slightly distorted mirror-image of the other.

Marky's fingers contact and curl the hard muscle of Jeffrey's naked arms. Marky's head bends forward, and his tongue flicks within licking distance of both cockheads. His tongue lathers their mated coronas.

Marky's one lick, though, isn't nearly enough. Using his handholds on Jeffrey's arms as leverage, Marky more fully bows his head. He swallows both cockheads.

"Jeeeesus, you double-jointed sexual wonder!" Jeffrey says, his head bowed only so far as to speak into the platinum-blond hair of Marky's head.

Marky's secure mouthing of their cockheads calls for a wide yawn. Were his lips chapped, they would likely crack under the strain of encompassing such a preponderance of joined pulpy cockflesh.

Marky's tongue washes the tips of their dicks. The resulting tastes, individually, and combined, are familiar but, nonetheless, aphrodisiacal. He sucks their cockheads as greedily as he ever sucked a dual-headed lollipop. His efforts draw not only their cockheads into his throat but a good two inches of each supporting cockshaft.

"Oh, fuck, Jesus, Marky!" Jeffrey says. "You're . . . oh, Jesus, Marky . . . you're . . . oh, oh . . . ohhhhhh . . ."

He groans low and loud as Marky endeavors to out-perform every cocksucker that ever was.

Marky's view is down the back of Jeffrey's powerful dick. Jeffrey's corn-yellow pubic hair grows not only on taut lower belly but on the first thick inch of Jeffrey's cockroots. Marky dives for that hair-grown inch of cockroots and for the corn-yellow nest of curly pubic hair. On the way down, Marky smells the musky aroma of Jeffrey's healthy and sweaty body. Once down, Marky shakes his head and their cocks, like a dog worrying a single hard bone.

"Nice as your cock feels, joined with my dick, up your throat, buddy," Jeffrey says, "I want it rammed far and wide up my asshole. I want to sit my butt over your stiff peg, until your cockhead plugs my throat from the inside-out."

What Jeffrey wants is what Marky wants.

Marky unswallows their saliva-soaked dicks. Marky's released prick springs back and strikes his hard-naked belly with a resounding whack. Jeffrey's stiff prick almost hits his belly, but his cock's swollen weight means it simply rebounds, then droops slightly . . . rebounds, then droops less slightly . . . like a castle drawbridge unsure whether or not to span an existing moat.

Jeffrey rubberizes Marky's stiff cock with a swiftness that would grab top honors in any who's-the-fastest contest, then raises his ass off Marky's thighs, still kneeling. His right hand dips beneath his raised butt, and he expertly grabs Marky's rubberized erection. He tugs Marky's prick into position beneath the overhang of Jeffrey's muscled ass.

The head of Marky's prick travels the crack of Jeffrey's ass to the spot where Jeffrey's pucker waits.

"Contact!" Jeffrey says. The bulbous tip of Marky's erection not only rests against the small anal pucker but slightly concaves it.

The elasticity of Jeffrey's sphincter prepares to open fully around Marky's dick.

"Going down," Jeffrey says and begins to sit.

"Going in," Marky says. He arches his head back against the trunk of the tree. Ecstasy floods him and makes concentration on anything but their sex pretty much impossible.

There are no bumps, humps, bulges, or other irregularities, anywhere along the length of Marky's erect dick, but the yawn required of Jeffrey's butthole to accommodate the smoothly golden phallus is a big one.

"Are you ripping my asshole, you motherfucker?" Jeffrey says, as if Marky is in position to see the last inch of his dick about to disappear into Jeffrey's descending behind.

"It's just my hard pecker preparing your asshole for all of those fresh-air dicks, sprouted from all those hairy bellies of northwest lumberjacks, probably lined up even now to take you on in Seattle," Marky says.

Jeffrey is in no real pain when his ass finally reaches ground zero, and he wiggles to make sure every iota of Marky's dick is thrust as deeply inside as is possible.

"Ahhhhh, yesssss!" Jeffrey says.

They pass for Siamese twins, Jeffrey's ass joined to Marky's crotch, the two apparently sharing but the one cock that juts so impressively from the base of Jeffrey's lower belly. It's as if Marky's stiff dick penetrates all of the way through Jeffrey's butt and comes out, in thoroughly impressive display, on the other side. Each belly is sexily sweaty within whatever its shallow and muscle-parenthesized creases.

Jeffrey's jugular notch is an attractive indent. His chin thrusts upward. A flick of his long and snake-like tongue, glosses his lips with spit. His nostrils flare attractively. He breathes. His chest moves. His ribcage expands and contracts. His stomach moves in and out. His cock moves in and out of Marky's fists. He swallows. His Adam's apple moves — up, then down. His ass moves up and down Marky's stiff dick.

"Fuck my ass," he says. "Whip my dick."

The spring-like flexibility of his bent knees allows his torso its bounce up and back. His asshole smoothly slides the length of Marky's submerged (then reappeared) inches.

"Let your stiff cock have at my tight asshole," Jeffrey says, and he has Marky's full cooperation.

Marky beats Jeffrey's dick closer and closer to ejaculation.

Jeffrey increases his ass-over-cock movement and momentum.

Jeffrey holds to Marky's sweaty shoulders. Jeffrey's asshole lifts farther than usual along Marky's dick. Jeffrey's sphincter gums an encirclement of Marky's cock where Marky's cockhead flares Marky's cockshaft.

"I am going to miss you, Marky . . . stud," Jeffrey says. "Miss how your hard-on always knows just what my asshole needs. Miss how your hands always know just what my stiff cock needs."

Marky delivers a fast and furious series of tight and hearty cockstrokes. "Oh, Marky, Marky, Marky!" Jeffrey says.

Jeffrey really gets into the rhythm. He rides the hard and uplifted cock hard and fast.

Marky's dual-fist tugs upward along Jeffrey's steely cockshaft, then down-slides and mashes Jeffrey's compact scrotum.

It seems a defiance of all known physics that Jeffrey's sweaty and muscled torso manages its rises and pauses atop Marky's boner. As powerful a shaft as it is, Marky hard cock seems painfully insufficient to support so much of Jeffrey's obviously muscled weight.

Less an apparent defiance of gravity is each drop of Jeffrey down the entire length of Marky's erect penis. When Jeffrey fully sits, Marky can't see his own balls, but he knows what they're doing. Their sac is no more flaccid than the compact mass Jeffrey's scrotum has become.

One of Marky's hands leaves Jeffrey's cock to cup Jeffrey's nuts. Marky's fingers massage Jeffrey's gonads and provide the manipulation that puts them on a collision course.

"Ohhhhhh, yes, squeeze my nuts . . . squeeze my balls . . . squeeze my cum-bloated marbles!" Jeffrey says appreciatively.

Rivers of perspiration drool pectoral cleavages. Beads of conjured moisture form on foreheads and cheeks. Necks go shiny with dewy slick.

"Marky, I'm going to come, buddy," Jeffrey says from somewhere beyond Marky's now closed eyelids. "You and your cock make me come, bastard. Your hand on my dick, your fingers on my nuts . . . make . . . me . . . come!"

"Come!" Marky says. "Fuck, yes, come your spunky wet cream!"

As if Jeffrey has only awaited Marky's command, his nuts let go. Thick and juicy comets fly to set-down on and eventually drool Marky's chin.

"Yesssss . . . . Jesus, fuck . . . yesssssss!" Marky says as his own nuts let go their spurts of goo.

Jeffrey burrows his cum-filled butt deeper over Marky's cum-spewing erection and into Marky's sensuously couching lap.

"Oh, buddy!" Jeffrey says. "Goddamn, I'm going to miss you."

"Ditto," Marky says by way of echo.

CHAPTER FOUR

Jorge looks up. He is finished with Steven for the moment.

Steven, completely naked, is still belly-down. He seems to be napping. There's a smile of contentment on his face. There's a veneering of sex-produced sweat glossing his lily-white ass.

Jorge has shifted most of his attention to Jason who is back in the room. What attention he has left, he devotes to languidly stroking his recently butt-fucking dick.

"You ever dock that impressive white-man cock of yours with a red-man's pecker?" Jorge asks.

"You offering?" Jason is pleased when his cock, until then extended straight out, suddenly provides a couple jerks to take it more toward the vertical.

Jorge sits up in bed, his legs over the side. It's indication of the great physical shape he's in that his belly doesn't crease all that much. His cock, still gently being caressed, juts to an upward stance that puts its head higher than the his indented navel.

"Come on over, and let's see how much elevation I need if I stay seated," Jorge says.

Jason obliges. His cock is an impressive metronome that tick-tocks before his belly. He walks up to, and in between, Jorge's open thighs.

"What say I taste the merchandise while I'm at it?" Jorge says.

Jason thinks: "Why not? It's your money." What he says is: "I'd like that."

He does like it. Jason's cock obviously isn't the first white-man's dick siphoned up this red-man's vacuum-producing face. The suction applied to Jason's cockhead eases the dick into Jorge's mouth, slow and easy, easy and slow, one sweet getting-spit-wet fraction of an inch at a time.

"Mmmmm," Jorge hums over the swallowed inches, and it sends vibrations all of the way to Jason's cock roots from which droop Jason's balls.

Jason's nuts roll within his scrotum and becomes more compact.

Jorge's free hand slides Jason's left hip, glides Jason's honey-colored ass. Jorge's fingertips delve the tight crease formed by Jason's mated buttocks. One fingertip connects with Jason's feeling-very-vulnerable pucker.

Jason's hands go, one-to-each red-man shoulder. They touchdown lightly, as if surprised by the warmth of the skin. His fingers walk inward from the swell of the Indian's biceps to the red-man's neck. Fingertips entwine within the coal-black strands of the Indian's hair.

Jason has assumed the hair would feel coarse, but it's downright silky. His fingers wind more completely within the inky cascades, his concentration interrupted by the suddenness with which Jorge gulps down the remaining cockinches poked upward from Jason's belly.

"Nice!" Jason says. It's an understatement, if ever there was one.

Automatically, Jason's pelvis shifts and grinds, to assure — as if not quite certain — that all of his cock is gone inside, eaten up, devoured, consumed. "I'll bet you could make me cream without half trying."

He's hoping for a suck to creaming when Jorge's face begins its pull-back, slow and easy, suction still exerted in skillful counterpoint, up and along the just-swallowed inches. The cockshaft emerges wet and slick and slippery, easily mistaken for gold.

"Ohhhh," Jason bemoans the sudden complete release of his dick. Reflexively, his hands close in on Jorge's head and give a too-late try to put Jorge's face right back down over the prize.

The cock is free, though, and there's no getting it back without Jorge's cooperation. Made stiffer by its brief in-mouth-and-out, its slap against Jason's belly leaves a distinct spitty sunburst.

"Nice-tasting dick, but I was talking docking my dick with it," Jorge says.

Jason too much bemoans the lost opportunity of fucking Jorge's face to climax to make any reply.

"Need a bit of ass elevation, though," Jorge says. "Give me the damn pillow, sleepy head!" He pulls the pillow Steven has usurped for his nap.

"Be my guest," is all Steven manages by way of comment. Anyway, that's what Jason thinks Steven says. It comes out muted and modified by Steven's real or feigned sleepiness.

Jorge plumps the freed pillow. He folds it. He stuffs the result under his ass. His face is no longer at Jason's cock-level. What his mouth touches down on, this time, is one of Jason's nipples. The exerted suction plumps the budded nipple-center. Jorge's teeth bite down hard enough so that a slight pull-back of Jorge's head stretches the nipple center, but it doesn't stretch it so much or so hard that Jason complains of the pain. Jorge finishes off with a long lap that drags his rough taste buds over the nipple surface, like a tongue dragged over tasty ice cream.

Jorge looks up. His face is partially covered by cascading black hair. The luminous quality of his eyes is that of coal hinting of diamond-potential. His nose, unlike the Indian that Jason once saw on a collector's Indian-head nickel, isn't at all prominent. But, Jorge's cheekbones are Indian-high, and they make his cheeks slightly concave. His lips are sexy-full.

"Elevator going up," Jorge says. He repeats the fluff-and-stuff procedure with another pillow. Which pretty much positions his cock belly-to-belly with Jason's stiffy-in-erection. "Would you believe there are actually people out there, in the big wide world, who go through their whole lives thinking there are only circumcised cocks? Thinking that everyone's dick comes from the womb all rocket-like and naturally trimmed to unencumbered projectile status, like your exquisite white-man dick?"

It's not as if Jason is one of those unenlightened multitude. He's seen more than one unclipped dick in this time, even if he's hard-pressed to admit he's ever seen any foreskin quite like the one sported by Jorge's erection. There being foreskins and then there being foreskins. Jorge's one of the latter: thick-

thick, bulky-bulky, so-so copious an overcoat for one, albeit admittedly impressive, steely dick. Certainly, Jason has never docked his cock with anything so voluminous.

Jorge leans back slightly. He gives Jason a chance to look down between them to where Jorge's hand increases its squeeze on the Indian's dick and elevates to an even more pronounced snout — the loose skin he brings up and over the cockhead.

Jorge's foreskin is rivered with large blue veins. Aside from that blue, though, his cock is as naturally toasty brown as the rest of him.

"Nothing like docking your dick with another guy's foreskin," Jorge says. His is the voice of experience. "Especially if you're lucky enough to come across a guy with a foreskin like mine, in this day and age when most excess cockskin is clipped away as thoroughly as a Marine recruit's side-walls."

He moves his foreskin back and forth . . . back and forth . . . back and forth . . . over the solid inner shaft of his dick.

Each time, Jason is fascinated by the roll of snouted skin brought up and over the end of the prick.

Jorge's thumb and forefinger pinch off to emphasize his cockhead's latest fleshy overhang.

Aside for a short, possibly let-me-sleep snort, Steven has absolutely nothing to say about the sexual situation that develops without him.

"Step back just a bit," Jorge says. "We have to make enough room to lower our cocks."

Jorge's crotch and Jason's crotch are perfectly aligned across the gap between them.

"See," Jorge says. His thumb pushes his up-jutted cock to the horizontal. "My cock's gopher hole is suddenly ready for your snake to come on in."

Jorge opens his thighs wider. His partially compact scrotum is still flaccid enough to cascade his big and dark-haired balls over the upper edge of the top pillow. By comparison, Jason's gonad-sac has grouped into a seemingly solid and hairy ball attached to the roots of his stiff pecker.

Jorge's crotch has very little hair. Each strand is as straight, though not nearly as long, as any of those on his head.

Jason drops his dick to the horizontal. He shifts slightly to one side so his cockhead more directly aims at Jorge's cock.

"Time to bump cockheads," Jorge says.

Jason's feet move him the distance that positions his cockhead within a mere fraction of an inch from Jorge's awaiting and open-end foreskin.

Jorge's free hand slides between Jason's legs, palm-up. His fingers curl Jason's balls. Jason shivers from the pure sensuousness of the resulting touch and squeeze.

Jorge scoots the slightest distance to bring his suddenly unveiled cockhead into direct contact with the head of Jason's dick. Jason's cock-cupping hand rotates the length of his hand-held meat so his prick's blunt head screws itself against the tip of Jason's erection and remains firmly pugged there.

Jorge releases Jason's balls, but Jason doesn't move. No way, of his own accord, does Jason go anywhere but right where he is. This cock-docking with Indian dick is getting better and better.

Jorge's hand moves along his cockshaft toward Jason's prick. Jorge's hand tugs foreskin along with it. Jorge's other hand provides the additional maneuvering that allows his foreskin to yawn wide enough to swallow Jason's projected cockhead and glide the distance, up and over, into the groove formed by Jason's coronal flare.

Jason watches and feels. His cockhead has donned its first foreskin since circumcision.

The excess flesh from Jorge's dick flows farther. It rides over Jason's erection like a tunnel over a train. Its soft and sensuous all-enveloping snugness is made snugger by Jorge's skillful fingers constantly manipulating and squeezing to assure progress so far along Jason's dick, toward Jason's hairy belly, that the two cocks seem merely one.

"'Rattle-rattle' says your snake in my gopher hole," Jorge says.

Jorge's foreskin seems more and more like one of those Chinese fingercuffs that get tighter whenever anyone tries to remove one of the fingers entrapped at either end.

Jorge's palm more securely curls the cocks mated-in-foreskin.

"Your snake not likely to find a more commodious gopher hole," Jorge says. "Had my mother let a doctor clip my prick, I would have ended up at least a pound lighter."

Jason believes it. Jorge's fleshy tunnel buns Jason's wiener as thoroughly as any hotdog bun ever wrapped its frankfurter. Jason envisions his cock claustrophobic within confines so snug, so clinging, so soft, and so — ever-so-slightly — moist.

"Whoa!" Steven says from the bed. He sits up. His movement bounces the springs and bounces Jorge's pillow-supported ass, and shifts Jorge's cock against Jason's cock up the foreskin tunnel. "You two planning to let me sleep through this marvel-to-behold?"

Jason has trouble focusing on Steven, or on what Steven says. Jason has trouble focusing on much of anything except the way his dick . . . and Jorge's dick . . . are wrapped . . . wrapped . . . wrapped by cozy foreskin.

Steven slides off the bed. His fat pink cock is more impressive for its girth than for its length. Its pulpy knob borders on scarlet. Blond-to-invisible pubic hair, including the scanty growth that covers his scrotum and climbs the crack of his ass, bears witness to blond not originating in some bottle.

"Don't you studs move," Steven says. "I'm thinking, maybe, about feasting on sweetbreads."

"Thymus glands?" Jason asks. He once held the same anatomical misconception as Steven.

"Balls, my man," Steven corrects. "Big, hairy-to-black balls. Your balls. Indian Jorge's balls."

He comes at them from one side. He drops to his knees. He peers between them, like someone peers between two stalwart brick shithouses to check out the heavily insulated pipe that connects the two.

"I've seen jellyrolls less impressive," Steven says. "You really turned on by all of this, aren't you, Jason?"

"What do you think?" Jason says. His voice is breathless to his own ears.

"I know, from experience, my man, that when your big nuts pull as far up into your lower belly, as they are now, you're primed to let go one of your genuinely manly big loads. Only a foreskin the size of Indian Jorge's likely big enough to hold the soon-to-be-released discharge. Except, even his fleshy tunnel is going to be hard-pressed to do the job if Jorge's scrotum-hugged balls are any indication of his about-to-shoot cum-load. You about ready to let 'er rip, Jorge?"

"Why in the hell don't you just shut the fuck up and either fondle my priming nuts or suck on them?" Jorge says.

"Let's confirm just how cum-bulged your red-man testicles really are," Steven says.

His hand extends between the two bodies. His fingers scoot beneath Jorge's balls. They ride in along the edge of the pillow. Gently, Jorge's gonads collide with each other on the palms of Steven's hand, as Steven's hand slides farther along beneath them.

"Oh, yes!" Jorge says. His hands wrap the penile bridge. The contained two-cocks-with-foreskin bulk is too big for Jorge's fuck-finger to meet his thumb curled toward it from the other side. But the grip is firm and sufficient to pull loose foreskin back toward Jorge's belly, almost to the point where the head of Jason's cock is no longer contained within it.

Steven tries to figure the best way, and the best timing, to stick his head between the two studly bodies and somehow suck-claim Jorge's Indian balls. If he waits very much longer, Jorge's cum-swollen gonads will release their load without him. Already, he's waited too long for Jason's load.

"Oh, sweet Jesus," Jorge says. "Who thought fucking docking dick could be so fucking . . . so fucking . . ."

Steven opens his palm around Jorge's scrotum and pushes his fingertips farther along the pillow and up between Jorge's asscrack to the sweaty pucker of Jorge's anus.

"Hey, you sonofabitch!" Jorge says. "Don't, Jesus, don't . . ."

But Steven already squirrels his finger, albeit only to its first knuckle, into the protesting-with-spasms interior of Indian Jorge's ass.

"Fuck . . . fuck!" Jorge says. His hands go even more firmly around cocks and foreskin.

Steven crooks his anal-inserted finger in the direction of Jorge's suddenly exploing gonads.

"Unnggghhh!" George grunts. His cum, not Jason's is the first to cream-fill, then overflow, all of the available space within the cocks-encompassing prepuce.

Jason's cum, though, isn't far behind. As if the squeeze and massage of Jorge's gripping fingers aren't enough, there's something sensuously orgasm-triggering about the sudden wet-warm wash of Jorge's ejaculated spunk flooding . . . flooding . . . over and around . . . over and around . . . the stiff contours of Jason's cock-in-foreskin.

There's major spermal overflow, creamy and partially opaque. Its rich Jason-Jorge combination of sex-juice butters both dicks and oozes pearly streamers into and onto the black hair that grows at the base of both bellies.

CHAPTER FIVE

Talbot's wet-dream-in-progress is based on actual events: guys he's found attractive, would have made a move on, only to have his desire somehow shift into lower gear and/or flutter out completely.

Gerald McTalon is one such guy. Talbot genuinely was attracted to Gerald, even planned his let's-get-it-on moves. The wealth of Gerald's family admittedly makes the guy a tad uppity, but uppity in Talbot's book can be a major turn-on. What cools Talbot's ardor is Gerald's sudden penchant for running marathons which has, almost overnight, turned the guy cadaverously thin. Skin and bones a turn-on for some people, but not for Talbot.

Peter Flanner is one of these guys. He still comes under the category of hot-hot-hot, but Talbot rejects him for fun and games, because Peter works for Talbot's father. He won some kind of prestigious student-architecture award while a senior at Yale, and a lot of firms had been out to get him. Talbot would love "to get him", because Peter fills his pants far better than any poured cement fills its construction form. That said, Talbot has a policy to steer clear of even the studliest of his father's employees. Maybe, something about mixing business with pleasure, although the business won't be Talbot's for a long-long time. There is, also, the possibility that tricking in-firm increases the possibilities of the elder Crane finding out that the likelihood of his one and only son producing heirs is next to nonexistent. While Talbot expects that whenever his father does find out he will eventually accept the inevitable and be supportive, Talbot isn't in any hurry to usher in that day.

Kane Clydesdale is one of these guys. He retains his stud-rating since Talbot first spotted him. He, too, though, works for Talbot's dad. He, also, works for his own father who runs the national security service hired to watch all of the many Crane, Benbrook, and Toriglee properties. Kane was hired by Ralph Clydesdale just the year before, after Kane's graduation from some east-coast high school. Immediately, he was shipped to the Los Angeles branch office. No one denies nepotism, in this instance, provides Clydesdale Security with someone who genuinely looks the part. Kane is handsome in an attractive in-the-rough, old-beyond-his-years, seen-more-than-he-possibly-ever-could-have kind of way.

Funny how circumstances conspired to put Talbot in a situation wherein he re-appraises his feelings for all three.

All because of old Helen Glindel Health and Beauty Spa building. The building is an old beach-front landmark turned prime real-estate property in the face of all the commercial build-up all around it. The Spa having had its heyday when Helen Glindel was still alive and successfully persuading rich ladies that they couldn't make it through any day without a steam bath, a sauna, a pore-cleanse, a seaweed or sea-salt exfoliation, an exotic-oil massage, all before lunch, followed by a manicure, a pedicure, a hair-do, cocktails with accompanying chamber music, and maybe even a movie, or a play, or a lecture, or preview of the latest French haute-couture fashions.

The Spa stayed open for a couple of years after Helen died but, in the end, it was Helen who proved to have been the glue to hold the whole corporation together. There is a power struggle for control of the estate by Helen's heirs. Nasty. On-going. Never-ending. Until the point that whoever wins will end up with nothing. The Spa itself entangled in a Gordian knot of resulting legal machinations that included lawyers suing for unpaid fees. The Spa's future all the more uncertain when the California Society for the Preservation of Historical Buildings declared the building an historical monument and therefore imposed so many restrictions upon any eventual renovation that everyone with any interest ran in another direction. All except Talbot's father who stepped up to the plate to do what he did best whenever he finds a project that really catches his eye and interest; he somehow finessed his way to shovel through all of the bullshit and cut all of the red tape to put the Spa into Crane, Benbrook, and Toriglee's real-estate portfolio.

It was just an accident that Talbot drove by the building as Gerald and Peter disappeared into an adjoining alley. Talbot was really not surprised that Gerald and Peter were together. Peter had graduated Yale, Gerald was headed for Yale in the fall, Gerald's father was a Yale alumnus. Peter had even stayed with the McTalens when he'd been in Los Angeles for job interviews the year before.

Why was Talbot's curiosity aroused not only by Peter letting Gerald in the back door of the Spa but by Peter going around to get himself let in by the security guard?

In Talbot's dream, as it had been in reality, Kane Clydesdale looks up from the security desk when Talbot gets around to tapping on the front door. Kane gets up. He comes over. He unlocks the door.

"I don't know if you remember me . . ." Talbot says.

"Mr. Crane's son," Kane says.

"Right. My father thinks he may have left some papers here the other day." Peter is disappeared into the back of the building; Gerald is already back there. "Dad said, you have any questions about my stopping by to check to see if the papers are where he thinks he left them, you should give a call."

Kane steps back, but not so far that Talbot is kept from slight physical contact on his way in.

Does Kane know just how sexy he is, all decked out in his security-guard uniform? Talbot wonders, and for not the first time, just what Kane looks like stripped down . . . without his uniform . . . without his underclothes (if he wears any) . . . bare-ass naked . . . with stiffly erect cock.

"Mr. Flanner is in back," Kane says.

"Peter Flanner?" Talbot is all innocence.

"Something about his needing to recheck the structural integrity of some walls in one of the old locker rooms. Just thought I'd let you know, in case you hear some banging around and think it's a ghost."

Talbot sure as hell would enjoy some banging around with Peter and/or with Kane. Although with Talbot's resolve to steer clear of his father's employees, that isn't going to happen.

What is happening, by the time Talbot stealthily runs across it, is a good banging of Gerald's ass by Peter's stiff and ramming pecker. Peter's asscheeks all dimply on each and ever insert of his cock, all of the way, up Gerald's gyrating and grinding behind. Peter's basketball balls are suspended in black-hair scrotum and are grouped into Brillo-pads at the base of the award-winning young architect's fucking boner.

"Faster! Jeez harder! Please!" Gerald sounds more than a little breathless. Talbot can't blame him. Peter's dick is enough to take any fucked-by-it guy's breath away.

"It'll be better, slow and easy," Peter says. "You and I both know that."

Talbot has all intentions of sticking around to wait and see just how good is the promised slow and easy. He's in a good position, behind a row of rusted lockers, side-on view of the two through the gap. There's a breach of about three inches through which he spots Gerald, belly-up, on a bench, Peter, belly-down between Gerald's opened legs.

Initially, Talbot's viewing space had parenthesized merely Peter's cock working Gerald's ass. It was only when Talbot had moved in closer that more of the whole picture came into view.

Gerald's hands are around Peter's neck. Gerald's legs are up and his ankles locked over the backs of Peter's calves. Gerald's head lolls this way and that.

Gerald doesn't see Talbot. Gerald doesn't see much of anything. Except maybe for stars. His eyes, mostly shut, are, when they do open, downright unfocused. Gerald is really riding high on the sensations Peter's prick makes happen inside his gripping bunghole.

"Ah . . . ah," Gerald says.

"See, see," Peter says. "You've got one expert butt-fucker, riding your tight asshole."

Meanwhile, Talbot's whanger starts going hard in his pants. Talbot thinks, "Hold on here, Talbot, get a grip! This is Peter Flanner, employed by your father, and skinny-to-the-point-of-unsexiness classmate Gerald McTalen, here. Nothing you want or need your pecker to get all that excited about."

Except, Talbot's pecker obviously thinks differently. His cock hasn't gotten this hard, this fast, since the advent of puberty had suddenly allowed him the novelty of cock elongation.

Talbot's swollen dick meets with a twist in his undershorts that keeps his dick bent as it tries to figure out how to straighten completely. In the end, it requires some deft maneuvering by Talbot's right hand to get his prick un-kinked. That chore accomplished, his fingers stay on his extended length of stiff pecker.

What to do?

Not "what does Peter do?" He keeps right on pumping Gerald's behind. Not, "what does Gerald do?" He keeps right on taking Peter's pumping cock and begging for all the more of it. But, "what does Talbot do?" He stays put and keeps watching.

"I think I'm going to come," Gerald says.

Talbot wishes just about anyone but Gerald was on the receiving end of Peter's stick. If Talbot had once found Gerald physically attractive, that time is passed. Hell, Talbot can readily count each and every one of Gerald's ribs. He can readily see Gerald's predominant hipbones. Talbot wonders if there's enough padding on Gerald's whole skinny ass to offer any kind of cushioning for the thump, thumb, thump, of Peter's belly fucked against it.

"You aren't going to come, yet" Peter says, and it isn't a question. "Hear me, Gerald?"

"Oh, oh, sorry," Gerald says and creams his load. "Jesus, sorry! Jesus . . . Jesus . . . sorry . . . sorry."

"Goddamn sonofabitch!" Peter says and increases his humping tempo of the orgasming Gerald.

Peter's hips drop his crotch into one final and loud mating with Gerald's skinny ass. The full weight of Peter's hips keep his submerged cock anchored for his continuing ride.

Both of Peter's asscheeks dimple really deeply, as if twin balloons are simultaneously deprived of air. Each buttock collapses, along Peter's asscrack, until the anal valley is just a shallow, sweaty line that extends from his compact and hairy scrotum to the sexy small of his back.

"I'm squirting my spunk!" Peter says. "Ugh, ugh, ugh . . . I'm feeding my pearly, pearly jism up our tight, tight, tight asshole butt!"

Talbot takes that as his cue to exit. An exit made somewhat difficult because his cock is so damned stiff in his pants, like a third leg with no pants leg into which to put it.

Talbot is out of the Spa locker room as quickly as he can manage. He heads for the front of the building, and exit, literally bumping into Kane.

It's like colliding with a fucking brick shithouse, even for Talbot who plays enough high-school football to have banged into some of the best physically toned bodies the school system has to offer.

"You okay?" Kane says. His hands clamp Talbot's shoulders to keep Talbot from careening any farther.

"I'm fine," Talbot says. He's no longer as worried about the collision as he is about the obviousness of the boner in his pants. "Really, I'm . . ." He angles for a quick bye-bye, with the attending hope that it all happens so fast Kane hasn't noticed, and won't notice, the ridge of his stiff pecker.

"You're sure?" Kane says and sounds as genuinely concerned as anyone who has just about knocked the boss's son to the floor.

Talbot's inclination is still to run for the hills. Too late! No telling how he knows, he just suddenly knows, his boner is no longer any more a secret to Kane than it has, for a long time, been a secret to Talbot. Maybe, that message telegraphed by just how quickly — as if Talbot is suddenly hot as magma — Kane withdraws his steadying handhold.

Silence. Pregnant silence. Anticipatory silence. Talbot . . . Kane … anticipating just what?

Now is the perfect moment for Talbot to make his retreat. Kane will let him go, no questions asked. By the expression on Kane's face, he'll be more than glad to do so. Kane appears as if he may well have bitten off more than he can chew.

Talbot is locked to the spot. Why is he locked to the spot? Why is he excited by the knowledge that he has a big hard-on and Kane knows he has a big hard-on? Why his resolve never to trick with an employee of his father suddenly fading faster and faster? In that, does he actually have a chance of sex with this stud? Or, is all he reads in Kane's defensive stance, in Kane's expressive and handsome features, something other than the sexual desire Talbot would give just about anything to find there.

"Did you know Pete Flanner is in the locker room fucking some guy's asshole?" Talbot says, his voice in a low whisper.

"None of my business," Gerald says.

"Peter let the kid in the back door," Talbot says. "What do you think my father is going to have to say about that?"

"I'd say, whatever he has to say, it's between your father, Mr. Flanner, and whomever Mr. Flanner is fucking."

"You don't find it disgusting, what he's doing back there?"

"If they're doing what you say they're doing that's their business. My business is to make sure the property stays secure. Does Mr. Flanner fucking some guy's ass make the property any less secure? I think I can successfully argue that it doesn't."

"So, you don't care?"

"Mr. Flanner is on the list of people who have twenty-four hour access to the building. He wants in, I let him in. You want in, I let you in. After that, what either of you do remains none of my business, as long as it doesn't compromise building security."

"How liberal of you," Talbot says.

"You want to complain to your father about Mr. Flanner and what he does, or about how I handle or don't handle it, that's your prerogative."

"None of your business, likely none of my business as well," Talbot says, magnanimously. "I guess I'm just a little confused by how my seeing Peter and guy doing what they're doing gives me this." One hand parenthesizes his boner jutted down one pants leg.

"Not a conversation either of us should have," Kane says. He licks his lips. They're dry? He's nervous? He's excited? All of the above?

Is that a definite stirring Talbot spots in the crotch of Kane's uniform trousers, or just tricks of shadow played by the really bad lighting?

"Why isn't it a conversation we should have?" Talbot asks, as if he doesn't know. "I mean, if neither of us sees any harm in the kind of stuff Peter and his friend are up to, here, this evening . . ."

"You're my boss's son," Kane says.

"So what?" Talbot comes across as if he never, ever, made it a policy not to pursue any attraction he felt for anyone working for his father.

"Never a good idea to mix business with pleasure."

"So, that is how you'd see it, then? Pleasure?"

"Don't twist what I say, Talbot."

"And, if I'd consider it pleasure, too?"

"You and I know it will be better for the both of us if you just head on home now, with or without the paperwork you father sent you for."

"And, if I don't head on out? If I stand here for a few more moments? Would your cock swell even bigger? Could we measure, maybe, to see which of our cocks extends the farthest down its pants leg?""

"Not a good idea."

"So, why do I find it so exciting?"

"I work for your father," Kane says, for not the first time.

"Which makes your hardening cock any the less real? Which makes my boner's increased hardness something other than it is? Which makes me find you any the less attractive?"

"Jesus!" Kane says. "We should have sense enough not to get ourselves involved in a situation we know is going to be a real complication for the both of us."

CHAPTER SIX

Jorge is still a little peeved at Steven's finger having found its way, even partially, up the red-man's butt. He warns Steven against any attempted repeats. Steven's half-ass smile prompts Jorge to warn him again. Apparently, butch, he-man Indian stud that he is, as interested in fucking butt as he is, Jorge isn't all that eager to offer up his own anus for fucking, by finger or otherwise, at least while he's paying the bill.

Jorge isn't bashful about saying what he does want for his money-paid. "How about Jason and I tandem-fucking your ass, Steven?" Jorge says.

Jason isn't at all certain Steven is going to go for that. Steven's ass accommodated Jason's cock, on occasion. Steven's ass accommodated Jorge's cock, not all that long ago. But Steven take on Jason and Jorge's hard cocks, one at the same time?!

"Just use a lot of lube," Jason says and shrugs acceptance.

Jason is more than a little awe-struck that Steven is so blasé. No way Jason will take a simultaneous assault by Jorge and Steven's cocks. Jason doesn't care how much money Jorge is willing to add to the kitty.

"Guess what I have here?" Jorge says. He produces two condoms out of seeming nowhere and two sachets of lubricant. The guy is some kind of magician. He tosses half this conjurations to Jason.

"So, how do you want me?" Steven says, matter-of-factly.

"I worked on that last fuck, didn't I?" Jorge says. "So . . ."

"Worked?" Steven interrupts.

"Whatever," Jorge says. "I want to just lie back and enjoy this one."

He goes belly-up on the bed. The mattress compresses beneath his weight. The bedsprings compress, as does the mattress, the former singing protest. A slight rebound of the coiled springs produces a small but noticeable bounce.

"Come sit your ass right down over this," Jorge says. The crook of his thumb hooks his cockshaft and levers his dick to a shoot-for-the-ceiling launch position. His cock, already gone off in Steven's ass, once, and already gone off while kissing Jason's cock up foreskin, looks more than ready for its third time around.

Jason is as much impressed by his own continued erection as he is by Jorge's cock refusing to go soft. After all, Jason had been dubious, considering all his pre-fuck drinking, that he'd be able to get his dick up at all. No doubt the gallon of cum he'd erupted to join Jorge's discharge inside Jorge's foreskin might, some other time, have sent his prick into softness, but not — for whatever the reason — this time. Not only is Jason's cock hard, but it goes even stiffer as he marvels at that stiffness.

Steven crawls up on the bed and into a kneeling position over Jorge's studly body. Jason hardly believing Steven isn't having second thoughts.

Steven assumes a sitting position, facing the same way as Jorge, between Jorge's open thighs. He lies back and hoists himself up along Jorge's body, so the two assume one-on-one matching supine positions.

"Anyone ever tell you your sexually stimulated Indian nipples are sharp as little thumbtacks?" Steven says.

He shifts the back of his legs off Jorge's legs and drops them into the space between Jorge's open thighs. He bends his knees slightly. He puts more pressure of his body to Jorge's torso. His hips lift.

"Need Jason to give you a helping hand getting your big red-man dick positioned?" Steven asks.

His question is answered before it's even completely asked, by Jorge's thumb having hooked his cock and elevated it into position beneath the sudden overhang of Steven's lily-white ass.

"You just bring that asshole of yours right on down," Jorge says. As Steven obliges, the crease of his ass slides open for the entering dick and puts cockhead to pucker.

"Ready or not, here I come," Steven says. His ass drops, but his asshole and Jorge's cock aren't quite properly aligned.

"Wait, Jesus, wait!" Jorge says. He manhandles his eager cock the tiny bit required.

Steven feels the time is right. His butt descends over Jorge's cock from cockhead to mid-cockshaft without even trying hard. A fraction of a second later, his asshole as easily gobbles up those inches remaining of Jorge's impressive erection.

"Oh, but I do seem to have something rammed up my butt," Steven says. He screws his asshole more firmly into place. His asscheeks become striated with indents caused by steady and intense contact with the nest of Jorge's black pubic hair.

"Feels to me as if we're going to need a little bit of help from Jason before we've completely stuffed full your asshole," Jorge says.

"Maybe," Steven says. "Why don't we invite Jason on in?"

Once again, he dances his plugged asshole over the hard cock that plugs it. The revolutions of his ass would likely twist off a less firmly anchored erection.

"I think it's time, Jason," Jorge says.

The bedsprings sing additional protest as Jason ventures at least getting near enough to the two men to do the requested deed. He's still uncertain the dual-fuck is destined for success.

"Legs up, Steven," Jorge says. "I want to see the expression on our friend's face when his dick joins mine up your asshole."

Jason gives Steven's leg-raising an assist. Jason scoots forward to position the backs of those legs up against Jason's chest.

"Ride that rubberized belly of your dick right on in on the belly of my butt-plugging pecker," Jorge says. "Don't get put off by any of Steven's pig-squeals, either. He's up to this, and he knows it, no matter how much noise he may decide to make."

No way, though, Jason fucks when and if Steven squeals too much of a fuss. No way Jason helps split a friend's asshole for whatever Jorge may assume is the going rate.

Jorge sees Jason's reluctance and says, "Steven, please, tell Jason that we've been this route before. Jason's cock impressive, to be sure, but not, do you think, nearly as thick as Claymore's cock which once joined mine up your ass."

The only Claymore Jason knows does have a cock that's bigger than Jason's. Actually, it's enough to give Jason a small-cock complex. Comparing Jason's cock to Claymore's dick is like comparing a frankfurter to a beer can.

"That, now, was a real tight fit," Steven said. "Almost too tight."

"'Almost' the key word, here," Jorge says.

"It's okay, Jason," Steven says. "I've always had an exceptionally elastic asshole, even back in the Ice Age when it was still virgin." By way of illustration, his back weight again pressed fully into Jorge's chest for leverage, and he pushes three fingers of his right hand into his butt, along with Jorge's stuffing pecker. He does so without any protest or groan.

So, Jason maneuvers for the ideal cock-insertion position that will join his dick with what Jorge already offers by way of butt-fuck.

The pressure exerted by Jason's oncoming shoulders and chest against the back of Steven's legs causes Steven's ass to lose the lowest couple of inches of Jorge's erection. The gripping anus hikes the lubricated condom up along the suddenly emerged inches, as well. The sudden slip out provides a thick hunk of cock sparsely grown with the same black pubic hair that grows the sac that contains Jorge's big balls.

The exited inches of Jorge's cock have become the runway that invites Jason's cock to make touchdown and slide right along to the point where the only thing separating Jason's dick from inside Steven's asshole is a barrier of gripping pucker.

"Just keep your dick right on sliding," Jorge says. "My dick is getting mighty lonesome and needs some cuddly company."

Jason, though, is still a little uncertain. Nonetheless, he goes through the final shifts of his body, and the manhandling of Steven's uplifted legs and ass, so that Jason can lean forward and . . .

He feels the resistance offered by the seemingly non-space available for insertion of his cock. He's not sure which will happen first: his cock bent to breaking, or successful cock-run up along Jorge's awaiting cockbelly into the depths of the asshole. For a painful while, it feels like it will be his cock breaking. His dick, no matter how steely, converts to a slight bow.

Then, suddenly, as if Steven's butt actually is a mouth able to open all the wider, the asshole gulps not only the let-me-in cockcorona but a good three inches of Jason's dick.

"Ohhhhh, sweet Jesus," Jason groans in accompaniment to the sudden vise-like snugness provided by Jorge's cock and by one half the circumference of Steven's asshole. He's helpless to control, let alone contain, the drool that forms at the corner of his mouth. His spit flows as far as near drop-off from his chin before he can get a hand into place to wipe it away.

"Good start," Jorge says. He gives an appreciative wiggle. He's really not in a position to control much of the action, other than by voice command. But, he does provide the shift necessary to allow Jason's cock to sink in deeper. "Now, what say we really get on with the main show?"

Jason is suddenly eager to oblige. The clamp his cock experiences inside Steven's butthole demands whatever cock-stretch-butt movements he can provide to achieve a more comfortable accommodation of the two dicks.

Jason's buttcheeks dimple as his hips push to slide even more of his dick in . . . in . . . in . . .

"Both rockets have landed!" Jorge says, as all but two inches of Jason's big dick falls into place, belly-to-belly against Jorge's prick, inside Steven's butt.

Steven's sphincter is like a double-wrapped rubber band as it presses to both men's cocks where the thick bases of those cocks protrude from the asshole. Movement of cock against cock, cock against asswall, is like the movement of resisting geologic tectonic plates, one against another against another, finally revving for a devastating climax of earthshaking proportions.

Steven arches his back to press his shoulders all the more tightly against Jorge's steely chest. His hands clamp his own ass, one to each of his cheeks, and he manually widens the expanse of his asscrease.

"Oh, oh, oh," Jason says. Progress has been made, but he still doubts the final end will be achieved. How is it possible one guy's obviously tight asshole can manage the stretch necessary to take on not one big cock but two?

Jason grits his teeth and centers all of his concentration on his pelvis region and the final push he plans to muster behind the base of his dick. He's rewarded for his efforts by an additional slide of cock along cock, of cock along asshole, of cock inside asshole.

"Give me a second!" Steven says, breathless. What else can he be but breathless, under the circumstances?

Jason obliges with a pause, even as Jorge says: "Don't know about giving you that second, Steven. I'm mighty anxious to have what's left of Jason's dick fucked full belly-to-belly against mine.

"Just let me . . . ah, yes, there."

It's genuinely miracle potential the way Steven's asshole suddenly just kind of yawns. It's outward expansion just enough to allow the final insertion of Jason's cock up funky corridor, without any help except gravity.

"Ohhhhh," Jason says when his cock bumps up and over the flare of Jorge's concealed cockhead.

As quickly as Steven's butt yawns, it clamps down with a vengeance. It seems destined to metamorphose two cocks into one.

"Oh, good, good . . . fucking good!" Jorge compliments.

Jason's mouth opens and shuts . . . opens and shuts. Little growls exit with more drool.

Inside Steven's ass, the pleasure and the pressure cause both plugging cocks to leak sticky pre-cum juice.

Though Jason provides an additional shift of his hips to screw himself even deeper, there's no more of him capable of entering the butthole. His balls hang, as if waterfalled from the mouth of the asshole. His scrotum is against Jorge's scrotum. The black hair of his balls is entwined with the black hair that grows Steven's sac.

"I do believe I am butt-stuffed," Steven says. No one present to argue his point.

"And, by way of additional reward to you, for services rendered . . ." Jorge says and squirrels his hands between Steven's uplifted legs. One hand to Steven's cock, one hand to Steven's balls.

Steven's cock is made harder than usual by the pressure exerted by the dual-fucking cocks, through anal wall, against the submerged segment of his erection. His cockhead is glossy with clear and juicy pre-cum discharge. Jorge's fingers play within the gloss, smear it farther, slather it all of the way down Steven's cockshaft.

"Your nuts are like two fuzzy new tennis balls," Jorge says. His hand is so positioned that he's able to speak directly into Steven's ear. "Ball one!" He squeezes one nut. "Ball two!" He squeezes the other.

Steven gives an automatic fuck and fuck-me response. It lifts the length of his cock upward through the tunnel formed by Jorge's cupping fingers. It slides his asshole up along the two stiff cocks that so thoroughly plug his anus.

Jason starts to fuck in earnest. The bits of movement provided by the shift of Steven's ass, by the jiggle of Jorge, simply aren't enough even as Jason's each and every pull-back seems to stretch his dick to twice its usual length. Jason's dominating sexual needs require him, quite beyond his conscious control, to pull ... push ... pull ... push ... fuck ... himself and whomever else wants t come along for the ride ... to climax.

"Ohhhhh," Steven moans appreciatively. There were pleasures for him in just his stuffing. But, Jason's cock in movement is all Steven assumed it would be when Jorge first suggested the tandem fuck of Steven's ass. It's better than Claymore's even bigger cock had ever been. Some guys just knew how to fuck better than others. Jason is one of those guys who fuck better, whether his cock does it alone or joins in the fun and games with another.

"That's the way to do it . . . yes . . . yes . . . stud . . . stud!" Jorge says, in one-hundred percent agreement — and then some — with Steven's evaluation of Jason's prowess. And, Jorge has fucked a helluva lot of asshole tandem not just Steven's, so he knows when he's really lucked out on a good time. To think that he'd almost balked when Steven had suggested Jason come along. Jorge, after all, more into blond blue-eyed surfer types.

For Jason, the fucking gets easier as it progresses. Cock and assholes adjust . . . adjust . . . adjust. Asshole suddenly seems as if it is designed specifically for these two dicks, the one dick sliding up and back . . . up and back . . . causing a pleasant friction-spawned heat along the belly of the other and against the wall of the asshole.

Oh, so quickly, they're all three fully engrossed in the fuck. Not much Jorge can do, pressed down beneath the combined weight of Steven and Jason, but enjoy. Steven able to do only a bit more than Jorge: a torquing of his pelvis, a flutter of his asshole. Jason leading the way. His cock the magic wand, the conductor's baton that says what happens and when, that determines how much pleasurable miracles are visited upon Jorge's cock-stroked cock and Steven's dual-cock fucked ass.

How quickly Jason is able to forget that he'd ever had doubts that what happens could happen. Steven's asshole is plenty large enough for the task. Jorge's cock no longer seems too huge to admit, even welcome, the company. Jason's cock seems more and more able to maneuver the tight confines provided for it. In no time, Jason's basic in-and-out strokes take on a certain sophistication that includes slight torques, varying degrees of penetration and withdrawal, fast pokes, combined with slow. Jason's fucking repertoire no longer is in any way inhibited by a role for which he no longer seems anything but ready-made.

Jason's ass sweats along its crack. His asshole hair is flattened by the sweat, as well as by the pressure exerted by each inward squeeze of asscheeks against it, as his cock slides again and again up Steven's asshole.

Jorge enjoys just lying there. It's an acceptable form of passiveness where cock up his ass still isn't. Not that cock up his ass will forever be out of bounds. Guys like Steven just seem to have too much fun, their asses on the receiving ends of hard cocks, for Jorge's curiosity not to get the best of him eventually.

In fact, lying on the bed, not much to do but bask in the increasing level of pleasure each slide of Jason's cock against his cock provides him, Jorge can't help wonder what it would be like to go belly-down on this very bed and invite Jason's white-man cock up Jorge's tight and virgin a-hole.

The fantasy-image of Jorge suddenly skewered by Jason's white-man cock flashes powerfully across Jorge's mind's-eye as Jason's cock, already having done wonderful things, conjures even greater sunbursts of pleasure within Jorge's groin.

Steven says his asshole has been elastic from the Day One, but Jorge isn't sure his own asshole is, or has ever been, elastic. He's experienced some bad times just passing extra-large turds. But, a cock can be lubricated, where a ...

"Oh, lovely fucking cock!" Jorge can't help but compliment. It is so lovely. It does so keep getting even lovelier. No doubt, now, from where the term love-stick. If ever there was a love-stick, Jason's cock is the love-stick. It's one wonderful ... wonderful ... stuck love-stick.

Jorge closes his eyes. Again, he pictures himself on his belly, Jason kneeling in the bed between Jorge's open legs. Jason's cock hard, ready, willing, and able to explore Indian stud's virgin asshole. Jorge actually inviting ...

"Yes. Yes. Yes!"

"Feels so ... so ... so good!" Steven says and increases Jorge's inclination to fantasize someday ... maybe not today BUT someday ... Jorge will experience cock up his butt is as wonderful . . . wonderful . . . wonderful . . . as Steven says . . . as Steven seems so truly to believe. Can Steven fake such sincerity? Jorge has been around long enough not to be fooled by any whore . . . male or female . . . pretending passion.

To enhance his accompanying get-fucked-up-his-own-butt imaginings, Jorge does something he's only very seldom done. It's the very something for which he'd so shortly before chastised Steven. His hand slides between the squash of his ass and the mattress. He snakes his fingers into the crease of his ass. He locates his asshole.

Yes, there was a noticeable increase in Jorge's pleasure by his having made simple fingertip contact with his pucker while his cock, up Steven's ass, is being sensuously massaged by the friction-heated belly of Jason's exquisitely pumping dick.

Will there be pleasure if Jorge just, for a moment, for just a little bit, pushes his fingertip in through his guarding pucker and . . . ?

"Ohhhhh!" Of course, there's pleasure! He knew there would be. Which is why he is so often disconcerted — yes, disconcerted — by guys like Steven, with poking cocks and fingers, who try to take advantage, especially blond surfer types like Steven. Although, up until only a few minutes ago, Jorge had no inkling he would ever imagine how it might be — how it could so easily be — to give himself over to someone dark-complexioned as Jason, especially when Jorge had almost rejected Jason for this threesome just because the stud was so dark-complexioned, having always assumed his own preference was unwaveringly for blonds.

How strange Jorge, collecting so many notches on his belt for sex with the blond and the beautiful should find himself, in the end, turned on so much by the mere fantasy of being screwed up his Indian ass by the big cock of a white man without a blond hair on his body.

Jorge makes his fantasy nigh on to complete by unmercifully jamming his finger deep . . . deeper . . . deepest . . . up his asshole. His fingertip collides with and butts against his prostate. Jorge's body proceeds into wave after wave of delicious shivers.

"Jason!" Jorge says with accompanying grunt.

"Jason!" Steven says with accompanying grunt.

"Fucking shit!" Jason says and fully buries his dick, one final time, into the space already pretty much filled.

Steven's fat pecker squirts a streamer of pearly slime that is so large and wet that it's touchdown, within the cupping jugular notch at the base of his throat, would have been readily audible if not so buried beneath the three-part harmony sung by the three studs caught so securely within the helplessly enjoyable web of their shared spermal-discharging ecstasy.

CHAPTER SEVEN

Talbot still dreams. His sleep-induced fantasies remain no-less wet-dream for having already played out in real life.

His erotic dreamland is so happening-right-now, as it has Kane and Talbot stepping out of the more public Spa hallway and into the comparative privacy of a small auditorium whose aisles slant away toward a small stage, it seems as real as did the real. Certainly, Talbot's in-dreaming anticipation of upcoming events is no less pleasurable than when it actually happened.

"Just out of curiosity," Kane says, "say you pull out your cock; although what with its obvious present state of stiffness in your pants, I'm not at all certain getting it out through an opening as small as your pants fly is at all possible. Say, I pull out my cock which, if it gets much harder in my pants, will no more likely come free than yours is likely to. Then what?"

Talbot wants to fuck Kane's studly ass. That's what Talbot really wants to do. Talbot has a mind's-eye flashback of Peter's boner turned loose inside Gerald's bung; at which time, Talbot's dick thereby stiffened to just about the tensile strength of steel.

Or, Talbot wants Kane to fuck Talbot's ass. Suddenly, something tells Talbot, as surely as he stumbled on Peter stuffing Gerald's asshole, that Kane knew all the ins and outs, ins and outs, ins and outs, of a good bum-fuck.

"Maybe, we could start off cockbelly to cockbelly, like the Greeks used to do," Talbot says. "You know, beat the two-head, two-neck monster we create, until the thing spits."

Kane's response is a half-ass grin and a fingers run-through of his black hair.

Talbot unzips his pants, but he knows that just unzipping isn't going to do the trick. Not with the boner the size of his. Getting his erection out through his fly requires the same miracle as the Biblical camel through the eye of a needle.

Talbot unfastens his belt and pops the top button of his trousers. His fly, releases along its total length, peels open in a sexy white V of his undershorts.

His hand fishes between his belly and his underwear waistband. His fingers slide the soft red down that fuzzes his lower belly. They proceed right along to the thicker, more wiry, wedge of wooly red hair that grows the thick roots of his dick.

His cock is swollen downward, along his left leg. His index finger hooks beneath the bow of his cockneck, between his cockbelly and his red-hair balls. He gives a tug. The circumcised head of his dick, securely wedged, up until then, into high relief between hugging denim and his leg, chafes as it slides a mere fraction of an inch out of entrapment.

He bends his legs slightly and finds it easier to dislodge the totality of his phallic meat while in that position. Even then, it isn't a task easily accomplished. Normally not much room for even his leg in his trouser leg, his dick has stiffened into all available space remaining, like a nail into a piece of pitchy wood.

Nonetheless, his efforts are rewarded, finally, by a whipping to attention of his cock that would have knocked silly anyone within striking distance.

"Jesus!" Kane says appreciatively.

To make the presentation of his cock even more impressive, Talbot drags down the waistband of his shorts and hooks it beneath his balls so his scrotum waterfalls the lip of the elastic. Kane has a look-see from the final drop of impressive nuts to the tiptop of heart-flared cockhead.

Talbot continually remains surprised by just how anxious he is for the security guard to drop his drawers in reciprocity. Less than an hour ago, the idea of Talbot seeing Peter, or Kane, any time soon, naked as a jay, seemed highly unlikely. Since which, Talbot has been turned on by Peter screwing Gerald's skin-and-bones ass, and he almost creams, then and there, as he waits in anticipation of what Kane will do next.

"Shall I put this Clydesdale back in its stable?" Talbot asks, referencing his cock. "Or, is your horsy coming out to play?"

"I can't believe any of this," Kane says with a slow shake of his head that shifts his black bangs this way and that.

Talbot isn't sure if Kane continues to marvel at the size of Talbot's cock, and the way Talbot talks dirty, or whether the security guard merely marvels at Talbot's moxie.

"Neigh!" Kane says.

At first, Talbot thinks Kane says, "Nay!", and Talbot is damned disappointed by the turnaround. Then, the Kane repeats, more drawn out, "Neee-iiiiggghhhh!", and Talbot gets the hint that the security guard's horse, in its stable, isn't going to be there much longer. Kane Clydesdale's Clydesdale is about to come on out for a romp with the other stallion presently on display.

Talbot wonders if he will be disappointed if Kane's cock isn't as impressive, unveiled, as it appears in the security guard's pressed uniform trousers? Talbot doesn't think so. It isn't — nor has it ever been — the prospect of enticing into view a big cock that has Talbot's juices flowing. It is merely the enticement of a fellow dick come on out to play that has Talbot so riled and excited. He wants to see Kane's prick — small, medium, or large — as much as he's ever wanted to see the equipment between the thighs of anyone.

Kane begins to undress. The removal of his shirt reveals just how well-muscled the security guard is. Kane's chest is not to be believed. Square pecs. Dime-size nipples. Serrated pectoral cleavage. Skin hairless, except for around his navel. His bellybutton more innie than outtie.

He unfastens the waistband of his pants. His trousers hang precariously from his narrow hips, and hold out so much illusion as to what might yet be revealed that Talbot actually trembles.

The flat of Kane's right hand runs the washboard plain of his belly. His palm over his navel, his fingertips dip beneath the material that clings to his hips like a survivor clings to the slippery slopes of a steep cliff.

"Come here," Kane says and gives a sexy beckoning jerk of his head. "In a bit closer."

Talbot's pants, more down than up, make Talbot waddle like a duck.

"Quack, quack!" Talbot says and is rewarded with one of Kane's most winning smiles.

Smiles, though, aren't the only reward Talbot is after. Not at that stage of the game.

"How did I get myself in this predicament?" Kane says. "One I told myself I'd never get into. Plenty of cock out there, in the big wide world, I tell myself. No need getting myself in any way involved with any cock belonging to a boss's son."

Talbot asks much the same questions. Why there? Why then? Peter's naked, hairy, and fuck-bouncing ass somehow the catalyst that opens an entirely new playing field?

Kane's pressed uniform trousers drop all of the way to the floor. Just like that. Up, one second. Down around his feet, the next second. So quick, Talbot is hardly aware they've slid. The swing of Kane's cock, from downward-jut to upward-thrust is a semi-circle blur that leaves prick weaving metronome-like in finale.

Jesus, lovely, fucking, dick! Not as big as Talbot's prick, but big nonetheless. Not circumcised as Talbot's cock, but nonetheless beautiful. With pulpy corona that not quite extends all of the way beyond the cowling prepuce. A mere bit of Kane's cockhead visible. Its coronal flaring, within its covering, gives the loose outer veneering of foreskin decided definition, like the outline of someone's head covered within the confines of a sleeping bag.

Two veins, like two blue Nile rivers, arise at the roots of Kane's cock, meander the belly of his dick, and meet up at the very lip of his loose-skin penile cowl.

His whole cock is a deep brown in color, in direct contrast to his background body which is golden, or possibly bronze. His pubic bush is not only curly but as black as the hair on his head.

He plays duck this time, without quack-quack sounds, and waddles, up close and personal, in nothing flat. There is nothing between his dick and Talbot's cock but a fraction of an inch of empty space.

Kane is the taller. Talbot hasn't noticed that before now, but he notices it now. If Talbot looks straight ahead, he sees Kane's Adam's apple, sexy as hell.

Kane touches Talbot who shudders.

"Cold?" Kane thinks it's absence of heat that is the matter.

In reality, Talbot burns. The spots of Talbot's skin, directly beneath the security guard's fingertips, are singed. Talbot begins to sweat. Moisture runs the crease of his ass, slides the jugular notch at the base of his throat, meanders through the hair of his crotch and within the hair beneath his arms.

Kane's hands slide over Talbot's arms, all of the way to Talbot's fingertips. Then, they slip around Talbot's ass.

"God, you are so dangerously seductive to this poor sucker who can't seem to pass up trouble when he sees it," Kane says. "Tell me you're not trouble just waiting to happen."

"I'm not trouble," Talbot says.

Kane squats slightly. The repositioning drops his balls to alignment in front of Talbot's nuts. The belly of the security guard's dick is up against the belly of Talbot's cock. The swing of the security guard's scrotum follows through. The security guard's scrotal hair mingles with Talbot's scrotal hair. The spongy flesh of Kane's scrotum contacts Talbot's scrotum.

"Sweet, sweet Jesus," Talbot says.

Kane double-hands Talbot's dick and his own, as if the two cocks are one and the same handle of a butter churn. His thumbs hook the back of his cock. His palms wrap the sides of their cocks. His fingertips almost, but not quite, touch across the back of Talbot's up-thrust erection.

His handholds pull upward.

"Lie down on the floor," Kane says.

"Here, you mean? In the aisle?" Talbot too much enjoys where they are to contemplate somewhere new.

"I'll do it," Kane says and frees their cocks. Talbot's dick feels like a bride deserted at the altar.

Kane slips out of his shoes and socks. He steps out of the pool his trousers make around his feet. Completely naked, he drops to the aisle and spreads out. His body tilts slightly downward toward the distant stage.

"All your blood is going to drain to your head," Talbot says, suddenly worried the sanguine tidal flow will drain Kane's cock and leave it less hard.

"No way my cock goes soft!"

Talbot slips out of his shoes. He steps out of his clothes.

"Bring that dick of yours right down to mine," Kane said. "One of your knees to each side of my thighs."

Talbot sits on him. Talbot's scrotum, although not as baggy as usual, manages to puddle Kane's compacting bag of nuts.

Kane's thumb hooks his own dick and pulls it to a position aimed straight toward the ceiling.

He doesn't have to curve his fingers for Talbot's dick. Talbot positions his own dick, belly-to-belly with the security guard's pecker. Though their adjoined pieces of jigsaw meat still aren't the same size, they seem a perfect fit.

"Feels good," Kane says in response to Talbot's automatic masturbation of their combined dicks.

Talbot likes the view. The way Kane's muscles still seem solid and well-etched, despite Kane's obviously relaxed position on the floor.

There's a defined line, a slight indentation really, that extends from the security guard's navel, through the washboarding of his abdominal plain, to his pectoral cleavage, through the serrated depression of his cleavage and to the jugular notch at the base of his neck. Kane's Adam's apple is emphasized by the way his chin is upthrust, his head positioned slightly laid back. His arm muscles bunch as he puts both of his hands to the space still available above Talbot's handholds on their erections.

"Pump for cream," Kane says. He increases their masturbatory rhythm.

Talbot feels pleasure. He can't believe he's there, doing what he's doing. How short a time since he spotted Peter's naked ass dimpled as his cock fucked Gerald's bag-of-bones ass!

"Oh," Kane says. "I can't tell you how many times I've dreamed of your dick squashed up tightly against mine."

Kane slowly and steadily increases the pumping momentum. He provides a slight torque on the upswings and on the down. The slight raising and lowering of his hips adds icing to the sexual cake.

Talbot wants it to last — forever. It was just that special, that unique, that gut-meltingly pleasurable. However, it is, in the end, its very specialness, its very uniqueness, its very pleasantness, which decides how short it will be.

"I'm going to come," Talbot says apologetically.

"Come ahead, buddy," Kane says.

"Oh, Jesus, fucking, yes!" Talbot says.

Kane's cock pulses its eruption so nearly the same time as Talbot's cock that it seems as if streamers of cream come from but one and the same double-coned volcano.

As their cocks explode, Kane manages a sitting position, beneath Talbot. The downhill slant of Kane's body causes the security guard's abdominals to crunch, as if he performs his sit-up on a Roman chair. He clamps one hand to each of Talbot's hips, for balance. He curves his spine to get his head all of the way to both their still cum-spitting dicks.

"Jesus, fuck!" Talbot literally screams as Kane's open mouth actually swallows Talbot's cockhead, then Kane's own.

It's almost too much pleasure for Talbot to endure.

"Oh, Kane! Kane!" Talbot screams.

*　*　*　*

Outside the tent, Jeffrey curiously turns to Marky.

"Kane?" Jeffrey asks, trying to put a name to the certain someone obviously so predominant in Talbot's ongoing, and very loud, wet dream.

Marky shrugs.

CHAPTER EIGHT

It's just after dawn when Jason leaves the seedy Florida motel room.

He feels good after a whole night of fucking and sucking.

He feels good with the twenty-five dollars from Steven added to the money in his pocket, plus the twenty-five bonus Jorge threw in for Jason's job obviously well done.

Both Jorge and Steven have asked Jason to stay on. Already the two are beginning a morning round of sex and games. Jason, though, has graciously declined their invitation, even when Jorge offered to put more money on the table. Jason professed an early-morning appointment that he just can't cancel.

The truth is that Jason still feels a certain something on the wind. At first, he thought, maybe, his roll in the hay with Jorge and Steven was it. But that wasn't it. Whatever is upcoming, though, he's more than willing to head on out and embrace it. As fun and lucrative as his life can be, as last night proves, he can't help thinking he is in some kind of rut from which he's destined, hopefully, soon to be extracted.

He sniffs the air and wonders if he might smell something floating on it. There are actually people who have been in Florida for a while who swear to God they can smell the four distinct seasons, feel them in their very bones to the point of having to pull out coats in official winter time. Apparently Jason just hasn't been in Florida long enough to distinguish such atmospheric subtleties, because it smells the same as any other day. It certainly feels like any other day. It even looks like any other day: a clear blue sky with indications of balmy temperatures. Pretty much always summer time, as far as Jason is concerned. Maybe, because he's from Colorado. Having really experienced the cold of that state — in winter and, sometimes, even in summer — Jason has a hard time attributing Florida's occasional winter dips to near freezing temperatures with anything but weird summer anomalies.

"It's bloody endless summer," he says to himself and stretches on the motel landing. "I don't care who tells me it's only spring."

The shortest way home is down Broadmore, a fairly busy thoroughfare, even at this time of the morning, then right on Kilpatrick Street to Jayne.

He spots the hitchhiker on Broadmore long before he reaches him. It doesn't exactly take genius IQ to tell someone with his thumb stuck up and out into the roadway is looking for a lift. Broadmore runs north and south and is a good street for anyone looking to head north, up the Florida panhandle, or south to Key West. A lot of the cars on Broadmore, at any one time, head for the north-south connects with Interstate 95, and someone Jason knows, Caneley Johnson, once made it all of the way north to Jacksonville in one hitch.

The hitcher whom Jason spots looks clean-cut compared to most Jason has seen. Many an on-the-move guy who thumbs this stretch of roadway wouldn't have got a lift from Jason on a bet. Undoubtedly, it's less easy to keep up appearances while on the road, but does anyone want in his car someone who looks and smells like he's just mud-wrestled a hog?

This guy has brown hair, a bit shaggy over his collar and ears. It's obvious he needs a haircut, but it's equally obvious he hasn't needed one for all that long. His hair bangs his forehead, and he tries to comb it back with his fingers as Jason approaches. Immediately, the shifted strands flop back. Not that the hitcher looks any the worst for having his hair almost into his eyes. Quite to the contrary.

His tan is the toasty kind, noticeably attractive even in the state of Florida which daily boasts millions of tans.

He wears a tight black T-shirt and tight blue-faded-to-light-blue jeans. Both his shirt and pants emphasize, to good advantage, his obviously well-chiseled body. He shows a nice basket that impressively plumps the crotch of his jeans. Helplessly, Jason can't help wonder if the guy's dick is circumcised, and if not, whether it would be more fun docking dick with it than with Jorge's big-cock foreskin.

"What's happening?" the guy says when Jason is almost to him. Jason expects him to follow up with a request for a cigarette or for some spare change. He doesn't ask for either.

Jason wonders if the guy really wants to know "what's happening". Like-wise, he wonders how the guy would react to hear Jason has just spent a hot and horny night of sucking and fucking.

The guy stands there. He smiles. He even lowers his thumb and out-stretched arm. He genuinely looks as if he expects Jason to respond with some-thing more than, "Not much happening at all!"

Jason fumbles for something to say that will come off less than complete-jerk.

A Mercedes pulls up to the curb. A window rolls down.

The hitcher turns his attention from Jason to the man in the driver's seat. When the hitcher squats and leans inward on the open car window, he displays an ass, in tight-fitting jeans, that's really one of the most muscled and compact butts Jason has ever seen.

Jason is surprised when the hitcher turns his head from the window, still maintaining his lean-to posture, and says, "Louis, here, wants to know where you're headed? Says he has plenty of room and is going as far as St. Augustine. Great for me, since I'm overdue at New Smyrna Beach to meet a buddy. Sound good to you?"

Jason is so confused, by this unexpected turn of events, he thinks he's being asked to comment on the hitcher's travel arrangements. It's only on second thought that Jason realizes the query has been a variation on the origi-nally asked, "What's happening?", as regards Jason's plans.

Does Jason say, "Tell Louis I'm headed home, but I'll be glad for the lift to save on shoe leather"? Or does he say . . . ?

Jason calculates how far north he can travel without being stranded in the middle of nowhere, no way to get home. He has some money in his pocket. These days a bus ticket to (or back from) just about anyplace in the mainland U.S. is dirt cheap. As a result of having worked part time a couple of weeks ago, driving part time for a pizza place, Jason's rent is pre-paid (for three months, no less), for the first time in ages.

Is this the beginning of that "certain something" he's been expecting to happen?

Jason figures he'd better pick a destination somewhere before New Smyrna Beach, where the hitcher is scheduled to get out. Jason has read too many things about what happens to unwary hitchhikers, these days, to embark upon any little adventure on his own. The way he figures, there's little chance of the driver pulling a fast one as long as there are two passengers on board.

"Titusville," Jason says, after realizing the hitcher eyes him strange-like. Maybe the hitcher figures Jason is a mute, or has a speech impediment, since Jason doesn't seem all that inclined to answer questions. "A ride that far would be great."

"Okay, then!" the hitcher says. He comes unbent long enough to offer Jason his hand. His handshake is firm. "Name's Tom, by the way."

"Mine's Jason."

"Well, Jason, this does seem to be our lucky morning," Tom says. He opens the car's back door.

Jason hopes Tom will scoot his studly body into the backseat next to Jason, but that's not how it goes. Tom shuts the door after Jason is in and opens the passenger door, in front. He climbs in beside the driver.

"Louis, this is Jason. Jason, Louis."

Louis turns back over the seat, by way of greeting. Jason gets his first really good look at the driver. Up until then, Jason has concentrated all of his attention on Tom.

Jason doesn't expect the nice-looking businessman-type, complete with white shirt unbuttoned at its collar, and loose-knotted tie, who sits behind the wheel. Louis has a full head of short-cropped black hair, combed back with no part. He has dark eyebrows, long dark eyelashes, dark eyes. He has a nose slightly upturned above lips that are neither so thin as to seem invisible, nor so thick as to appear rubbery. He has a very nice smile.

Jason expected an ape-man kind of guy, muscled enough and brave enough to pick up not one hitchhiker but two, while pretty sure he can handle the pair in any kind of nasty situation that might develop. Hitchers are some-times just as disreputable, if not more so, than the drivers who pick them up. No way ape-like, this driver must have a pair of balls big as they come or, maybe, merely possesses the daring-do gotten from a black belt in karate.

As soon as the three are off and headed down the roadway for the Inter-state-95-north connect, Jason's mind does a better-late-than-never wig-out. Maybe Tom is a decoy used to con just some know-nothing like Jason. Tom and Louis in cahoots. Rapists, killers. Perverts from the word go. Spiders entrapping this naive and careless fly. To do just what with and to him?

In less than four months, five women have been found dead on Interstate 95, between Miami and Jacksonville. Suspected hitchhikers every one. All the victims of "The Australian Serial Killer", so labeled by the press because his first and third victims were found just outside of Melbourne, Florida. Sexually assaulted. Mutilated. Garroted. Never any sign of a struggle.

Okay, neither Tom nor Louis looks like a serial killer. But who says serial killers have to look like serial killers? Quite the opposite, according to one local police chief who was on television less than a week before. Okay, Jason isn't a woman. Who says serial killers don't kill guys? What better way to have Jason let down his guard, and get Jason on board, than give him the illusion that he can rely on a fellow hitchhiker in the car with him?

Does Jason test his macabre theory by insisting Louis pull over, right then and there, and let Jason out? No. He rationalizes that if Caneley Johnson made it all of the way to Jacksonville, without ending up dead in some ditch, then Jason can safely make it as far as Titusville.

He convinces himself that he will keep constant watch for anything funny, either from Tom or from Louis, or from both. So firm is his resolve that he's scared shitless when he realizes he's fallen to fucking sleep, rocked by the motion of the car, Tom saying something to wake him.

"What?" is Jason's response. Not "what?" to whatever it is Tom has said, but to whatever has possessed Jason to swear himself an oath of constant vigilance and then throw caution to the wind by drifting off into never-never land.

"Louis thinks it would be nice if I unzip his pants and give him a blow-job," Tom says. His arm is over the back of the front seat, and he is turned in Jason's direction. He wears a what-about-that-? smile that makes him all the more handsome.

"While he's driving?" Jason says. His major concern is how Louis's driving might be affected by Tom's head bouncing over Louis's hard dick.

"I've a lot of practice on this stretch of the road," Louis says and locks eyes with Jason in the rearview mirror. "I drive this route all the time. Know it like the back of my hand. Pick up guys all of the time who don't mind doing a little something for the ride. Never lost control of my car yet. Neither of you likely to tell I'm shooting off, except for whomever gets the mouthful of my cum at the time."

"You think Jason and I are queer, Louis?" Tom asks but manages not to come off threatening.

"The blow-job is just a suggestion," Louis says. "You insulted by the idea, just say no. Do I look like someone who's going to force either of you into something you don't want to do?"

"I don't know, Louis," Tom says. "You look like you've a pretty well-muscled body underneath those businessman clothes. I thought from the very beginning, when I leaned my head into the car to take a good look at who was driving, that you looked pretty damned studly. Jason, you think Louis is muscled enough to take on the two of us if we're insulted by his proposal that I give him a suck?"

"Whether you suck my dick or not, I give you the ride," Louis says. If he sounds as if he considers anything Tom says as a threat, it's not indicated in the tone of his voice. "It's just a little something to pass the time. Kind of like, what's the harm in Jason pulling out his dick, and giving it a good whack, while my cock gets mouthed by his buddy to hearty climax?"

"You've been at this long enough, Louis, have you, that you can pretty much read the guys you stop to pick up?" Tom asks.

"Pretty much, yes," Louis admits.

"Sixth-sense, right? Something you just feel inside you? You're not telling me that Jason and I look like a couple of queers, are you?"

"Damned silly question, if either of you butch numbers looked in the mirror, any time, lately," Louis says.

"'Cause Jason doesn't look at all queer to me, Louis. You see something there, you feel something there, with that sixth sense of yours, that I don't?"

"All I do is ask the fun-and-games question," Louis says. "One or both of you say no, that's where it ends. I'm not so horny that I can't wait for someone more agreeable."

"Well I have to admit that I, too, have been wondering just what Jason has in his pants that makes such a damned big bulge," Tom says. "I wouldn't be above a quick look-see at whatever the studly dick Jason sports in the backseat before my head goes a-burrowing over Louis's crotch, up here. What do you say, Jason?"

Tom laughs. He has a nice laugh. It comes down from deep down, like a loud purr.

"Cat got your tongue, Jason?" Tom asks.

"Come on, Jason, let us see your cock," Louis coaxes.

"Yeah," Tom agrees.

The two have ganged up to see if they can get Jason's dick out of his pants. Once again, Jason ponders the conspiracy theory. Louis and Tom prowling the streets looking for guys, just as stupid as Jason, to get in the car with them.

"Then again, if you don't want to, just say no," Louis says. "No one ever does anything in my car that he's not a mind to."

"Right!" Tom says. "I wasn't saying you had to pull your dick out, Jason. I was just saying that I'd be mighty happy to have a look at it. I mean, once I'm down over Louis's stiff dick, well . . . if I don't see your dick now, God only knows when I'll get a look, unless you oblige by leaving it out of your pants after I've finished sucking off Louis's pecker."

Suddenly, it's no longer a question of if Tom will go down over Louis's cock, but whether he'll do it before or after he has a look at Jason's dick.

Jason is only recently from a three-way, and here are two new guys asking him to pull out his cock so they can see it. Louis maybe watching while Jason plays an already overworked dick to explosion? Neither Louis nor Tom suggest Jason play train-in-the-tunnel with either of their pricks. So, if what they're asking is, in fact, all they're asking . . .

He unzips his trousers.

"Yes!" Tom says.

In the rearview mirror, Louis licks his lips.

So . . .

Jason reaches in through his open fly and hauls out his dick and balls. Despite what his dick has been through the previous evening, it isn't soft. It isn't as stiff as it can be, but it's engorged with enough blood so that, when it slips out, it presents an impressive package.

There's enough natural lighting to provide ample viewing.

"Jesus, look at the size of Jason's horse-like balls!" Tom says.

Jason's scrotum isn't as sagged as it can be. It has contracted. Though, not to the point that prevents its impressive cascade over the lip of his open fly. His sac pools the soft and expensive leather of the car seat between his thighs.

"Pull down the central armrest, Jason," Louis says. "Sit on it."

Jason pulls down the backseat's central armrest and lifts his ass to straddle it. Which elevates him to where he has to bend his head to keep it from banging the roof.

He's concerned that his elevated position makes him, his cock, and his balls, readily accessible viewing for any Peeping-Tom in any car passed or passing.

Louis reads his mind. "The windows are tinted. No one sees in."

To believe or not to believe!?

Suddenly, Jason sees his cock and balls in the rearview mirror, just as clearly as Louis sees them.

"Goddamn!" Louis says. "How lucky you are, Jason, to have good looks, giant cock, and Titan balls!"

"Like what you see, Louis?" Tom asks. "I certainly do."

"Love it," Louis says. "Makes me hot. Makes my dick stiff."

"Stiff dick to the rear of me, stiff dick to the side of me," Tom says. "Stiff dick in my pants. Goddamn, this is my lucky morning!"

"Play with your dick, Jason," Louis says. "Can you do that for me while Tom goes down so deep over my cock that his nose snorts my pubic hair?"

"Sure," Jason says.

Jason's hand strokes his dick in the bumpy ride provided by the glide of his fist over and along his knobby cockhead.

"Mace-head dick: that's what you've between your legs, Jason," Louis says. "I didn't see anything as impressive in the armory at Windsor Castle."

"Visiting the queen, were you?" Tom asks. "And, here I thought you preferred us butch."

"The more butch the better," Louis says. "You and Jason the most butch and the best."

"You going to let me unzip you and let me free your dragon, so I can play St. George and have at it?" Tom asks the driver.

"Just be careful as you fish the monster out," Louis says. "It's hard as glass and just as likely to shatter."

"Never fear, Louis," Tom says. "I've manhandled my share of stiff dick, and I've yet to break one."

Tom's handsome face disappears behind the front seat. Jason watches Tom's torso bend in on Louis's crotch.

"Pecker, pecker, where's the pecker?" Tom says.

Tom's fingers expertly work the zipper of Louis's pants.

"Not a speck of underwear, by the looks of it," Tom keeps up his running commentary. "Almost as if Louis expected us for these fun and games, Jason. Were you expecting us, Louis?"

"Actually, I just lucked out," Louis says.

"I'll just hook my index finger into the breach, and slide it around the far side of your sizable erection, Louis."

"Ohhhh, easy. Please easy," Louis says.

"Pecker, pecker, here comes the . . ."

"Jesus, careful!" Louis says as Tom succeeds in popping Louis's sizable cock from the man's open trouser fly.

From where Jason sits, astride the armrest, he imagines, rather than sees, the boner Tom released.

"Nicely streamlined cock," Tom says. "Nicely circumcised. Neither webbed nor discolored by scarring. Not a vein in sight. Just a wide expanse of golden cockbelly, golden cockback, golden cocksides, golden cockhead, golden cockroots. Just call me Midas, hungry for this man's gold."

"Ahhhhh, yes," Louis says. "You do know how to do it, don't you, you stud bastard? Just . . . like . . . that . . . all of the way down . . . down . . . down . . . Jesus, down . . . to my . . . ohhhhh, yes . . . all of the way down."

No denying, Jason wants to hop the front seat for a better look. He wants to see just how Tom manages swallowing Louis's cock in such a way as to provide Louis so much pleasure.

"All of the way down, and not even one gag," Louis compliments. "Tom does know how to suck cock, Jason. And you, Jason, do know how to beat your sweet willy to climax, don't you? That is what you're doing for me, right, Jason? Beat your knobby-head dick so it'll cream your fingers just as my big cock creams the back of Tom's sucking throat?"

"Yes," Jason says, although he doubts he can coordinate any explosion of his having-already-exploded-all-night dick to match up with Louis's eruption. Jason does, though, feel the swelling of pleasure inside of him, on the increase. Faster than if he were beating his cock in the privacy of his own bedroom.

"Tom's taut lips glide my prick, Jason," Louis says. "Feeling oh-so-good . . . oh-so-very-very-good. Tell me how your hand feels gliding the stiffness of your young and sexy boy-dick."

"Feels good," Jason says.

"Has to be more than just 'good', though, doesn't it, Jason?" Louis persists. "This is different than just pulling out your pud and whipping it to climax on your own. After all, here I am, just a car seat away, getting my dick blown. After all, here's Tom, just as close to you as I am, giving me head. Two of us in the front seat, locked cock to mouth, mouth to cock. You in the backseat, beating your stiff erection. When was the last time, if ever, you found yourself choking your monkey in the backseat of a fast-moving car while two handsome studs went at it in the front seat?"

"Not lately," Jason admits. Although, he feels like telling Louis to ask when was the last time Jason docked his circumcised dick with an Indian's foreskin. Because, Jason has recently had his pecker playing snake so deeply up Jorge's gopher hole that it had looked as if the Indian and Jason were Siamese twins forced to share the same connecting erection for time and eternity.

"Your steely cock," Louis says. "Your skyscraper cock. Your too-thick-for-your-fist cock. Getting whipped like sixty by your stud-fist. Getting beaten like crazy by . . . sexy . . . sexy . . . cock-pumping sonofabitch'n . . . sexy . . . bastard . . . stud."

"Oooooh, feels good," Jason says and strokes the neck of his cock even harder and faster. "Make it feel better for me, Louis, by telling me how your dick feels inside Tom's sucking mouth and throat."

"Warm," Louis says. "Wet. Hugged. Petted. Tongue-whipped. Cheek-fluttered. Stretched. Massaged. Eaten. Chewed. Swallowed whole."

"Mmmmmmmmmmmm," Tom says, his face buried all of the way over Louis's stiff erection.

"Vibrated," Louis says.

"Mmmmmmmmmmmmmm," Tom repeats.

"Played like an oboe," Louis says. "Blown like a trumpet."

Tom rears his ass skyward as his face dives yet again over Louis's prick. He presents wondrous viewing of just how his buttocks well-fits the seat of his jeans to stretch-denim capacity. Jason can tell just exactly where Tom's nearest buttcheek dimples then undimples beneath the material as Tom moves his sucking of Louis's cock into even higher gear.

Jason matches the piston-like pumps of Tom's head, over Louis's cock, with fist-pumps of his own dick.

For a moment, there's seemingly nothing, by way of sounds, in the car, but the sounds of sex in progress: Tom slobbers over the dick he services; Louis helplessly grunts; Jason gasps as he gets nearer and nearer orgasm and hopes to hold off just a . . . little . . . while . . . longer.

Jason's resolution to ride the cresting wave to his climax, at least as far as Louis rides his, isn't helped by his sudden fantasy of Tom's head, instead of Jason's hand, over Jason's dick.

"Eat cock! Eat cock! Eat cock!" Jason commands.

"Yes . . . yes . . . yes," Louis agrees. Wrongly, he assumes Jason means Tom's face over Louis's stiff dick, when Jason means Tom's phantom face over Jason's cum-primed erection.

Jason's nuts are thoroughly vacuum-packed within his shrinking scrotum. His black-fuzz scrotal skin nets his nuts and hoists them to where Jason's balls become lost inside his lower belly. Those nuts are plump with creamy cum no longer capable of containment. Whatever sperm raced from his dick, when his snake blasted to fill Jorge's gopher hole, as completely as any whipped cream ever filled the barrel of a puff pastry, and whatever was shot after, during the course of that motel-room three-way, all of that runoff is long-since replaced by fresh cum.

"Fucking . . . creaming . . . load!" Jason bellows in description of the magmatic mess of jism suddenly set loose from the inadequate containment his balls have become. "Blasting . . . blasting . . . Jesus . . . blasting . . . cum . . . sweet-Jesus . . . cum!"

The first rocket of Jason's coagulated cream is airborne as far as the top of the front seat. When it lands with a resounding splat, some of it drools the front of the front seat, some the back.

His next few spermal comets splatter the back of the front seat, like exploding galaxies splatter the inkiness of night sky.

All that remains is a tardy lava-like flow that oozes from his cockhead and smears his fingers with goo.

Tom comes to a full kneel on the front seat and turns in Jason's direction so swiftly that he takes Jason completely off-guard. Tom's mouth is wet from Louis's spent cum.

"Give me your hand," Tom says.

Jason hesitates.

"The one with the spermal icing all over its fingers," Tom says.

Tom reaches over the seat. He takes hold of Jason's wrist. He gives the tug that pulls Jason's fingers free of his dick. Tom's tongue, when it snakes out, licks Jason's sticky palm.

"Jesus!" Jason says. He doesn't know why he finds it so strange that someone who has swallowed Louis's load of cum, has no qualms about sampling Jason's stale spunk. Certainly, he doesn't know why he finds the rasp of Tom's tongue against palm so goddamned sexy.

Tom turns Jason's still-curled fingers over and licks their knuckles free of clinging cream.

"Open your fingers, one at a time," Tom says.

"Come on, Jason," Louis says.

Jason has forgotten Louis. He's surprised to find Louis not only there but knowing what goes on.

Jason thanks God the car, with all of them in it, remains on the road, no worse for Louis having blasted his wad. The possible consequences from Louis having orgasmed as the car barreled down the highway could have been fatal. That Jason had been so far gone, the moment of his own ejaculation, not caring whether or not the car skidded off the road, is scary in aftermath.

Tom isolates Jason's index finger from the rest of the stud's fingers, sucks Jason's it all of the way to its second knuckle. When his face comes back up, his tongue continually wraps and unwraps his mouthful. He leaves Jason's finger wet with spit, all of Jason's stale cum thoroughly dissolved and washed from it. Jason surrenders his fuck-finger, which Tom similarly sucks and cleans without the slightest hint of a gag. There's something sexy about the suction Tom provides Jason's fingers. Whether it's the sexiness, alone, or whether Tom sucking fingers is merely part of the totally unique package, Jason's cock remains stiff.

Tom licks the back of Jason's hand and sucks thumb. Finished, he pushes Jason's hand to one side and snakes partially over the front seat. Tom's hands, one to each of Jason's thighs, push Jason's thighs wider. Tom's head butts Jason's chest, then slides Jason's belly.

Jason is pushed back in such a way that, in combination with the downward pressure Tom exerts to his thighs, his hips slide forward and his crotch elevates slightly.

Tom's mouth opens over Jason's cock and swallows stiff prick all of the way to cock's balls.

"Grrrunnghhhh!" Tom growls over his mouthful.

For Jason, the pleasure of this unexpected moment is made excruciatingly intense by so complete and so thorough an engulfing of his cock by Tom's face . . . by the gumming of Tom's taut lips around the base of Jason's dick . . . by the fluttering of Tom's cheeks against the entire length of Jason's erection.

Jason's guts erupt an orgasm more spontaneous than any he's known. It comes very close to being more painful than pleasurable. The reflexive cum-pumping mechanism activated inside him has so very little cum left to siphon from his already cum-depleted balls. The vacuum formed within each of his nuts seems on the verge of imploding his gonads with the same intensity of dying stars collapsing upon themselves.

"Ahhhhh . . . ahhhhh . . . . ahhhhh," Jason says, his hands on Tom's head.

With one final suck that completely drains Jason's cock and balls of whatever cum remains, Tom slides his head back up the length of prick. His lips release cockhead with a resounding, "Pop!"

His hands still anchor hard and fast on Jason's thighs. His lower body still hangs the front seat. He lifts his handsome face to look Jason directly in the pleasure-dilated eyes.

"Goddamn, but I do love the taste of stud cock and cum," he says with a very wide and mischievous smile.

CHAPTER NINE

Something wakes Marky.

It's morning. Soon-to-be-summer sun filters through the surrounding trees and turns the tent canvas opaque.

The wind? Not the wind. Waves? Ocean sounds are usually more muted, on this side of the bluff, in among these trees. The acoustics of the place, though, are hinky, so sometimes . . .

Yes, ocean waves. Marky is sure of it.

"What?" Jeffrey asks sleepily from beside Marky.

On the other side of Jeffrey, Talbot softly moans something undecipherable.

"Waves," Marky says. "Sounds like big ones. Want to take a look?"

"Want to sleep," Jeffrey says.

"Wear you out last night, did we?" Marky says.

The three had fucked and sucked up a storm.

"Need to piss," Marky says and scoots out from under the covers.

"Take one for me," Jeffrey says.

Talbot moans another something.

Marky takes his clothes into the sunshine that makes it through the canopy of surrounding trees. It's surprisingly warm. He stands naked in the sun. His have-to-piss hard dick sticks out in front of him. The sunshine is a sexy caress. Warm. Toasty. Intimate. Had Marky lived in pagan times, he would have been a sun-worshiper.

He wants to stand there longer, but he isn't kidding when he says he has to piss. He sits on a log along one side of the gutted camp fire, but only long enough to pull on his socks. Only long enough to put on his boots, but he leaves them untied.

He takes one of the pathways into the woods. In anticipation, his cock loses much of its hardness. By the time he stops in the underbrush, his cock flaps against his leg.

He pisses, long and hard. His release of urine is almost sexual. He enjoys every squirting drop, most of which he aims at the gnarly trunk of a tree.

Not even the splash of his piss, though, masks the continuing rumble of waves on the other side of the rise. He steps out of his boots long enough to slip on his shorts. He doesn't bother donning his T-shirt. He pokes part of it in his front pocket and lets the rest hang down his leg. He steps back into his boots and squats to lace them, then heads uphill through the trees.

The beach that greets him, on the other side, down the cliff, is unique for two reasons. One, the size of the waves that crash on the shore beneath a totally cloudless sky. Two, the surfers who were there the night before have obviously struck their tent and left before the sizable waves commenced. What a fucking missed opportunity for someone really into big waves!

The curls aren't as large as the ones Marky saw at North Beach in Hawaii, but they're certainly as big as any waves he's seen here . . . at this time of year.

He's proved wrong in his assumption that all surfers prematurely left the area, in that there's a sudden movement on the water, just beyond the surf break line. One lone figure, on one lone surfboard, expertly maneuvers to catch a particularly nice wave. The surfer stands on his board and begins a long and graceful diagonal slide across the belly of the curl.

It's a long ride. It's a graceful ride. No glitches. No falls. No early ending. No erratic cresting of the wave. The slide that began out to sea ends almost on the beach.

Immediately, the surfer turns his board back toward the incoming water and paddles out.

It's hard for Marky to distinguish much of anything about the surfer from the distance, except generalities. The guy obviously is a good surfer. The guy obviously is dark-complexioned. Black hair without a trace of sun- or peroxide-bleaching. Well-tanned. Well-muscled. Wearing not the typical baggy shorts of a U.S. surfer but European bikini briefs.

Marky heads down the steep seaside cliff that separates him from the sand and the sea and the surfer. Whether a remnant of the wave-causing storm at sea, or something that merely hitched a ride later on, a breeze stirs Marky's blond hair. It's not a cold breeze, but it's cool enough to keep Marky from sweating on his none-too-easy descent to sea level.

By the time Marky reaches bottom, the surfer has ridden two more waves and is headed out to catch a third. All his rides have been as skillful, and as graceful, as the first. All have taken him from beyond the surf break line almost to shore. The last time in, the guy was close enough so Marky could tell he's genuinely attractive. A flash of sunlight even revealed, in a quick moment, the guy's blue eyes.

Marky chooses a convenient spot, close to where the final splash of the waves runs the sand. He sits and watches as the surfer, once again, catches a wave and heads toward shore.

There's something magical about the warmth of the morning. About the cloudless sky. About the cool but not cold breeze. About the loud sounds of the large waves splashing the shoreline. About the white sand. About the beach deserted, except for Marky. About the water deserted, except for the lone surfer who gracefully stands his board and glides nearer and nearer.

The surfer rides all of the way onto dry sand. He's only a few yards from Marky.

He's older than Marky but only by a few years. He has a square jaw line. He has a dimple in his right cheek. He has a cleft in his chin that's really more of a thin etch. His body is to die for. His square pectorals, his washboarded belly, his muscled legs, his sensuous back, are all a sun-golden brown.

The crotch of his bikini swim wear provides telltale cock-and-balls lumps.

"Damned bitch'n waves!" the surfer says. He has an accent. French. "Where's your board?"

"Those babies are way too big for me," Marky says. He's not ashamed to admit it. Most surfers appreciate someone who knows his limits. Someone who doesn't know them is likely only to get in the way.

"I should have brought a wet suit," the surfer says, admitting limitations of his own. "If I don't sit out a few waves, I'll freeze my you-know-what off."

"And, wouldn't that be a crying shame," says Marky and means it.

Damn studly ass the surfer has. Solid muscle that burrows a place for itself in the sand next to where Marky sits the beach.

"André," the surfer says and extends a large hand. "From France."

His grip is firm and holds far longer than Marky expects but not nearly as long as Marky would like.

"We don't get waves this big in France. Not that I've ever seen."

"We don't usually get them this big, here, this time of year," Marky says. "Must have come a long way, or more surfers would know about them and would have shown up to take advantage."

"Ohhhh," André says, shifts position, and manhandles the lumps his cock and balls make in his swim-suit crotch. "Excuse, please, but this all gives me a very big hard-on. My friend says, 'Take my surfboard, André. See Baja for a few days on your own. But, you'll find bigger waves in the bathtub.' Ha!"

Marky, too, has a hard-on, but it isn't to do with any thing more, nor less, than the studly Frenchman immediately adjacent him on the sand.

"Water should be cold enough to shrink my dicky to disappearance, yes?" André says.

Marky hears him clearly. A weirdness of acoustics makes it possible to hear over the roar of the waves.

"My dicky, he gets this cold, he usually disappears," André says.

Marky thinks the Frenchman exaggerates. What Marky sees evidence of, in the man's swim-suit crotch, doesn't look easily disappeared, with or without benefit of cold water.

"Something in the water, do you think?" André says. "Something on the shore, maybe?"

"Maybe," Marky says.

"Big-cock American, maybe?"

Marky feigns looking, this way and that, as if in search of a recently arrived big-cock American.

André laughs.

"Such talk doesn't scare you?" André says.

"Such cock doesn't scare me," Marky says.

Again, André laughs. His blue eyes sparkle.

"Can it be?" André says. "Not only waves to die for, but . . . ?"

"I'm the life-saver here to see you don't lose your dicky-boner to the cold," Marky says.

André's cock is so hard, there's little left to the imagination. It's aimed upward and pointed toward André's left hip. It's possible for Marky to determine, even through swim-suit material, at least one large vein that runs the Frenchman's cockbelly.

"I think I must dream this, yes?" André says.

"Let's make it a wet dream, then" Marky says, "starting off by getting you out of that swimsuit."

André doesn't wait more than a fraction of a second before he hooks the waistband of his swimming trunks and peels them off.

"If your dicky has been in any way shrunk by the cold water, I can hardly imagine how big it must be when it's normal," Marky says appreciatively.

André's cock is uncircumcised. Its hard core shoots through the open end of his foreskin, like a wrist shoots through the cuff of a suit coat. It's a long cock: possibly close to ten inches. It's a thick cock: unlikely to allow Marky to close his fist around it. It's a cock latticed with veins, some delicate, some large and well-delineated. It's a cock with a pisshole that is more drilled than slashed. Closed as the hole now is, it seems more a slight scar on the head of the dick than it does a bona-fide exit for piss and cum.

André's balls are perfect accompaniments. They're large and furry. They droop so far between his thighs that a good inch of their hang becomes as sand-covered as the muscular globes of his now naked ass.

Marky moves in for a far better look. He crawls right in between André's legs and pushes them farther open as he goes. He bows his head down real close. André smells of sea, of wind, of sun.

Unable to prevent himself, Marky licks the head of André's cock. The thick and long dick tastes of the ocean and all the briny things that live therein. It's a nice taste, a refreshing taste, a give-me-more taste that impels Marky not only to give another lick of the fat cockhead but to oval his lips around it and slide on down a good six of the available ten inches.

"Oh, *mon dieu*!" André moans. "I do so love America!"

Marky decides he genuinely likes Frenchman and Frenchman's cock.

"I do so love American dicky," André says. "No reason you can't give me yours, at this one and the same time, yes?"

The only reason Marky can think of is that he is enjoying his partial suck of the Frenchman's cock too much to go to the bother of changing position. Though, as it turns out, André takes the decision away from him.

"I've got to have at your dicky!" André says. He slides out from under Marky. "I want to see and eat it, just as much as I want you to finish eating my dicky."

Having been deprived of André's thick nice-tasting boner, Marky figures he can now spare whatever the extra time necessary to drop his drawers before getting back to French gourmet dining. He helps André's decidedly clumsy efforts to get Marky stripped and, in no time, Marky is as naked as the Frenchman.

"Beau! Beau!" André says.

Marky hasn't taken French in school but thinks André calls Marky's revealed big dick Bo-Bo (the Clown?).

"Beautiful! Beautiful!" André provides translation and makes Marky feel a little ridiculous in thinking, even for a moment, that André names cocks as some guys name their cars.

Nor has André been kidding when he says he wants to have at Marky's cock. He is so quick in gobbling up most of it that Marky is taken back by the swiftness which leaves his own mouth still not returned to the Frenchman's thickly luscious penis.

Marky moves quickly to reclaim the prize all of this shifting and stripping on the beach has kept from him. If the sand is a tad inconvenient, in its tendency to stick to even dry skin, Marky pays no mind. He zeros in on André's thick prick that's eagerly waiting. Although, he only just manages to regain the initial lost six inches of the Frenchman's dick when André's sucking face gums Marky's cockroots where impressive prick grows thickly from a bush of platinum crotch hair.

Some sex just isn't destined to go slow and easy. This is that kind of sex. The two simply become animals obsessed with enjoying a pure, unadulterated rut. Forgotten is the soon-to-be-summer sun, the sand, the glory of the morning, the crashing waves that get more large and impressive by the moment. André is no longer a surfer out to ride the biggest wave. He's a cocksucker, pure and simple, out to ride the biggest dick, besides his, on the beach. He's hungry for it. He's starved for it. He has to have it. He'd eat more of it, if only there were more. His hot and heavy suctioning claims even that portion of Marky's cockshaft usually hidden beneath Marky's muscled belly. So great is the vacuum, Marky is momentarily afraid his dick will uproot and slide André's throat like a sled slides a luge run.

Marky is driven to give tit for tat. Braving a choke on the mouthful the Frenchman's cock offers, Marky dives on down. His gumming lips reach bottom and press deep into the bushy nest of black-black pubic hair. His mouth borrows deeper, pushing inward on André's lower belly and gaining whatever additional cockshaft is found there.

Still buried all of the way over Marky's prick, André manhandles Marky goes to supine on the sand as André, in a kneel, straddles.

Marky's hands hard-clamp the aimed-skyward spheres of André's butt. The Frenchman's rear is so well-muscled that Marky's fingers barely make an indent as they hold for dear life to keep Marky's face elevated upward and deep into the overhanging crotch of the cock-feeding Frenchman.

Each starves for the other's dick and for the meal of thick cream that dick can offer. For this time around, the most pleasure is seen to be gained from feeding on cream, not on doing the feeding. Therefore, Marky is less concerned with how far André sucks cock toward climax than in how close André's fat and long cock is sucked toward spurting cum that Marky can swallow, drink, guzzle and enjoy. André hardly cares how close this big-cock American has sucked French-cock toward ejaculation — he's too intent upon siphoning squirts of creamy breakfast destined to be fed him through the large and tasty phallic straw sucked deeply into his face.

The two progress into frantic bouncing of faces over cocks.

On each slide up André's thick prick to massive cockroots, Marky's nose pokes all of the way beneath the Frenchman's scrotum which has compacted to baseball-size. So far up does Marky go on each gulp of the Frenchman's stiff dick, that Marky's nose contacts the crack of André's ass. Had ass not been so recently, and for so long, submerged in seawater, it would provide musky aromas instead of the sea smells that meet him on each and every head-lift into the overhang. Marky has a good view of the asscrack, but he closes his eyes to avoid the sand that constantly dislodges from André's butt and drifts the beach like carnival glitter.

André can't believe his wonderful luck. Of the spectacular waves and Marky with the big cock, he considers himself more lucky to have at the latter. There is nothing — NOTHING — André finds comparable to dining on dicky. That this dicky is big and fat and tasty and belongs to a studly American blond is just a bonus. André will always be a cocksucker before he's a surfer. He'll always get more jollies off by going down on stiff prick than by going down on the glassy face of some wave. He craves the taste of spunk, where swallowing seawater sometimes makes him puke.

Wet-wave sounds are replaced by wet-sex sounds. André and Marky's world narrows even farther as each concentrates more and more on coaxing thick, rich cream from the spit-soaked prick of the other.

André's hands scoop between Marky's ass and the sand. His handholds pull up on Marky's hips each time the Frenchman's face dives the long length of that dick. Each time André's face slides up the phallic totem, Marky's hips fall more firmly back against the man's cupping hands and the underlying sand.

Simultaneously, the two go on automatic pilot. Each has coaxed the other so close to the brink of orgasm that the resulting pleasure is self-evident, even above the continuing need to have at the other's cum.

Marky still maintains his handholds of André's overhanging body but slides one of this hands so that his fingertips contact the opening to the Frenchman's hair-haloed rectum. Marky thinks that if he can poke but a portion of one finger into the hole maybe that will trigger the eruption of cum Marky is so hungry to eat. He's right.

"Aggghrrrunngh!" André groans over his mouthful. His lower body collapses, and his exploding cock nails Marky's feeding head to the sand.

It's the vibrations of the Frenchman's ecstatic groans that provide the hair trigger that detonates the barrier holding Marky's cream securely locked within his balls.

Their sex becomes a feeding and being-fed frenzy. On the beach. The sun overhead. The wave-curled ocean stretched to the horizon. The cliff abutted to the landward side. Seagulls spiraling in wide circles in the blue-blue soon-to-be-summer sky above.

The more cream they're fed, the more they want. Even as each prick squirts the last of its meal, André and Marky suck for even more. So greedy are they, their nuts are drained of each and every drop of available cream. Even the usually stray drools of semen, left inside the shafts of erupted dicks, aren't left behind this time. Even when the boners are as clear of cum as any gun barrel reamed and cleaned and polished after firing, the cocks are sucked with destined-to-failure hopes for even more.

CHAPTER TEN

Nothing wakes Talbot! Not even Jeffrey's loud, "For Christ's sake, come on out of wet-dreamland for some real cock!"

Talbot simply enjoys where he is too much, at the moment, to be summoned back to reality, even by sexy Jeffrey. Lately, he has a whole repertoire of sexy wet-dream potential, straight from his real life, which oblige by replaying almost — if he's lucky — nightly.

In this one, Talbot feigns a stomach ache at the end of gym class. Just as he had feigned a stomach ache at the end of one gym class in real life . . .

He heads for the can. No way he pulls down his jockstrap and has everyone point fingers and spread the mistaken word that his Peter-Gerald-produced boner results from close quarters with his male classmates in the school shower room.

He whips his dick to creaming in the can, helped along by remembrances of Peter fucking Gerald's ass, not to mention of Kane and Talbot "doing their thing" on that Spa's auditorium floor.

When done, he's surprised to find Gerald waiting outside the stall.

"You okay?" Gerald asks. "Some of the guys said you have a belly ache."

Someone really should tell Gerald to eat more. It isn't like his parents are on welfare.

"I'm fine," Talbot says. Possibly, he should lecture Gerald on the definite advantages of a good plate of steak, mashed potatoes, gravy, and calorie-ridden biscuits. Rabbits must get more to eat than run-his-marathons Gerald.

Gerald accompanies Talbot to the bench in front of Talbot's locker. He sits when Talbot sat. Since Talbot's cum-depleted cock isn't swollen even a bit from Gerald's presence, Talbot is convinced his successful beating of it, in the can, combined with Gerald's skinniness being such a turn-off, won't see him get another stiffy within the next few seconds. It was never Gerald's ass, naked and skinny, getting fucked by Peter's big and probing prick, which was a turn-on, rather the naked and masculine fucker laid out atop Gerald's naked and skinny butt.

Talbot pulls off his shirt and unties his tennis shoes. He stands and drops his shorts. There is certain dampness, other than sweat, that nestles inside his jockstrap, along with the curl of his cum-depleted pecker. Luckily, there is only a slight spotting of wet that soaks through to the outside of the elastic pouch. Lest he unveil a dick with a stray drop of tardy cum drooled from its mouth, he removes his jockstrap by grabbing its elastic sock and pulling outward and down so that, as the pouch comes off, it first wipes clean whatever the leftover residue on his pecker.

"Something I can do for you, Gerald?" he says, more confident.

"The rumor is that you've applied for Princeton," Gerald says.

"Isn't a rumor," Talbot says and reaches for his towel which is folded inside his locker. He is so confident another boner isn't immediately forthcoming, he doesn't bother to conceal his pink dick behind a wrap of terry-cloth.

"I've a cousin who goes there," Gerald says. "He's visiting next week. My old man knows some of the big wigs on the Princeton administration board, even though Dad's a Yalie and expects me to be the same. You want to come on over and maybe get a few pointers from my cousin?"

Talbot wonders if Gerald spotted him spotting Gerald on the other end of Peter's delivering boner. Granted, Gerald and Talbot know each other since junior-high school, but they have never exactly run in the same social circles. Gerald's dad makes far more money than Talbot's dad.

"My cousin is a real bore," Gerald says. "I'm looking for someone to occupy him so he won't put me to sleep. The only other kid in school I know who's applied to Princeton is Wayne Donald, and he's more of a bore than my cousin."

"Okay," Talbot says. He isn't going to look this skin-and-bones gift horse in the mouth. One editor of Princeton's *Alumni Weekly* was often quoted for having said it imprudent of Princeton, in view of its dependence upon gifts from alumni, to isolate itself from the upper classes by admitting too many common high-school graduates. Although the school advisor constantly reassures that soon-to-be-common high-school graduate Talbot that his grade average and his extracurricular activities put him on the fast track for admission to Princeton, Talbot would be foolish not to hedge his bets. Especially since his going to Princeton means a whole lot to his father; probably more than it even means to Talbot. If Talbot's father has made a well-respected name for himself, in the field of architecture, and achieved a status wherein he's now hiring ivy-league grads (Peter a prime example), it isn't through his having graduated from any ivy-league college (he attended ?San Jose State), and/or through his having had access to any of the benefits of a good-old0-boy system. Talbot's father has worked his ass off, clawed and scraped, to get where he is today. If he somehow — for whatever the reason — sees himself even partially validated by the cachet of having his son accepted into one of *the* prestigious universities, who is Talbot to do anything that might deprive him of that opportunity?

"You just let me know the when."

"Okay," Gerald says.

As Gerald leaves, Talbot again remembers him before Gerald got so goddamn cadaverous. Once, Gerald had been a genuine good-looker. He could still look good if he only gained back even a few of the pounds he'd lost by running marathons.

"You okay?" Sam Nimms says. He's just outside the building when Talbot leaves the school. It's genuinely balmy out of doors. Summer definitely is on the way.

Sam is handsome and sexy, in a blond all-American sort of way.

"Someone said you had a belly ache," Sam says.

Talbot figures if Sam follows up with a request for Talbot to meet his cousin that something fishy is going down.

"Someone else said you had merely been dumping a load, after which he'd seen you head in for a late shower."

"I can't tell you how happy I am there are those, among us, who keep such close tabs on my daily bowel movements," Talbot says.

He heads down the sidewalk, and Sam falls in beside him.

"Something I can help you with?" Talbot says. Sam hasn't been waiting around just to repeat reports of Talbot's belly ache or dump in the toilet.

"Terry is trying to get me to come to one of your club meetings."

Terry MacQuire is the unofficial president of The Red and Blue Circle. TR&BC, a very unofficial school social club, consists entirely of guys, like Talbot, Jeffrey, and Marky, whom Terry has, at one time or another, persuaded to sample the joys of whipping off dick with a few other guys doing the very same thing. More than once, Talbot has been subjected to Terry's hopeful: "Yahoo, wouldn't I like to check out Sam Nimm's weenie shooting off its load!"

"You're thinking of pledging TR&BC?" Talbot says.

"Terry says I can expect some — you know? — touching and stuff."

"You don't want to be touched, no one touches you but you," Talbot says.

"Terry's kind of aggressive," Sam says.

Talbot doesn't say anything. What is there to say? Terry is aggressive. His aggressiveness helped decide, not prevent, Talbot (and Jeffrey, and Marky) to join Terry and others in pulling out cocks and doing a bit of show-off.

"I wouldn't mind doing 'it' with you," Sam says. "You know, just the two of us. Kind of ease me into doing it in front of Terry and the others."

That brings Talbot up short.

"You think Terry too aggressive, you'll want to stay far away from me," Talbot says. "What I see you and me doing isn't our pulling out our dicks and watching each other beat to climax. I see my prick buried to my cum-filled balls up your tight asshole." Talbot's mind's-eye flashes Peter fucking Gerald's skinny butt. He substitutes Sam for Gerald, and it's a far far sexier picture. He goes one step farther and pictures himself fucking Sam. He's about to go whole hog and fantasize his dick deep up Peter's dimpled butt, but Sam's expression distracts him.

"What?" Talbot said.

He hasn't a clue what Sam is thinking.

"Look," Talbot says, "Terry is an okay guy. He likes you. He's not going to expect you to do anything but unzip your pants, whip out your dick, beat your prick to climax, and see if you can outshoot him and the other guys. If he fists your cock, or you fist his, or if you're both jerked off by someone else, everyone gets off, no one turns out any the worst for wear. However, if you think having a little fun and games with me will ease you into the process, by all means let's do it."

"Let me think about it, a bit more," Sam says.

"You do that," Talbot says and heads on home.

His cock gets all the harder with thoughts of potential hot sex with sexy

Sam, combined with continuing thoughts of sex with Kane and even with Peter. By the time he reaches home, he's glad his dad and mom aren't there. There's no missing the bulge his swollen prick makes in the crotch of his pants. Even though, it's hardly likely his parents would make comment. Then again, Talbot doubts his father and/or mother would approve of their son fooling around with Jeffrey, and Marky, and Terry, the guys in the TR&BC social club, as well as with Kane. As for Talbot's ongoing fantasies about Peter and Sam . . .

He goes to his room and shucks his clothes in front of the full-length mirror that runs the length of his closet doors.

"Look what I've got for you . . ." He picks a name out of the hat. " . . . Peter," he says. He gives a little sway of his hips to set his stiff dick into metronome motion. "For you, too, Kane and Sam!"

What he has for Peter, and for Kane, and for Sam, he would have liked to give them, right then and there. Just the thought gets his stiff dick stiffer.

He's disappointed more sex with Kane has to wait until the next night. Kane, although he and Talbot have done it once at the Spa, balks at doing anything more there. He works there, and he doesn't want to be caught doing it there. What with Peter carrying on in the Spa locker room, after hours, Kane thinks the place too crowded for anyone's good.

So, Kane and Talbot will next screw around on Kane's day off. Kane has suggested a secluded bit of park, since the weather has been so summer-warm. If the weather gets chilly, or if it rains, he says he'll think of somewhere else for them to go.

Talbot prefers the spontaneity that had Kane and him on the floor of the Spa auditorium. He hopes they get back to that.

"Tomorrow, tomorrow," he sings to his naked reflection. He's determined that, come tomorrow, Kane and he are going to come.

In the meantime. . . .

He's enthralled by the physical dexterity Kane exhibited in achieving a sit-up, from supine position, on that down-slanting auditorium floor. He's fascinated by Kane having elaborated upon it by tightening the curve of his spine and actually feeding on their cocks. Since the first time he saw Marky's similar flexibility, Talbot has tried, several times, to duplicate it. He knows there was a time, in his not-so-distant past, when he would have been able to perform what he now wants to do. Unfortunately, between then and now, he has been too sexually ignorant to keep as limber as required. Alas, as one gets older, flexibility is lost, even by those who make a specific effort to maintain as much of it as possible.

As he bends from his waist, lowers his head, anchors his hands to his calves and gives a pull, his mouth still comes up short of the head of his dick.

He asks: "Was I still flexible enough to eat my own dick when puberty first set in — had I only thought of giving it a try? Or, had I already, by then, lost my ability to dine on my cum while leeched to my cockhead?"

The very idea that he may have lost his ability to eat his own meat, purely because he hasn't had the imagination to give it a try, leaves him perturbed as all hell.

He tries mouth-to-cock again. This time on the bed, his legs thrown up and over his head, one knee to one side of each cheek. The position puts him closer to his goal, but closer doesn't win the ball game.

He waits. He holds his present position. He knows, from his experiences on the playing field, that the body stretches farther when warmed up. If he maintains his present position for a couple of years, admiring the droop of his balls towards his face, the hairy trail of red fuzz traveling the crack of his ass to halo his pink anus, will he, sooner or later, achieve the sufficient bend necessary?

How wonderful if only his mouth could attach to the head of his dick. The idea of tasting his cum, mingled with Kane's spewing sperm, at the exact moment of their mutual blasts-off, makes him all the more frustrated.

"Shit!" he concedes defeat for the moment. He can't expect a quick return of flexibility, after so long without it. He's ask Kane if the Kane realized early-on the possibilities of self-fellatio, and has always maintained his ability to do it, or if Kane lost the necessary flexibility, at least for awhile, and has since worked to regain it through special stretching exercises. Marky's flexibility is maintained via a continual and long-lasting regimen of gymnastics and yoga-stretching.

Thoughts of studly Kane are followed by thoughts of Kane's studly cock, by thoughts of Kane's studly ass.

"May I fuck your ass, please?" Talbot asks his for-the-moment fantasized lover. "Kane, my man, how I wish today was your fucking day off for fucking."

Talbot imagines his languidly cock-stroking fist to be Kane's anus suddenly wrapped around Talbot's butt-fucking primed dick.

Talgot shuts his eyes and experiments with substituting a phantom Peter's ass around his cock. Will Peter's asscheeks dimple as easily, while getting fucked, as they had while Peter fucked Gerald's bag-of-bones asshole? The sudden vision of Gerald's scrawny butt, impaled by Talbot's dick, does absolutely nothing for him.

He doesn't know when he substitutes Sam's imagined asshole for Gerald's asshole. Probably pretty damned fast, because Talbot's cock is still hard as a rock, not having been in the least depleted by the momentary unsexy flash of Gerald's skinny butt.

He marvels at how he came right on out and told Sam how sex with Talbot would mean Sam fucked by Talbot's exploring cock.

He curls his legs farther over his head. Not in another attempt to eat his cock but to watch his fuck-finger play the pucker of his asshole.

Such a small butt entrance! It's hard to imagine it ever successfully taking Kane's big cock, Jeffrey's big cock, Marky's big cock. It's hard to imagine it taking Peter's cock. It's hard to imagine it taking something as small as Talbot's fuck-finger.

Talbot's attempt to stick his finger up his ass doesn't work all that well. It's as if he pushes on taut latex.

He retrieves his fuck-finger. He smells the redolent muskiness of his bung-hole on the tip of his finger. He doesn't find the heady aroma any more distasteful than he does the smell of his own farts under the covers.

Spit-wet and returned to his asshole, his finger has an easier time. Once it's stuck up his rectum to its first knuckle, it tells him, by mere feel, that a genuinely virgin asshole isn't likely to be any the more tight-fitting than Talbot's butt.

How many cocks has Gerald's ass taken to make it so accommodating of the stiff pecker Peter fed it? Does Talbot dare ask him? "Hey, Gerald, happened to catch your bum getting screwed the other evening by Peter's hard prick, and I was wondering, 'How many cocks have made that very same trip up your skinny behind?'"

"Sure, Talbot," he says to himself. "You can make it part of the dinner conversation. Right after Gerald introduces you to his cousin from Princeton and suggests to his old man that dear dad might want to put in a good word for you with the people he knows at the university."

He twists his finger deeper. The tip of it punches his prostate.

"Fuck my ass, Kane!" he says.

Kane's phantom big cock delivers another playful jab to Talbot's prostate.

Talbot's squirts a gridiron of goo on his face.

"Ah . . . ah . . . ahhhhhh!" he moans and punctuates with additional sounds very much pig-stuck-on-lance.

He tastes his cream but wishes he hadn't wasted so much of it as a face mask.

He catches a glimpse of himself in the mirror. He sees gossamer splashes of cummy streamers caught in his hair. He decides, right then and there, to master the technique of getting his mouth to his cock, if just to make clean-up a helluva lot easier and faster.

* * * *

"Talbot, for God's sake, wake the hell up!" Jeffrey commands.

"Whaaaaat?" Talbot groans sleepily. He's only vaguely aware that his hand, in his sleeping bag, is filled with cream from a particularly exciting dream.

"You have me feeling as if I'm sharing this tent not only with Marky and you but with a crowd that includes a Kane, a Peter, and a Sammy Nimms. Which wouldn't be so damned bad if you weren't so fucking noisy about it."

"Sorry," Talbot apologizes.

"You actually been screwing around with any of those guys?" Jeffrey asks. "Peter somebody? Kane somebody? Sammy Nimms?"

"Jeffrey, for Christ's sake! Have you physically fucked everyone who appears in your dreams and gives you a handful of cream?"

"You have been fucking around with them, haven't you?"

"Where's Marky?" Talbot asks, attempting to delay the inevitable.

"You've been fucking around with them and holding out on giving the details to your good buddies," Jeffrey accuses. "What kind of a friend are you, for Christ's sake?"

"I have not fucked around with Sammy Nimms," Talbot says. "I only want to screw around with Peter who I already think I might have mentioned to you works for my father."

"This Kane the one you mentioned, too, as working for your father? He's a security guard or something, yes?"

"What's up?" Marky asks, pushing back the tent flap and coming on in. He's in a really good mood and is anxious to tell his tale of sex with the French surfer on the beach.

"Jeffrey here has been screwing around with just about everyone under the sun," Jeffrey says, "and I'm not talking just in his dreams."

CHAPTER ELEVEN

Peter sees the old Helen Glindel Health and Beauty Spa building as the architectural equivalent of a Fabergé egg. A masterful piece of artwork as a whole and filled with decidedly lovely and equally masterful smaller treasures. Like the exquisite Dodges' Dining Room with its faded tapestry-like frescos of Venice canal scenes. Like the Pump Room with its gargoylesque health-water dispenser looming Hieronymus Bosch-like from a central iron platform cast in the shape of a Chinese dragon. Like the Ladies' Salon on the third floor with its acres of mirrors long broken, fragmented, and fallen like rare crystals, scattered upon the floor.

The building's architect, Mary-Anne Quantylico, was definitely ahead of her time, if her time ever came. Her only major construction project was the Spa, a no-argument-one-of-a-kind, after which Mary-Anne gave up her career in architecture to make her real fame and fortune as a designer of exquisite and intricate pieces of costume jewelry.

Although the facility's style and decor were loved to distraction by Helen Glindel, who commissioned the building, and by its paid membership who frequented it in droves, the Spa's main appeal was to the women in a time when men not only still ruled the roost, or the vast majority of roosts, but controlled the vast majority of the purse strings that financed the erection of most buildings. "Quantylico panache", as the Spa's style eventually became known (not to mention the notion of any woman architect), simply didn't appeal to the masculine gender of that day and to few of this day. Such men preferred and prefer their erections a tad more rugged and straightforward.

Put the question to the present day members of the California Historical Society who put the building on its official register of historical buildings, and it's almost a straight female-male dividing as regards whom really likes and dislikes the "look" of the building.

Peter is delighted that Canton Crane is one of the few men who is so certain of himself that he can not only publicly admit that the building is a true gem that warrants being restored to its original grandeur, but can put all of the expertise and financial clout of his company behind the building's purchase and reconstruction.

It had been Crane, Benbrook, and Toriglee's acquisition of the property which persuaded Peter, prestige-award winner architectural student and straight out of Yale, to come to work for them instead of hire on with any of the many other firms that had been hot to have at him.

Peter, architect connoisseur, is also into good sex, and his sex with Gerald in the old Spa building is some of the very best. Surprising, how it turns out being that way. Upon their first meeting, Peter in Los Angeles for job interviews and staying at the McTalen house, Gerald's father the head of the California Yale Alumni Association, Peter had found Gerald sexually appealing but certainly not to the degree he did once Gerald took up marathon running, shed all excess weight, and then some, and converted his physique into Peter-genuinely can't-resist greyhound-athletic.

Peter hasn't a clue why that particular body-type is such a turn-on for him. He has no memory of anyone of such appearance having existed anywhere, let alone exerted sexual influence, within his sexually formative years. It wasn't until Ethan Stanton came along that Peter had even a clue as to the effect such a person could have on him. In the animal kingdom, Peter is sure the condition is called "a rut". It leaves him hot as hell and slightly breathless. It elevates his need for sexual satisfaction to a considerably higher degree, even to the point where he (usually, blasé and waiting for it to come to him), will actively pursue it. And, the resulting sex, if and when it occurs, is genuinely the best ever.

Luckily, Peter's penchant hasn't reached fetish proportions. While someone with a foot fetish has a whole wide-ranging selection of feet from which to choose . . . While someone with a leather fetish has a whole wide-ranging selection of leather from which to choose . . . There isn't exactly a preponderance of gay greyhound-thin athletic types to be had for gay fun and games. In Peter's life, there has, thus far, only been Ethan Stanton, Toby Cornwall (Gerald McTalen's Yalie cousin, as fate would have it), and Gerald. In the interim, Peter can be quite satisfied with more ordinary gay sexual experiences. In fact, he welcomes them, in that his few-and-far-between ruts leave him mentally and physically drained. He'd even likely be more than happy to have sex with Talbot Crane, who has made it more than apparently obvious that he's interested, except Talbot is the boss's son. Peter has no intentions of pissing off Talbot's father to where the elder Crane fires Peter's ass and Peter loses out on the restoration of the Spa.

The Spa restoration shortly to begin in earnest, Peter is relieved that his sexual rut with Gerald is about over; he will be better able to focus all of his attention on his career and relegate his sex to maybe-yes maybe-no weekend status.

How does Peter know his present rut is about over? One clue: Just a few minutes ago, Gerald and Peter stripped down for their latest round, Peter (albeit subconsciously, when it happened) put the impending finale into words by saying, "You've gained a pound or two." It wasn't a question. He can see something not quite so razor sharp, not quite so well-defined, about Gerald's body. It's a softness, likely unrecognizable by anyone but Peter (after all, it was but a pound or two), but to Peter it's unmistakable. It isn't something he bemoans. These things happen. It isn't something he'll try to change. Such intense sex isn't something, even without the Spa project in the offing, to which he wants to become permanently addicted. It doesn't mean that he won't enjoy sex, even now, with Gerald. It doesn't mean that he won't enjoy sex with Gerald even a few times more.

"Since my sprained ankle keeps me from running, I've dropped my mara-thon-runner's diet as well," Gerald had confirmed. "Little helped by my father who's on his sudden let's-try-to-fatten-up-my-son project."

"And, the weight-training?" There's a definite new bulge to Gerald's biceps. Again, likely unnoticeable to anyone but Peter.

"Yeah, a bit of that." Has he actually thought Peter wouldn't be able to tell?

They're in Peter's very favorite room of the Spa. *The* primary jewel surprise within the Fabergé egg. The swimming-pool room. The natatorium. A simply glorious enclosure of brightly colored walls wherefrom marvelously Edenesque flora and fauna materialize, quite by magic, from the jigsaw mosaics of highly baked tiles. Gazelles and antelopes leap. Zebras and buffaloes graze. Storks and ibises strut. Giraffes and elephants feast on the leaves from high treetops.

The pool is empty but filled with sea-water blue tile, giving the appearance of ocean, in which swim mosaic dolphins and manta rays and seals and starfish and octopi, and in which exist all sorts of curlicue shells. Walking the pool's high-dive board, which Peter and Gerald now do, stark naked except for the condom and lube packets they each palm, makes them participants in the illusion that the pool is a real-life aquarium that they might enter, at any time, by merely stepping too far forward, to the left, or to the right. Peter plans that the two of them fuck on the end of the high-dive board. It's a feat that could be downright scary if Peter hadn't already checked the structural integrity of the board, of the platform, and of the anchorages of both, to assure that old-age hasn't made any of the long-standing equipment incapable of the weight and movement of weight soon to be put to it.

Peter remains a little worried about Gerald's sprained ankle, as Gerald walks such dizzying heights, but Gerald insists it's hardly painful at all unless he attempts running long distances on it. In truth, it's less a sprain than it is Gerald's excuse to give up the racing regimen and diet program of which he has grown exceedingly weary.

Peter proceeds to a spot short of board terminus and sits. He faces Gerald who remains between him and the platform. Peter lies down on his back. His head is pretty much at board end. He opens his legs and lets them fall, as far and as wide as possible, one to either side. It's a position he has enjoyed many times before, without a fuck in the offing. There's something almost mystical about the tiled ceiling. Whatever the magic, it's unaffected by the preponderance of tiles which, over the ages, have fallen to shatter and splatter the natatorium floor. The fake sky (any real sky viewable only by cutting a hole through three floors and a roof), is a night-time wonder of yellow and white fiery-tailed comets; asterisk- and Christian-cross stars, many in recognizable constellations; ringed and unringed planets; all portrayed against a black backdrop that the years have covered with a milky-way-like film and dust.

"Fuck me," Peter says and lifts his knees slightly. His butt rocks more of his asscrack into visibility.

Gerald unpalms his condom packet and retrieves its lubricated rubber. He rolls the opaque tubing over and down the length of his dick then lubes it further. He knows his sexual moments with Peter are now short-lived, probably even more prepared than Peter to except the inevitability of moving on. Nonetheless, he's just as prepared as his partner to milk these last moments for all they're worth.

If the abrasive surface of the diving board is irritating to his knees as he drops in position between Peter's open thighs, the resulting pain is more stimulant than detriment to the pleasure he feels.

"Nice and easy," Peter says. "I wouldn't want you inadvertently launched into the wide-open spaces below us."

Gerald is careful alright. He's very careful. No denying it's a bit disconcerting to see Peter laid out against the board, like supine rider on surfboard, high above a seascape panorama that makes everything seem slo-mo underwater. For a moment, he's fooled into gulping for a breath of air that would have come as naturally as before if he'd only let it.

Peter begins a more pronounced lift of his legs, and Gerald gives the helping hand that completes the maneuver. Peter's ass rocks up even more, and his asscrack presents his anal pucker, somewhere within, for Gerald's taking.

Yes, Peter is excited by greyhound-thin Gerald's torso suddenly looming and parenthesized by Peter's lifted legs. Peter lifts his head slightly and looks down his chest, along his pectoral cleavage, over the ridged plain of his abdominals, along the length of his cock laid out, hard and stiff on his belly. His gaze travels farther than the clump of pubic hair at his crotch, to where Gerald's hard cock and sagging balls hang suspended, heavenly objects, not all that far from Peter's suddenly very vulnerable anus.

Peter's ass is some planet's moon; Gerald's cock is a rocket with blasters. The rocket prepares to land, or maybe crash-land, in that it comes in headfirst. A soft-landing, though, cockhead ever so gently into the leading pinch of one buttocks against the other.

Peter is excited by the streamline thinness of Gerald's chest and belly, by the way Gerald's nipples are so coppery-to-gold taut against the pale gold of Gerald's skin. He's turned on by the gathering of sweat, not yet dribbling, that is caught by Gerald's collar bone, by the faint gloss of perspiration that centers Gerald's chest and belly as far as his navel. There's even a faint veneering of wet to Gerald's scrotum within which cum-bulged balls hang directly from the base of an impressively poised-for-fucking erection.

Gerald savors the moment, on his own and knows just what there is that initially attracted him to Peter. Gerald's check-list for the perfect male isn't nearly as exclusive as Peter's, but he wants them studly, and Peter is studly; he wants them handsome, and Peter is handsome; he wants them sexy, and Peter is sexy; he wants them sexually versatile, and Peter is certainly that. Peter so studly, so handsome, so sexy, Gerald devoted — and still devotes — a good deal of time and effort to discover just how sexually versatile he is. Gerald has every intention to end their relationship, which is ending, with a satisfactory bang.

Peter's hands grip the cheeks of his upturned ass and pull them outward along their mutually shared crack. His buttocks are sweaty and pry apart as if stuck together by Velcro. His black asshair is damp and plastered to the curved sides of his opening-like-a-peach buttcheeks.

Gerald's cock prods the opening of Peter's anus and pauses there. Each participant enjoys the anticipation of cock-up-butt to follow.

Gerald's knees provide the pressure against the diving board that sends the board into a slight bounce. The upward end of the bounce brings Peter's asshole up to greet the cockhead that pushes forward to meet it. The whole head of Gerald's dick disappears into Peter's butt.

"Ohhhhh," Peter moans. Not in pain. Jesus, not in pain. Not really even in response to the pleasure of cockhead stuffed up his butt, although there is pleasure in the stuffing. He groans in eager invitation for Gerald to follow through and let cockhead lead the way for luscious inch after inch of Gerald's hot, hard, and ready prick. This time, he's the one who increases the spring of the diving board. It's his efforts which bounce his butt right on up and over another thick inch of Gerald's cock.

No way Gerald holds off the inevitable complete insertion of his dick up Peter's asshole. Gerald likes sex too much, still likes sex with Peter too much, not to want anything but to get on with it. His conscious mind, though, doesn't have much to do with it. Even at this early stage, all control of the fuck is pretty much turned over to some primitive part of his brain.

Gerald swings his downward-arching hips forward and plants every last additional inch of his stiff prick up Peter's butt. His complete weight follows through and concentrates at the base of his stuck dick to wedge in whatever inches of his prick may remain and keep the total securely in place while Gerald's senses adapt to the excruciating pleasure of vise-like ass enclosing the whole length and breadth of his erection.

"Fish speared by my pecker!" Gerald says. His gaze focuses beyond Peter to the seascape of the pool tiles aligned far below him. Some kind of bass peeks from Medusa-like tendrils of ceramic seaweed.

Like a speared fish, Peter's mouth opens, then closes, opens again. No sound, except for a small hiss of breath.

Gerald actually expects Peter to start flopping like a wounded fish out of water. Gerald pushes more securely against the base of his secured cock in order to keep his fucked dick in place whenever the out-of-water spasms begin.

Except, the only spasms that occur are the up-and-down vibrations of Peter's anal wall that massage the length of Gerald's inserted prick.

Peter is able, despite the condom packet still palmed in his one hand, to pinch both of Gerald's nipples. Between his tweaking thumbs and forefingers, the little nubs turn all the more erect and plump. He pushes his head back hard against the surface of the diving board, his chin aimed directly toward the mock-night sky above. He licks his lips. His body demands that Gerald provide more than just simple cock insertion. Peter wants, needs, has to have movement of that cock inside his ass.

"Screw me, stud!" he says.

Gerald is quite unable to remain still, even if he wanted. And he doesn't want. He needs his cock at work, plumbing the depths of Peter's tight asshole, as much as Peter needs it.

His hips swing up and drag behind them almost the entire length of his powerful erection. At the far end of that swing, his cock is free of the ass except for his bulbous cockhead which remains held firmly in place by the elastic-like pressure of sphincter into the groove formed by the flare of Gerald's cockhead from the shaft of his erect pecker. He's fearful that even one bit of additional squeeze by the encircling mouth of asshole will pop his cockhead as thoroughly as any pursed lips popped ripe cherry free of its stem. To avoid any possibility of the imagined catastrophe becoming fast reality, he re-inserts the total length of his dick into Peter's butt. Suddenly, he's faced with a still-squeezing buttmouth that threatens to munch his dick completely off at its base. The resulting pleasure-pain is so exquisite his eyes squint, his jaw locks, his teeth gnash. He drools spit that forms a slim and glossy filament that stretches all of the way to touchdown on Peter's chest before finally breaking free.

Peter claims the resulting small pool of Gerald's escaped saliva and transfers it to the length of Peter's stiff prick that lies his belly from his balls to his navel. It takes some effort, at making full use of the small supply, but eventually he has its slick wet veneered to the total length of his prick. The stickiness of the soon-evaporated spit makes the friction of suddenly cock-pumping fingers greater than what would have been achieved without it.

"Yeah, flog the hog!" Gerald says. He'd like to do it for Peter, but he's frankly afraid his doing too much, beyond the fuck itself, might interfere with their precarious balance. The high-board has obviously been made wider than usual, possibly to accommodate ladies wider than usual, but it's still a potentially dangerous perch upon which to perform the kind of sexual gymnastics. It takes a concentrated effort to remember they fuck on a diving board over a drop. Reconfirming the danger comes with its own masochistic rewards that make it all the more difficult to concentrate.

"Sweet, sweet," Peter says. No other way to describe the ecstasy from this cock, up his butt, finally starting more earnestly to move in-and-out . . . in-and-out . . . combined with the pleasure had from his own knowledgeable fingers working the entire length of his own spit-sticky swollen pecker.

They make seascape sounds: sighs like sea-borne breezes; gravelly groans like water moving stones; sweaty-skin-sticking-to-sweaty-skin sounds like a clam digger's wet boot pulled from the wet sand of a receding tide; slap-of-belly-against-ass sounds that mock waves-knocking-rocky-cliff-face. Perspiration runs their bodies like water runs the piles of an ocean pier. From deep inside each emerge high-pitched sounds, almost like those of seagulls.

Their shared ecstasy-on-the-rise is more heavenly than the fake sky, more celestial than any real sky. They're more enveloped by pleasure than any magnetic field envelopes its planet . . . more contained than any atmosphere contains its world . . . more turned gluttons by their sexuality than any gaseous cloud cannibalizing itself in its conversion to white-hot sun.

They're a super nova in the building. Each increasingly more frantic pump of cock up ass, of hand over erection, of fingers rolling and colliding cum-bulging nuts, stores more and more build-up of pressure within their bodies; pressure that needs release.

Gerald sees the swimming-pool mosaics, made wavy by sweat in his eyes. He imagines himself Neptune on the verge of yet again supplying sufficient spume to frost all of the waves of the Seven Seas.

"All of the waves," he says.

Peter thinks he says (and thereby echoes), "All of the way . . . all of the way . . . yes, yes, yes . . . all of the way!"

Peter's pleasure about pushes to its limits.

The high- board bounces all the more frantically, even more dangerously. Peter and Gerald, ignorant of anything except what their bodies now demand, slide upon the board. Everything ignored except the can't-be-ignored urgency to manage the last few movements, no matter how perilous, to tip them over the edge — not into the empty pool but — into the heady shudders of sexual release.

Peter's hand-fisted cock provides wet and soupy cum-comets that exit the pulsing lips of dick and splatter his face, his neck, his chest, his belly. His blasted cum drools, like stalactites, from Gerald's overhanging face, neck, chest and belly.

Gerald licks the splatter from his lips. The taste is aphrodisiacally that of salty seas.

The exciting flavor, combined with the suddenly even more intense wringing of Gerald's totally submerged neck, by Peter's ass gone into convul-sions as a result of Peter's climax-in-progress, shoves Gerald into shuddering orgasmic accompaniment.

"AAAggghhhhhrrrunngggg!" Gerald is at the mercy of sexually storm-tossed sea.

Peter thrusts his butt up as high as possible in order that his hole might gobble up each and every drop of liquid that Gerald is prepared to feed . . . feed . . . feed . . . it. It seems Gerald's cum manages the trip from Gerald's exploding dick, through Peter's accepting body, to replenish the sperm that still, miraculously, continues its eruption from Peter's hand-strangled and throbbing penis.

Only later, much later, do they realize how precariously close they came to literally tumbling into oblivion.

CHAPTER TWELVE

If Talbot thinks a sex-saturated long weekend with his buddies in Baja has sated him with enough sex and wet dreams to distract him for his wild fantasies of sex with Peter, of real sex with Kane, of potential sex with Sam, he's sadly mistaken. If anything, his time at the beach only increases his desires.

"Tomorrow evening, six o'clock," Gerald says.

Talbot is so consumed with thoughts of this Saturday afternoon's planned sexual romp with Kane (Talbot arrived at the public library with a boner so large that he's not gotten it down to a size less-than-obvious within his pants), he hasn't a clue what in the hell Gerald talks about.

"My boring cousin from Princeton," Gerald says.

"Right," Talbot says. Had Gerald suggested Talbot drop by that specific Saturday evening to say hello to his boring cousin and well-connected dad, Talbot would have had to tell him, cousin or not, old man with connections or not, that he couldn't come. Talbot is so keyed by the possibilities of more sex with Kane, not to mention more sex with Kane's impressively large cock, his priorities are askew. He knows they're askew. His acceptance into Princeton far more important to his future than Kane and/or Kane's hard cock, but he can't help momentarily focusing on Kane and Kane-cock.

"Just dress casually," Gerald says.

"Right," Talbot says. His cock has itself in some kind of painful impasse within the maze of his undershorts, and he has to realign it pretty soon, or it'll snap.

"Sam Nimms find you?" Gerald says. "He's looking for you."

"He caught me after I showered after gym the other day."

"Maybe he did," Gerald says, "but he's looking for you this morning."

"Well, here I am," Talbot says. "Maybe if he looks harder …"

"You don't like Sam?" Gerald says.

It's an everyone-likes-Sam-so-why-don't-you-? sort of question.

"I like Sam, sure," Talbot says. "I like Marky. I like Jeffrey. I suspect I'll even like your cousin, and your father." Actually, Talbot has met Gerald's father and found him a bit distant. "Hell, I even like you."

"I hear you think I'm too thin," Gerald says.

The kid has more information sources than the CIA.

"It's all the marathons and training for them that gets my weight down," Gerald says. "Burns off calories like they don't exist."

"Very seldom see a fat cheetah," Talbot says.

Gerald smiles. His doing so makes him look somehow less cadaverous. Maybe he's actually gained a bit of well-needed muscle, despite all of his marathon running.

"Tomorrow. Six," Gerald says and starts to leave. He limps.

Even as unobservant as Talbot can be, he sees Gerald limps.

"You okay?" Talbot calls after. Unlike everyone's conception of quiet-conscious librarians, not a one tells him to shush, although the one at the front desk frowns, whether or not from Talbot's loudness is hard to tell, since she doesn't bother to look up.

"Oh, the sprain, you mean?" Gerald says. He's stopped for a moment and has turned back in Talbot's direction. "I'm fine, although out of any marathon running for awhile. In fact, I've taken up some weight training to fill my suddenly excess time. "Figure that since I don't need to keep down the weight for running, I might try to bulk up just a bit."

"Sounds like a plan," Talbot says.

"See you," Gerald says and heads on off.

Talbot, his lap concealed under the desktop, tries his best to put his dick into a more comfortable placement, within the small space offered within the confinement of his under shorts. He wants to stand up and walk without all eyes turned suddenly in his direction. In the end, he scoops up his books and lowers them into position directly over his crotch. Even then, he's sure everyone notices he's in possession of an obelisk bigger than any Cleopatra ever had excavated from the quarries along the Nile.

He gets home and successfully lugs his by now painful erection up the stairway even as his mother calls out: "Sam, called for you while you were gone. Did he find you at the library?"

"I'll call him back," Talbot says. He's hoisting his boner up the rest of the way to his room, like someone suddenly grown a third leg without any coordination to use it.

Once in his room, his door shut, neither of his parents the kind to come barging in without a knock and an invite, he seriously contemplates a quick jack-off to get his obviously raging testosterone under control. He can't imagine his cock staying as swollen as it is for very much longer without exploding.

He drops his pants and undershorts, just to give his stiffy more freedom. He goes so far as to fist the thing, so needful is it, and so needful is he.

On second thought, he unhands his pecker and lifts his dropped pants and under shorts. He traps his dick in a more comfortable stand-tall position. At least, for the moment, it seems adequately disguised by his having left out his shirttail to drape over it.

"I'm going to the park to toss Frisbee," he says, headed down the stairs. He's left the Frisbee in his bedroom.

"Did you call Sam?" his mother asks from somewhere in the nearby kitchen.

"I'll probably meet up with him in the park."

"Don't be too late, will you, dear? We're having the Wilsons over for six o'clock, and I know Sally will want to see you."

Talbot likes Sally. Really. Not sexually, of course, but she's always fun to be with. Right now, though, fun with Sally is the very last thing on his mind. Actually, there's only one thing on his mind.

He does go to the park. It's a big one, and it gives him the privacy he wants, as long as he keeps away from the regular hang-outs. There are a couple of guys he knows sunbathing on the edge of an expanse of lawn, several others are playing soccer. He thinks one of the "skins", presently passing the ball, is Sam, but he can't really tell from the distance. He doesn't get close enough to find out, either. If he can tell it's Sam, Sam can tell it's Talbot, and a conversation with Sam, about the pros and cons of pulling dick with Terry, with Talbot, and/or the with rest of the guys, is not how Talbot wants to spend the time between now and his meeting up with Kane.

Except he really hasn't a clue how to occupy the time. He needs something to distract his attention from the anticipation which keeps his dick rock-hard. On the other hand, there's a masochistic pleasure he derives from the painful state of his swollen erection, and from the fact that his balls are probably, even now, turning deep blue in frustration.

He finds a spot, in among a few trees, his back to a tree trunk, and he tries to doze. He thinks — hopes — he naps for an hour or so, only to check his watch and see it's only five minutes.

He keeps telling himself that he's working himself into a state that's going to see him likely disappointed by the actuality. Except, how can Kane ever disappoint, when just imagining it gets Talbot so hot and bothered?

As it turns out, Kane can disappoint, at the time of their rendezvous when he says, as he does say, "I've decided we really can't do this, Talbot, not even here."

"You're kidding!" Talbot says. His boner is so painfully hard in his pants, its aching stiffness almost makes him cry.

"It has nothing to do with you," Kane says. "Believe me. It has everything to do with is my old man."

"Your father?"

"He wants me to get married, have kids. He was so ticked when he caught me at this sort of thing before, he packed me up and shipped me all of the way here, across country."

"Even if that's true, you are, as you say, now halfway across the country."

"Which doesn't mean he hasn't hired someone to watch me to make sure this isn't happening. He's in security, for Christ's sake."

"But, you're in security, so wouldn't you easily spot somebody."

"My father has a whole group of people who just specialize in tailing and not being seen."

"But it's not like you're still underage."

"It's a little more complicated than my being old enough to suck cock and fuck ass and get my cock sucked and my ass fucked in return. My life pretty well mapped out for me. I go to work for my dad, then I inherit the company when he retires. I didn't exactly apply myself in the classroom. So, if my old man disinherits me, now, like he's threatened to do the next time he finds me fucking around with some guy, I don't have all that many career options."

"Shit!" Talbot says.

Then again, all of that true, Kane needn't have brought the blanket, needn't have spread it out all nicely as a nesting for the two of them. Making

Talbot suspect Kane had changed his mind after he'd showed up early.

Talbot should have showed up early, too, so as not to have given Kane any chance for second thoughts. God knew, Talbot hadn't been off doing anything important while Kane made his God-awful decision to pull out.

"I got carried away," Kane says. "Admittedly, you were just too much of a temptation. Too fucking good-looking. Too nice a bod, too nice an ass, too nice a cock. Too fucking seductive for my own good. To ready, willing and able."

Talbot takes advantage of the fact that, although Kane is fully dressed (maybe once undressed and now into full reverse?), Kane hasn't yet gathered up the blanket and is still there.

Talbot walks right up and unceremoniously trips on a root snag. Automatically, Kane catches him. Like he had at the Spa. Talbot couldn't have masterminded it better if he'd tried.

Talbot is encouraged by the way Kane keeps Talbot held close and doesn't immediately let go. When Kane does exert the pressure necessary to separate his body, Talbot holds on with the same stick-to-itness as a survivor from the Titanic disaster.

"You know what this is?" Talbot says and rubs his hard cock against Kane's thigh, like a dog attempting to hump Kane's leg. "I've saved this just for you, ever since you and I last creamed our balls."

"Look, Talbot, I . . ."

No denying Kane's boner, either. Its outline is hard evidence in Kane's pants. Talbot strokes its concealed length with his hand, all of the way from Kane's horse-size balls to the bulbous tip of Kane's uncircumcised erection.

Kane groans. That's all. He doesn't push Talbot away. He just stands where he is and groans, then groans again. They're sexy, deep-throat growls, closer to purrs, originating from somewhere very deep inside him.

That Talbot just possibly can exert power over this study individual has nothing whatsoever to do with the size or capabilities of the muscles God gave either of them, except for the love-muscles.

"I know you want to fuck me," Talbot says. He continues the rub of his hard cock against Kane's leg. "I know you want to. So, what are you waiting for?"

Kane buries his face in Talbot's hair, says something that sounds like "Jeeeez!"

He actually trembles, as if he's a small puppy having caught a sudden chill in the rain.

Talbot knows Kane wants him. He knows Kane just wants to be convinced that it's okay. And he's ready to do everything and anything he can to make it happen.

"I want you naked," Talbot says. Both of his hands wander into the front waistband of Kane's pants. "I want me naked. I want us both down on that blanket, fucking, sucking, and humping like rutting dogs."

"Oh, Jesus, Talbot." The way Kane says Talbot's name is a caress. He looks so turned-on/turn-on helpless, standing there, partially leaned against

Talbot, but mainly kept in place only because Talbot's fingertips curl so completely between Kane's hard belly and pants.

Talbot figures if he gets him naked, Kane will have even less of a chance to bolt. Like an Army general, Talbot maps out strategy.

Kane's belt comes undone easily. So does the top button of his pants. Talbot has concerns of the zipper getting stuck, but it comes open with a well-oiled sigh, letting his hands slide into the breached fly and around Kane's hips. Kane's pants accordion down around his ankles. He isn't going anywhere without a good deal of effort and coordination.

Talbot's hands slide up beneath Talbot's shirt and contact bare skin. Kane isn't wearing an undershirt and gasps enticingly as Talbot's palms caress Kane's nipple centers which are about as sharp as the points of tacks.

Talbot's fingertips run along Kane's back and dive beneath the waistband of his undershorts. Talbot slides the white cotton of the drawers down over the muscled contours of Kane's ass. He leaves them tucked up under the lower curve of buttocks, because the shorts snag, up front, on the shifted stiffness of Kane's erection.

Talbot drops in front of Kane and makes sure to anchor Kane's piled pants to the ground as he does so. Talbot's close-up view of crotch shows a large damp spot on Kane's shorts that bears witness to preseminal leakage. Talbot puts his mouth to the wet spot on the material and feels bulbous phallic cockhead beneath. He licks, as if the white cotton, and what's underneath, is a lollipop gone runny in the heat.

"Oh, Jesus fucking Christ!" Kane says.

For just a moment, Talbot fears Kane regains his resolve and is about to push off and waddle away. But Talbot has already succeeded in coaxing Kane too far to turn back. Kane is finally committed, all caution thrown to the wind. Things progress too hard and too fast for either of them to stop.

Like in the movies, Kane doesn't unbutton his shirt, rather inserts his hands into the front of it and gives a tug that sends buttons flying this way and that, like UFOs in the afternoon sky. His chest is bare muscle and skin. He shrugs off his shirt, steps out of his shoes and out of his piled pants.

He collapses to his back on the blanket, his knees raised slightly and filleted. One hand strokes the length of his hard cock. One hand massages his balls.

"Okay!" he says, utterly defeated. "Yes, yes, for Christ's sake, yes!"

Talbot is tempted to do a button-popping number of his own, but says, "Now that we're both committed, we have all the time in the world, so don't get your rocks off before I get down there."

"Keyed up as you have me, I'm not about to waste my cream in my own hand."

Talbot stripping slowly for Kane is entirely different than stripping for his own hand or for anybody else's hand. It's different than stripping for Marky or for Jeffrey. It's different than stripping for a shower, or for a physical examination, or for a change of clothes. He can't recall a hard-on of his being so hard, so big, so fucking heavy. As for his balls, they feel and look as if hung with fifty pound weights.

As each part of him gets bare, he can't help but make the comparison between his body and Kane's body. Not that Talbot isn't well put-together and doesn't know it. He has really good body definition: square pectorals, ridged abdominals, impressive biceps and triceps and . . . the whole ten yards. It's just that Kane's physique is more finely tuned. His muscles are more deeply cut, more cleanly cut, as if carved by a sculptor a tad more skilled than whomever shaped Talbot's body from one and the same block of stone.

"My bad luck God made someone as sexy as you," Kane says when Talbot is completely naked and on full display.

He gives one more languid stroke of his hand down the full length of his stiff dick before he opens both of his arms in invitation for Talbot to come on down.

There's a paradox in the meeting of flesh and muscle: so hard, so soft; so hot, so "cool".

There's a sensuous slide of belly against belly, chest against chest. Arm against arm, leg against leg, cock against cock. Punctuated by stuck-together moments.

Talbot's left cheek is against Kane's chest. The top of Talbot's head is against Kane's neck. Talbot hears Kane's heartbeat, hard and fast, somewhere deep inside Kane's chest.

Kane hands run the length of Talbot's torso, from shoulders to butt. Each of Kane's hands is large enough to cup one of Talbot's buns, and it does so. Kane squeezes his handfuls gently. Simultaneously, his hugging arms exert pressure that unites their bodies all the more tightly.

Talbot finds heaven on earth, no denying it. There with Mr. Kane, in that nesting of park trees and shrubs and bushes, the heat of the afternoon supplementing the furnace-like conditions within them, Talbot has all he's ever wanted. Anything that comes after this is merely frosting on the proverbial cake.

"God, I do so want to fuck your ass?" Talbot says. He has a vague recollection of Peter's cock pulling and pushing within Gerald's asshole, but such thoughts are short-lived. Not so short, though, that he can't wonder if a naked Peter might yet play some active part in Talbot's dreams-can-come-true sex life.

"It's all yours for the fucking," Talbot says.

"Except, my cock shoved to climax up your ass, here and now, will likely be so good as to leave me limp-dicked forever."

Kane experience a head-to-toe shiver.

"So, let's save the fucking of your butt for later," Kane says. "How about I suck your cock, instead?"

"How about I suck your dick, instead?" Talbot says.

"How about we suck each other's cock?" Kane says. He puts one hand up Talbot's back, up Talbot's neck, all of the way into Talbot's hair.

For Talbot, there's pure, unadulterated sexual pleasure in doing nothing more than being skin to skin, muscle to muscle, hardly moving, hardly breathing, Kane's fingers ever so gently combing Talbot's hair.

When Kane rolls to a dominant position atop Talbot, it's done in seeming slow motion. Their body contact is never lost. The sensuality is increased by the slight slippage of one against the other.

Kane puts one hand to each side of Talbot's face. He licks a line from Talbot's forehead, down the length of his nose, to his upper lip, back and forth along his mouth. Gently, he puts his lips to Talbot's lips.

He kisses down Talbot's chest to his belly. He fills Talbot's navel with spit, then sips from the well until it's empty.

Kane's mouth is so near the head of Talbot's cock, Talbot feels breath, hot and heavy, along the top inch of his erection. Talbot expects Kane to gobble every inch, at any moment. He braces for the expected surge of accompanying pleasure. He's disappointed.

Kane kisses down Talbot's right leg, all of the way to Talbot's foot. He sucks big toe with the same force and skill he'd use on stiff cock. Despite Talbot embarrassed his foot may not be as clean, after the walk to reach this parkland nest, he finds pleasure in the toe-sucking. That pleasure increases, five-fold, when Kane's mouth opens to swallow the whole tip of the foot.

Before this, if someone would have suggested Talbot would find getting his toes sucked sexually stimulating, Talbot would have said the idea was crazy.

Now, he's disappointed when Kane transfers his attention to kissing up Talbot's left thigh.

"Shall I suck your balls?" Kane asks. He's positioned between Talbot's muscled but pliant thighs.

"Suck my balls," Talbot says.

Full of surprises, Kane chooses that exact moment not to swallow Talbot's cum-filled nuts but to swallow Talbot's dick, all of the way from blood-purple cockhead to cobalt-blue balls. So swiftly has Kane hoisted Talbot's boner to get at it, so skillfully and unchokingly has he made his miraculous descent down the total length of it, Talbot is temporarily unaware what causes the sudden fireball of lightning that explodes between his legs and expands, in every which direction, like an atomic blast.

"My God . . . my God . . . my God!" Talbot bellows, long before he realizes he's not only blasted several hot and heavy shots of cum into Kane's feasting face, but Kane has swallowed each and every drop of those and heartily sucks for more.

Talbot he should have moved faster to make this a sixty-nine. Kane's cock should have been stuffed to its balls up Talbot's face. Even now, there should be the aphrodisiacal nuttiness of Kane's exploded sperm on the back of Talbot's tongue and down along the length of Talbot's throat.

CHAPTER THIRTEEN

Kane's grin is all Cheshire-cat. Talbot sees it full-on as Kane shifts more fully onto Talbot in the aftermath of Talbot's sexual explosion.

"Pure ambrosia: your cum," Kane says and licks his lips. "Wonderful! Marvelous! Better than any seven-course dinner, but then I counted eight massive blasts of creamy cum, each one a serving for eight."

He supports himself in push-up position. Their bodies are pretty much united from their bellies on down. Kane's cock is harder than Talbot's dick only because the latter has gone a tad limp from having had so much cum blasted through and from it. It's sexy the way the naked Kane's biceps, triceps, and pecs are in high relief, a thin veneer of sweat covering his naked torso all of the way to where it disappears in its mating with Talbot's lower body. There's a beading of perspiration clinging to the lower edge of Kane's jugular notch; Talbot is tempted to raise up and lick away that teardrop of salty moisture.

"You don't think it even a bit rude that you ate without me?" Talbot says.

"Ah!" Only now does Kane realize why Talbot might, despite the overload of pleasure, be a little miffed.

"I really wanted an exchange of cum," Talbot says."

"Your cock, my virile and sexy stud, will undoubtedly be up and ready to go again in no time. And, I suspect I have plenty of cum to spare."

Kane rolls his belly against Talbot's belly. He leans slightly more to one side in order for Talbot's dick to get almost the full impact of Kane's shifting weight.

"Tell me I can't successfully predict your cock's full resurrection," Kane says. He's well aware, as is Talbot, that the latter's cock has regained most of the stiffness lost during its so-recent blast-off.

"About my meal from your with-plenty-too-spare-cum dick ..."

"Well, since you seem to be ready to eat, and since I seem to be ready for dessert . . ."

Kane shifts, rather like dismounting a horse to remount from the opposite direction. When he completes his maneuverings, his cock is right above Talbot's head. The dick, for which Talbot has been begging, is right there for the taking.

Talbot lifts his head slightly. He has a sexy, sexy view, beneath the drape of cum-filled balls, along the belly of stiff dick, to where Kane, even now, bows his head close to Talbot's resuscitated dick and looks back in Talbot's direction.

Kane doesn't wait for Talbot to start before he begins anew over his companion's revived dick. Quickly, he has Talbot all the more worried that his own nuts will spew dessert before Kane's sap gets coaxed out even the first time.

It's not as if Talbot has to grab ass, and hang from it like a monkey from a tree, in order to get his mouth around Kane's dick. All he has to do is take hold of the cock, like he'd grab a lever, lower that lever from its position and place its pulpy cockhead to his pursed lips. With his cross-eyed view, all along the vein-meandered belly of the dick, as far as Kane's impressively drooped balls, Talbot can suck away.

Kane's cock isn't perfectly round. It's flattened along its back and belly, like a pipe squashed slightly, but uniformly, along its entire length.

A small additional raise of Talbot's head feeds more than two inches of cock into eager face. At which time, he plays monkey and anchors his hands securely to ass. He does a pull-up and pokes Kane's cockhead to the very opening of Talbot's throat.

Kane leaves off licking dick to ask: "You want me on my back?"

Talbot shakes his head. He's certain he's not committing suicide, via strangulation on cock, but because he doesn't want even the slight delay that would result for yet another shifting of positions.

What Talbot imagines is what he's going to do and how it's all going to happen without a hitch. It's a mental technique learned early in sports, first taught Talbot by a PE teacher in grade school, additionally reiterated by every coach he's had since. Think the move through, follow through.

That said, Talbot is surprised when he suddenly has his nose poked so deeply into Kane's scrotum that he actually smells the heady fumes from Kane's asshole. Kane's cock is so completely disappeared from view, up Talbot's throat, Talbot is actually curious as to what's happened to it.

"Sweet Jesus!" Kane says, hidden somewhere beyond the masks Talbot makes of Kane's hairy nuts. Which says Talbot achieves a bit of sword-swallowing magic that definitely pleases.

It's when Talbot realizes exactly what he's done that he becomes more acutely aware of just what's inserted deep inside his mouth and throat to the point where Kane's cockhead is somewhere beyond Talbot's Adam's apple.

Talbot's face falls away. Talbot is fascinated by the reappearance of Kane's stiff prick, apparently out of nowhere, that the dick slips free.

The released erection's first eruption deposits a mess of goo directly into Talbot's mouth, through lips not yet completely closed behind the just-exited dick. The rest of the spunk, to Talbot's disappointment, is misdirected, hard and heavy, into milky splatters along both their bellies.

"Ooops!" Kane says and sounds more than a little breathless. "Sorry about the hair trigger, but you're just too much a natural-born cocksucker for me to have held on any longer."

Talbot reaches for Kane's dick which is sagged to offer an inviting drool of tardy cream beaded within the prepuce-couched lips of the cockhead.

Talbot raises for additional drivel from the sagged cock and takes on bulbous cockhead right along with it. He still sucks lovingly on the head of the dick when Kane lifts a leg to dismount their sixty-nine position. Kane's cock comes free of Talbot's face.

"I want your dick," Talbot complains and makes a mad scramble to retrieve it. "I want to suck up each and every inch of it. I want to siphon every last drop of cum you still have hidden within your horse-big balls."

"I figure the best and fastest way to get a bit of starch back in this pecker of mine, stud, is advantaging your skills of being as much a natural-born ass-fucker as you are a natural-born cocksucker," Kane says. "What say you come at me dog-style? Then again ..." He goes to his back and lifts both legs, flashing Talbot an enticing peek at an extremely sweaty crease of studly ass. "... I think I prefer seeing your handsome mug while you're screwing each and every inch of your big dick up my shitty asshole. Although, might I suggest a bit of lubricant to make the passage a little more convenient for the both of us? I just happen to have brought along one very lubricated rubber."

He rolls to his side and stretches for his discarded trousers. His buttocks dimple attractively. Talbot is reminded of Peter's ass doing pretty much the same while the Peter's dick probed the lengthy depths of Gerald's skinny ass in the Spa locker room.

Talbot wonders just how determined Kane had been not to have sex, here and now, if he'd gone to the bother of bringing a rubber along. Then again, if Kane's decision not to have sex had occurred only after he'd arrived on the scene, as Talbot had expected . . . And, what red-blooded American guy didn't carry a rubber or two in his wallet — just in case he lucked out?

"Here," Kane says. He tosses over the prophylactic packet. "Try this extra-large on for size."

It fits fine and provides stiff pecker with a veneer of industrial lubricant that will easily see Talbot's dick up Kane's asshole.

Kane returns to on-his-back, his legs lifted. A hand is on each asscheek tugs his hair-lined crack is wide to provide a provocative glimpse of a pucker that seems way too small for the ordeal set for it.

"Check out my dick," Kane says. He nods toward his recently exploded pecker that has had no problem regaining all of its lost stiffness. "See how damned excited you get me, even before the actual plug of your cock up my butt?"

Talbot kneels up against the backs of Kane's raised legs.

"You just scoot on in," Kane says. "I'll make sure the big cock of yours gets perfectly aligned for insertion."

He hitches his hips higher. His legs rest on Talbot's shoulders. He can't see all that clearly; he has sweat in his eyes without even having realized he sweats. Even through his blurred vision, though, he finds Kane handsome as all hell.

Once again, Talbot's crotch gives a couple of spontaneous humps that don't hit pay dirt. Talbot has the horrible feeling he's going to cream another load, this time along asscrack, before his dick ever actually gets inside.

"There," Kane encourages.

Where all Talbot's cockhead has encountered, before, is cockshaft-bending impasse, it can suddenly tell, even through the nozzle of its rubber, that it finally pokes, with Kane's patient assistance, a spot of resilient softness.

"Slow and . . ." Kane begins but goes all gaspy when another of Talbot's sorry-ass reflexes feeds a good couple inches of dick up rectum.

"Sorry, sorry," Talbot helplessly excuses, actually prepared to pull out and start over.

"Don't go anywhere, stud," Kane says. His hands clamp tightly to Talbot's ass and don't let Talbot pull free even a fraction of an inch. "You're just fine, right where you are."

Blinking clears Talbot's eyes of sweat. He's even more turned on by Kane now that he sees him properly. Looking downward between them, Talbot sees all the way to where his dick forms a seeming walkway between his lower stomach and Kane's cock-stuck ass. Kane's dick is as stiff as a board. Its fat cockhead pokes Kane's navel and leaks preseminal goo. Talbot is willing to bet that if he had the flexibility of Kane, Talbot would likely be able to suck Kane's dick even while his cock fucks Kane's asshole.

"You always been able to suck your own cock?" Talbot asks. A jiggle of his ass feeds even more of his dick inside butt. Goddamn, Kane provides one helluva tight asshole! For the life of Talbot, he can't think any shithole he's ever fucked so strangulation-tight. And that includes Marky's butt, Jeffrey's rectum, and everyone else's asshole.

"You've been giving self-fellatio a try, have you?" Kane says. "Want to have your cake and eat it, too? Simultaneously eat it and my dick? Simultaneously eat it and some other guy's dick? Maybe not impossible as you think, if you just go at attempting it a little at a time. Slow and easy, get your spine stretched out, like it once was. Slow and easy, like you're now going to feed me the rest of your lovely cock. Your cock likely more than big enough for you eventually to achieve a successful your-mouth-to-your-dick touchdown, even if you're probably never going to get as flexible as if you'd started trying self-sucking earlier."

"Oh, yes, you seductive stud! Do it! Do it."

Kane's hands flatten against Talbot's chest. He does it to have leverage, to give a push if the rest of the cock comes at him too hard and too fast, but his palms don't exactly exert sufficient pressure to accomplish that. They just kind of rest where he's put them, flattened gently over pecs. Then, his fingers tent and exuberantly pinch tack-hard nipples.

Talbot bites his lip. Not because the pinching causes him pain, but because he needs the pain of lip biting to counteract the pleasure of nipple-pinching and asshole garroting. Talbot doesn't want to cream before his cock is all the way inside. At the same time, even well aware that his previous orgasm should have better prepared him for the next one, he's going to let go any second now. Which means a cum-filled rubber, so awash with his cream that it'll provide danger of slippage up Kane's ass, and it will need replaced before any continuation of the butt fuck. Talbot doesn't want the delay.

"Try the multiplication tables," Kane says.

"What?"

"Whenever I want to take my mind off creaming too soon, I mentally do the multiplication tables. You know: one times one is one. One times two is two. Works for me most of the time."

"I can't imagine anything taking my mind off this butt fuck."

"Flattery will get you just about anything you want from me." He gives an upthrust of his hips that puts a good four more inches into asshole.

And, then, his ass meets Talbot's belly and grinds against it. Talbot's dick — somehow! — is up the accepting asshole as far as cock can go. Talbot's scrotum swings forward for a sensuous and powerful collision with the small of Kane's back.

The weight of Talbot's torso pries open and falls inward between Kane's raised legs. Talbot's chest falls hard against Kane's chest. Talbot's nipples dig hard against Kane's nipples. Talbot's belly grinds harder against Kane's ass. Both Talbot and Kane's cocks stiffen all the more, in direct result.

"Oh, stud," Kane says. He gives a grind that, had were there more cock for Talbot to give, feed cock to deeper depths of the asshole. "Sweet . . . sweet . . . big . . . big . . . wonderful . . . cock."

His sphincter exerts such a rubber-band squeeze around the base of Talbot's dick, down where the cock connects to Talbot's belly, that it gives every indication of snipping off the hard penis and sending it to no-return disappearance up the sucking asshole.

Talbot drools. Luckily, he's able to lick and swallow most of it before he covers Kane with more slobber than would a rabid dog.

Kane's hands, back on Talbot's ass and knead asscheeks. He rocks his lower body and makes his asshole seem, while no less tight, a bit more accommodating.

"Oh, sweet Jesus, give me a minute," Kane says.

Talbot puts his face directly over Kane's. Kane's eyes are such an attractive grey. Kane has the longest, lushest eyelashes Talbot has ever seen. He has this small sexy scar, crescent-shaped, on his right cheek. He has a small cleft dead-center his chin. His full and pouty lips are just made for kissing — by Talbot.

Talbot kisses. The pressure of his lips forces Kane's mouth open. Tongue touches darting tip of tongue.

Their lips still locked, Kane's handholds on Talbot's ass take firmer grip. Like a pro basketball player able to palm a ball in each hand, Kane palms Talbot's firm asscheeks. He lifts on the butt. Talbot's belly elevates to pull out some of the hearty inches of dick which, until then, have been snugly fit within hard-won anal territory. The slide is a sensuous ride of hard dick through the butt-tunnel. Anal muscles exert pressure along the entire length of the submerged dick. Pleasure dances within Talbot's balls. His scrotum tightens its grip on his gonads and hoists his nuts and the surrounding hairy skin even closer to the base of the stiff dick. Talbot's nipples go harder against Kane's manly chest. Talbot's tongue greedily explores Kane's mouth for more slippery tongue and wet-warm spit.

Whatever Talbot's illusions of control, they're gone. His conscious mind is taken out of the loop. He's definitely on automatic pilot. He's pushing and pulling his cock in and out of Kane's asshole, like a drill gone crazy, like a piston being tested for endurance, like a jackhammer with faulty off-switch.

Literally, he can't control any part of his body. Not the sounds he makes, which, even to his ears, are downright guttural. Not his sudden eagerness to swallow Kane's face. Not his bucking hips that perform at a speed which should leave him exhausted but gets faster by the second. Not the building pleasure in his balls that expands, then contracts, then expands, then becomes as concentrated within him as anything put in one of those powerful garbage compactors.

What goes off inside him has him believe his dick spews not only cum but guts, the resulting vacuum threatening to turn him inside-out by pulsing each and every last bit of him out of his cockmouth and into the rubbery tip of the condom lodged and stopped deep up Kane's greedily accepting asshole.

Talbot doesn't quickly come down from his high. He's left, by way of residual accompaniment, with helpless body spasms and jerks. He's disconnected from reality, without a clue as to where in the hell he is. His eyes may be open, but his vision is filled with exploding stars and flashes of colored lightning. He pants, like a bellows smelting steel.

"Oh, Jesus!" he says when a hint of reality finally creeps back in.

Kane takes so long to answer, Talbot thinks him possibly dead. It's hard for Talbot to detect Kane's breathing over Talbot's loud and gaspy sounds. Talbot leaves his face where it rests, against the side of Kane's neck.

Kane's voice comes from seemingly far far away. "Christ, but I've never been given a ride so fucking wild and wonderful in my whole life of been fucked by the best."

Talbot wishes he could better read the curious expression on Kane's handsome face.

"What?" Talbot asks intuitively.

"Fear," Kane says without coherent lead-in.

"Fear?" Talbot laughs nervously. He hasn't a clue.

"My fear of being so consumed with passion for you that I lose all sense of reason and of what's best for you and of what's best for me."

"Fuck the fear! You're what's best for me — and vice versa." Except does he really believe that?

There's no mistaking the huge lake of dampness Kane's exploded cock has spewed to sticky coolness on them. There's no mistaking the huge lake of cummy cream Talbot's exploded cock still has socked up Kane's dick-stuffed rectum.

CHAPTER FOURTEEN

Jason is at a crossroads. Literally. Ahead, the road extends through Louisiana, Texas, New Mexico, Arizona, California, finally ending at the roiling surf of the wide-wild Pacific. To his left, the road forks south, and the attending sign says, NEW ORLEANS 40 MILES.

He's amazed to be this far. All of the way up the Florida peninsula. Through Alabama. Through Mississippi. Into Louisiana.

Each time he'd been let out of a car, starting with Louis's car in Titusville, there has been another car and driver waiting to take him a few more miles down the road. Twice, he'd actually been headed for the bus station when, "Need a lift?" was asked through an open car window.

He'd sucked Stanley-from-Jacksonville's cock. Stanley was headed to Mobile, Alabama, to visit his mother. Stanley was handsome. Brown hair. Brown eyes. Brown tan. Pouty lips. Fat, brown cock.

Jason's cock was sucked by Wendell-who-had-business-in-Tallahassee. Wendell owned a burger franchise. He'd been in good shape once — college football, he'd said. He was beginning to go to pot — too much time at a desk, he said. He was a genuinely nice guy. Jason was more than willing to haul out hard cock when Wendell asked for it. The guy gave wicked head. Jason had ended up asking for more.

Standing now, beside the sign pointing him toward New Orleans, Jason wishes he had Wendell's hot mouth and hugging throat to take care of one helluva painfully hard erection.

A couple times, Jason got a ride without sex. Gordon-from-Jacksonville, Karl-from-Mobile. Each had merely wanted Jason to keep him awake. Each had been on the road a long time. Each was dead-tired. Each was finally close to home. Gordon hadn't seen his wife and kids for over two months. Kenneth-headed-to-Slidell was so anxious to get home, he'd let Jason drive. Kenneth slept the whole way. Not much hair. Spit bubbling his lips between almost-silent snores.

One ride, another, another. As if fate, or Manifest Destiny, took Jason up Florida state, turned him left, coaxed him westward as far as this New Orleans signpost.

Jason has never been to New Orleans. The city holds out the same fascination for him that it does for lots of people. His mind's-eye flashes Mardi Gras. Half-naked men and women dance in costumes and throw glass beads from balconies, or from massive papier-mâché floats. Liquor, in paper cups, is carried from bar to bar, in the French Quarter. Excitement. Perversion. Degeneracy. Sex.

He really should see the French Quarter bars. He can enjoy some Creole cooking, some praline, then catch a bus on back the way he'd come.

The car that stops isn't headed in any New Orleans' direction Something about the way its wheels return to straight-ahead after having angled the vehicle to the side of the road. Some sleek-as-a-submarine foreign model that looks like a Jaguar but isn't. Bright red.

Jason wants to see the car up-close.

The driver is fat. Really fat. So fat, the car seat as far from the steering wheel as it can go, the man's belly fills all the available space. The steering wheel chafes blubbery abdomen whenever the guy, or the wheel, moves. Roly-poly cheeks completely crowd the tiny nose they parenthesize. One, two, three chins. His wispy blond hair, too fine to do much else, bangs to his small bags-beneath black eyes. Not exactly a package designed to tip the scales, New Orleans stacked up as counterweight.

"Need a lift?" The smile does nice things for the fat man. It animates his features. Suddenly he's not gross flesh and blood but friendly cartoon character.

"If you're headed to New Orleans," Jason says. Fat man looks harmless. The car looks expensive. Forty miles is quite a walk.

"You don't want to go to New Orleans," the fat man says. His head shakes in emphasis. His three waddles jiggle. His belly shifts against the supporting steering wheel.

"Which means you're not headed my direction," Jason divines.

"Headed for Houston."

"Thought I might check out New Orleans. Being this close and all."

"The city will eat you up and spit you out."

"Sounds interesting. At least the eating part."

Fat man laughs. He appreciates Jason humor.

"Oh, they'll be lining up, fast enough, around the block to swing on your big dick," the fat man says. "I'll bet you have a big dick, too, don't you?"

Modestly, Jason shrugs.

"Problem is, they'll want your big dick for free," the fat man says. "You want paid, they'll look elsewhere for their hard-prick and hot-cum meals. Too much prime meat, too much rich cream, free and available, in New Orleans, for anyone, but the most desperate, to pay for it. Almost as many hard cocks there, on display, as there are in Hollywood. Between this very spot on the road and Houston, however, a sexy stud, like you, is as rare as gold. You get to say, 'It'll cost,' and I get to say, 'How much?'"

Jason sees where this goes, if only because his traveling companions, thus far, have been more than generous. He's never seen as much action in Florida in so short a few-hour period.

"I really kind of want to see New Orleans."

"'Really'? 'Kind of'? 'Want'?" says the fat man. Encouraged, he struggles to get a hand into the right side pocket of his pants.

Jason thinks the fat man tries to play with himself. Maybe the guy has clipped the bottom out of the pocket so his hand slides right on in and fists naked cock. His cock as fat as the rest of him? Or, a small dick made to seem smaller by all the overhanging fat?

The bulge that might be fat man's cock and/or balls is a wad of fifty-dollar bills, fastened by a couple twists of rubber band.

"I'm rich," the fat man says. His fat roll of money, on full display, momentarily has Jason's attention. "I'm generous. I'm horny."

"I'm flattered. Really. But . . . "

"How easily these fifties peel free of one another!" Fat fingers slip off the rubber band and maneuver the elastic onto the fat man's wrist. Skin completely swallows the rubber. "Why don't you tell me when I should stop?"

Jason is fascinated by the flip of one, two, three, four . . .

"How about these just to get you in the car beside me, and the car a couple miles beyond this New Orleans turnoff? How about another bill to get you a tad farther down the road? Then, another bill for a few more miles. Then, once you're comfortable and a little less shy, you can end up with a lot more money for a bit of just sitting back and relaxing."

Jason looks nostalgically at the road sign. He looks at the fat man who smiles all friendly-like. He looks at the fat wad of rolled fifties. He looks at the bills already peeled off and waiting Jason to get in the car.

"Come on, stud, you know a good deal when you see it. Can't tell me you're willing to give away your cock when you've a buyer, right here, willing to pay for it. Maybe, you won't even have to show me your big boy-dick. Maybe, when the time comes, you up and say, 'Pull the car on over. I want out.'"

"And you let me out? Just like that?"

"I've never forced myself down on anyone's cock. As for the money already spent, by then, on your companionship . . ." He shrugs. His waddles shift. His belly quakes. The car seat moans from the strain of all the man's weight pressed down on it. "I've access to plenty of money. In any city, I'd have access to plenty of big-cock far less reluctant to come along for the ride than you are. Out here, in the middle of nowhere, however, it's a decidedly seller's market. Don't mean to flatter you, but you're the best hitcher I've seen since I started this road trip."

"Houston, you say?"

"How about I sweeten the pie?" Fat man's fat fingers peel another fifty-dollar bill from the fat wad. He stuffs the mother lode into the pocket of his trousers. He folds the two-hundred-fifty and rubs the result against his chubby cheek. He extends the money toward Jason at the open window.

"Fuck New Orleans!" Jason says.

He reaches for the folded money. He takes it. He stuffs it in his front pants pocket and, simultaneously, realigns his stiffy dick to a more comfortable position. He walks around to the passenger side of the car and gets in.

Fat man greets him with another wide smile and another fifty-dollar bill. Jason fastens his seat belt. The only sound the car makes as it turns back into traffic is the soft sigh of rubber tires against roadside gravel.

"Have I given you enough money for small-talk, or does that cost me extra?" the fat man says. He laughs. It's high-pitched but not girly. It makes the man's whole body jiggle, as if made of Jell-O. "And, what should I call you, besides stud, that is?"

"Jason Summer."

"Well, Jason Summer, my name is Crandix Lecton. Call me Cran."

Finally, small-talk out of the way, Cran puts two new fifties on the dashboard. Jason unzips his pants. He hauls out his hard cock. He waterfalls his impressive balls over the lower lip of his open fly.

"Oh, sweet Jesus! Lovely bulbous cockhead!" Cran says. "Lovely . . . lovely . . . bulbous . . . bulbous . . . cockhead."

Only then does Jason takes the two fifties from the dash and add them to his increasing cache. Two more fifties appear.

"One, if I can fist your hard cock," Cran says, his eyes back on the highway. One, if you can bounce up and down so your hard cock fucks my hand. You manage a cream, somewhere in there, and there'll be another hundred for you."

"And the resulting mess?" Jason has no doubts his cock will give cream, the money a definite aphrodisiac. His cock is as hard as he's ever seen it. His balls are stuffed to bursting with spunk that wants out.

"There are tissues in the glove compartment," the fat man says. "If some of your mess slops, you're rich enough to afford a new pair of pants, yes?"

"Yes."

"So, my hand on your dick?"

"The hardness of my pecker says, 'Come along.'"

Cran's hand extends the breach, between them. His fingers curl uplifted cockshaft and clamp down.

"Lovely, velvety-hard cock," Cran says. "Nothing like it!"

Jason braces against his seat. Expensive leather crinkles.

Jason lifts his hips slightly. His mushroom-capped dick slides upward through Cran's vise-like grip. He keeps on up-sticking his pecker until the roots of his cock make snug contact where Cran's little finger and palm form the lower curve of the man's fist. When his ass drops back down, deep again into the cushion of his seat, his bulbous-tip cock is a hot rocket returned to its finger-curled silo.

"Love the feel of your sexy dick," Cran says. "Love the bloom of your massive cockhead."

Again, Jason's dick sticks upward through the tightness of Cran's fist. The cockmouth opens slightly as much of the loose skin that encases the sold inner cockcore is held back by the friction exerted upon it by Cran's fingers.

"Keep bouncing that sexy ass," Cran says.

There's air-conditioning in the car, most of the summer-soon-to-come heat held in abeyance outside the speeding auto, but Cran's forehead and upper lip are small-beaded with sweat.

Jason, too, feels a helluva lot warmer than just seconds before.

"Feel free to fondle your balls," Cran says.

Jason takes that as his cue to do just that.

Cran's eyes are dilated. His cheeks are flushed. His brow and upper lip are more and more sweaty. The hairless triangle of skin that shows at the open collar of his shirt is glossy with perspiration sheen. His tongue is damp and wet and glides to moisten and pinken lips already as darkly pink as the lips of Jason's pecker.

"It's like holding a lightning rod," Cran says. "Electric. Can you feel the electricity, Jason?"

"Sure," Jason says. It's not so much electricity as a pleasurable sensation that gets better and better with each slide of his stiff dick up and through, back and through, the fist Cran continues to provide for it.

"Only a dick perfect as yours comes with so much voltage," Cran says. "I know, because I've fisted my share of cock."

Just keep my cock fisted, Jason silently begs. Just keep your hand as firmly clamped down on and around it ... even as you now have ... for just a little ... little ... while ... longer!

"Bounce faster, stud," Cran interrupts Jason's train of thought. "I want to see your cream. Can you show me some of that? Can you geyser your pearly spunk? Can you grease my palm with your spermy quick-silver?"

Jason can sure as hell try. He can increase the speed of his cock sliding Cran's fist. He can fondle his balls more roughly, the resulting pain pleasurable in speeding Jason to a quicker rip-roaring blast-off.

"Oh, yes," Cran says. "Just that very way. Up and down. Down and up. Cock shooting its fat neck back and forth through my fist. Balls, cum-filled, worked this way and that by playful fingers. Cream filling testicles more and more and more. To bursting, stud? Are you and your cock and your nuts able to give me the creamy display of pearly pyrotechnics I want?"

"Sure." Jason has been on the verge of ejaculation enough times to know when another is upcoming. He's not put off by the man's fat. He's not put off by the fat fingers grabbed round his dick. He's not put off by the fat man's dirty talk.

"Oh, I want to see your cum," Cran says. "Creamy cum exiting your boner-hard dick at supersonic speeds. I've wanted to see that even before I knew you came with such a luscious bulbous-head dick. Before I knew you came with such a lovely large cock. Before I knew you came with such enormous balls. So many bonuses by way of truly big dick and balls, when either could have been small as a hummingbird's and it wouldn't have mattered to me. You so sexy, by the roadside. You threatening to waste yourself on those jaded shits in New Orleans. I had to have you. I had to have your cock. I had to see your cock and your balls. I had to make your sweet dick erupt its load where I could see it. It's sexy . . . sexy . . . load."

"It's going to be a big load, too," Jason promises. Without being asked, he provides more hearty bounces of his cock through Cran's hand. He doesn't doubt he can carry through on his promise. His cum-ballooned testicles are so full they'll turn blue if not soon allowed to release what stuffs them. "You've never seen a load as big and as thick and as juicy as mine. Or, you'd worry about this beautiful car of yours getting all cum-drowned. You'd worry about the thick and gooey cum-stalactites that'll soon drool your car ceiling, shot there by my cock. You'd worry about the road ahead disappearing behind all the slime my pulsating penis will spurt across the windshield. You'd worry about clothes so cum-stained you'll be embarrassed to go into a store to buy a change."

"Can you do all of that for me, stud? Can you do even half of that for me? Are you really able to cream with my fat man's hand wrapped round your studly fat pecker?"

Cran's hand has a skillful way of holding cock that provides fisting and fondling and petting and caressing and . . .

"Sure, I've come for you," Jason says. "Buckets full. Just for you. Because you asked for it. Because your hand feels so good as I fuck it. Because you know a damned good thing when you see it. Because you know just what to do, just what to say. Because I want to give you a blasting of my creamy load. Not just because you've paid for it, but because I want to."

"Oh, stud! Oh, stud!" Cran is breathless. His face is sweaty. His face is red. So is his neck. So, beneath his shirt, is his hairless girth of blubbery chest and belly. "Fuck my fist!

All Jason needs is a . . . few . . . more . . . up-fucks . . . and down-fucks . . . and . . .

"Please, please, please," Cran begs.

Comets of cum. Streamers of cum. Gushes of cum. Floods of cum. Never-ending tidal waves of the stuff.

Cran's hand goes juicy within the spermal onslaught. Jason's pants puddle with pearly lakes. The dashboard teardrops spurted spermal residue. The windshield gets splattered, inside-out, with nacre slugs.

Cum is in Jason's hair. Cum is on Jason's left cheek. More cum flies, geyses, explodes, erupts, spews, blasts . . .

"Yes!" Cran marvels. He can't believe the wondrous magnitude of creamy cream Jason squirts for him. "Fucking, yes!"

Cran's stiff pecker goes off in his pants. The suddenness of the explosion disconcertingly wets and fills the crotch of his underpants. His attending pleasure is so intense he almost steers the car off the road.

CHAPTER FIFTEEN

"I'll race you to the lifeguard station," Marky says. "I'll race YOU to the lifeguard station. I'll RACE you to the lifeguard station. I'LL race you to the lifeguard station. I'll race you to the LIFEGUARD STATION."

So many ways to say the line. So many ways to say any line. If he doesn't have that many lines, considering he's slated to play only a very minor role in the popular TV series *SandBox,* because of a favor owed his father by one of the network executives, there are still enough lines assigned him to make him wonder which of myriad possible readouts are the ones the director will want.

Although, at the moment, it's more a case of memorizing words. *SandBox* is already into the shooting of its next-Fall season. Marky's part is minor enough to be shot "around" until Marky shows up immediately after graduation. Once he sets down in Hawaii, on the set, though, he'll be expected to take very little additional valuable time making his transition to professional actor. His scenes will be all that's required to wrap several episodes. If he can only memorize his assigned words, ahead of time, there'll be a director, on the other end, to tell him which, if any, of those words need emphasis.

"I'll race you to the lifeguard station," he repeats as the cell phone rings on the pillow beside him on his bed.

"Yo!" he says to the other end.

"Guess who?" It's Jeffrey.

"Leonardo DiCaprio? How goes it Leo?"

"Don't you wish!?"

"Actually, he does very little for me."

"If you say so."

"Jeffrey Layins, now, he gives me a real hard-on."

"What say we find something to do with that hard-on he gives you? Terry is getting together some of the old gang for a circle-jerk. Not too many opportunities left to see who among us can squirt cum the farthest."

"I do need to do something with my presently stiff dick, but I can't take the time. I've lines to learn. I've a geometry final for which I'm totally unprepared."

"How often do you think you, as an actor, are going to be called upon to figure out the area of an isosceles triangle?"

"Hmmmmmmm. Never? Except, what if this actor shit doesn't pan out for me? I'll need a good education, not to mention good grades, to fall back on."

"I've a hard cock you can fall back on."

"That and fifty cents will get me a good butt-fuck and a cup of coffee. Not exactly a superb career move."

"You're going to be a big actor. Take my word for it."

"Like I took your word we were going to win our last tennis tournament against Grenwall?"

"You're too negative. Just such negative thoughts made us lose the game."

"That and too many of us out, the night before, playing who could get his cock beaten longest without creaming."

"Would you be interested in tagging along if I told you Sam Nimms might be there? Tell me you haven't wondered how big his dick gets when hard and how far it can spit cream once it gets all nice and stiffy."

"How long has Terry been hinting he's hooked Sam and is on the verge of reeling him in?"

"Apparently, Sam has been expressing some real interest as of late."

"Says Terry! Besides, even if Sam is there, I really can't make it. Pull your pud a few extra times for me, why don't you?"

"Okay. Be that way. I'll win jism-squirted-farthest, hands-down, without you there for competition."

"Unless Sam exhibits his as-yet-unverified potential."

"Right."

"Tell the other peckerheads hello for me."

"One last chance to change your mind."

"Really wish I could, but I can't."

Jeffrey rings off, and Marky is back to, "I'll race you to the lifeguard station." Such a simple sentence. Only seven words, for Christ's sake! So, why, no matter which way he says them, can't he make them sound right?

He hadn't lied when he says he has a boner. His stiff dick is even more of a distraction now that Marky has passed up Terry's planned circle-jerk. Marky's stiff dick wants Marky to go. It throbs its disappointment at his decision to stay home, memorize lines, instead of caress pecker — his and others. As far as studying for his geometry test, how can he find that more important than getting off his cum-filled nuts with friends?!

He moves his hard cock one way, then the other, in the crotch of his cock-swollen trousers.

"What am I going to do with you, once I'm shooting *SandBox* in Hawaii?" he addresses his stiff pecker, as if it'll answer him. "Just how is it going to look, you all hard and swollen in one of those skimpy skin-tight bikinis all of the characters wear on and off the beach?"

Granted, the days are over of the early-TV Superman, Batman and Robin, padding their crotches in order to smooth out bulges and come across totally sexless. *SandBox* focuses not only on T&A (tits and ass), but on C&A (cock and ass). Even so, those bulged men's bathing suits, paraded weekly through America's living-rooms, are never filled with too-blatant-to-be-tasteless erections. Nor, in a show watched more for its beautiful bodies than for its plot lines or its character development, is it likely any cameraman will long oblige by shooting an unacceptably bonered Marky just from the waist up.

If Marky hasn't a clue how he'll solve his boners in the future, he knows how to take care of this one. Especially since he's not prepared to devote the time and effort required to get off via self-sucking, or even via hand-whipping.

He tosses the script aside and heads to his parents' bedroom. His mother and father won't be back for a couple of hours.

He gets the hand vibrator from the cardboard box in their closet. The vibrator was bought after his dad was in a minor fender-bender that left him, for a long while, with a stiff neck. The vibrator helped relieve neck tension, although his dad needed assistance with it, because he couldn't reach some spots on his upper mid-back. Marky's mom did the honors until her hand started itching so badly she couldn't stand it. After which, Marky took over.

One haphazard scratch of his balls, the vibrator turned on and strapped to his hand, provided Marky wondrous insight into a whole new area of vibrator-relieved stiffness.

So pleasurable the sensations of that first vibrator-touch to his balls, it had been almost impossible to interrupt them. If his father wouldn't have soon wondered what the hold up was, Marky would have helplessly vibrated himself right on to climax, right then and there, on the spot.

Since then, there have been so many times Marky has gotten his rocks off by setting vibrations loose on his cock and balls, it remains a miracle the little machine hasn't given up the ghost. Marky always calls upon it for an assist whenever he wants his rocks off without bother or fanfare.

He brings the vibrator back to his bedroom and unwinds its cord as he does so. He pulls shut his bedroom door. He fucks the vibrator's plug into the wall socket behind his bedside stand. He lays it to one side and goes into the bathroom for a wash cloth.

Back on his bed, he unzips his pants. He hauls out his stiff cock and big balls. He curls the wash cloth around his uplifted pecker.

He straps the vibrator so its small motor rides the back of his right hand, held in place by two elastic metal straps that hug his palm. He turns on the vibrator. He wraps his cock with his shaking fingers and takes hold.

The jolt is intense and immediate pleasure. His balls immediately respond and lose whatever their remaining bit of flaccidness. Marky's nuts so closely hug the base of his dick, it's as if matching burls hug either side of a massive tree trunk. Burls and trunk experience an earthquake that trembles right on down to root level and up to flaring crown.

"I'll race you to the lifeguard station," Marky says. "We can go inside, and I'll fuck my vibrating cock so deep inside your ass that you'll feel my cockhead clog the base of your throat from the inside-out."

He improvises the written script. In actuality, sex on *SandBox* is more innuendo than blatant. More soft-porn than hard-core.

The scene has Marky's character challenge a fellow lifeguard, female, to a race. Lots of running on *SandBox*. Lots of jiggling tits and ass, jiggling cocks and ass. All filmed in will-you-look-at-THAT? slo-mo.

Marky does a mental rewrite. He X's Miss Tits and Ass and pencils in Mr. Cock and Ass. Specifically, he puts in the character Kyle (AKA studly actor Drake Stone). Kyle/Drake is tall, dark, and handsome. Marky prefers the bit-player's dark-complexion to the main stars' blond, blue-eyed too-perfect surfer-men image.

"How's it feel, Drake? My vibrating dick deep . . . deep . . . deep . . . and poking the shit up your tight . . . tight . . . tight behind?"

He shuts his eyes and intensifies the fantasy. Long ago, he first imagined how *SandBox* character Drake looks shed of stretch-Lycra swimsuit worn into America's living-rooms every week.

Drake's cock is nice, big, and fat. His swimsuit always fits so snugly his cock-size leaves little to the imagination. Its uncircumcised smooth lines, from cockroots to cockhead, make it more acceptable to censors (if TV still has censors), than would the bas-relief bump of a cock-without-cowling.

"Tight . . . tight . . . Jesus, tight!" Marky says. Drake's swimsuit never leaves any doubt the actor's ass is rock-hard and sexy. His ass is just made for Marky's fucking.

Marky hooks the back of his cock with his thumb. His hand angles downward to include his nuts in the St. Vitus dance caused by the hand-riding vibrator. The sensuous trembling penetrates deep into his balls. Like cream, subjected to the vibrations of a blender, Marky's cum gets whipped thick, then thicker.

"Oh, yes! Oh, yes!"

He transfers his vibrating hand entirely back to his penis. He places his other hand over his balls and brings it into contact with his other hand. Thereby, he provides sympathetic vibrations through his balls-couching fingers.

"Won't be long now. Never takes all that long, fucking your tight ass, does it, Drake? Because, you get me so hot and horny in all those C&A shots, provided by all those camera slo-mos that provide glimpses of your shifting uncircumcised cock as you run, run, run those Hawaiian beaches. Because, I'm so often with a stiffy cock that if I don't get it regularly softened up your mix-master ass, I'll have people screaming that my cock shows way too much stiffy to the not-yet-that-jaded American TV-viewing audience."

Oh, vibrator sex is so good, so fast. So very little effort required. Just grab hold and hold on. No pumping. No stroking. No pretzeling to drink from his dick. No head-bouncing. No tongue-licking. No hearty suck, suck, sucking.

"Ready for my hot cream, Drake? This potential TV star ready to feed you a butt-full. Gallons . . . and . . . gallons . . . and . . . oh, oh . . . sweet, sweet Jesus gallons . . . going, going . . . GONE!"

His vibrating erection is in impressive eruption. His vibrating cum whips this way and that as it exits his pulsing cockmouth. His creamy streamers of cum, airborne, are drooly and wet. They hit and mess the washrag that wraps his cock. They crash-land his shirt, all of the way to the jugular notch of his neck. The continual vibrations, in accompaniment, jiggle up and out the very last of that tardy cum within his cockneck.

"Ahhhhhh . . . agghrrunnnghhhh . . . ugh . . . ugh . . . UNGH!"

His cock is hyper-sensitive after explosion. Vibrations, once so pleasurable, are painful.

His cum-gummy hand unclasps. His cream clings unbroken, a spermal webbing, between his open fingers. The straps that hold the vibrator to his hand are soaked with coagulating slime.

Marky clicks off the vibrator. The only sound he hears is his own climax-over breathing.

CHAPTER SIXTEEN

Change is inevitable. Jeffrey knows that. If his school grades aren't all that good, and never have been, he's no fool. He's known all along that graduation will be a major turning point in his life, and in the lives of his friends. What he didn't expect is how much things would change even before graduation. He's expected Talbot and Marky and him (the Three Musketeers) to be together, having good times, until the very end.

So, where's Talbot? Off sucking and fucking with some security guard, for Christ's sake! No way Jeffrey thought to figure Kane Clydesdale into these last-days-in-high-school equation.

So, where's Marky? He and his big cock are home. He memorizes lines. Jeffrey is excited for his friend having landed a part on the popular TV series. But, why does that have to interfere with their last few days at Hoover High?

Of the three friends and fuck-buddies, Jeffrey seems the only one who manages to keep his next step, on life's big highway (his scheduled summer modeling job in Seattle), from interfering with the here and now. He's resentful Marky and Talbot have been less successful in doing the same.

"Better hope that expression doesn't freeze on your face." Terry joins Jeffrey against the railing of the porch.

Terry is definitely a jock stud. Not big, as in fat-big. Big as in tall-big and muscular-big. He's in a time warp where get-togethers with his peers, everyone present simultaneously whipping wienie, is the be-all end-all sexual experience. If he ever gets out of that rut, offers up his hairy ass for fucking, or offers up his stiff cock for sticking someone else's asshole, God only knows how much fun he'll have.

"Your expression will only bring on people wanting sex with someone mean or scary," Terry says.

"Think so?"

Jeffrey doesn't turn in Terry's direction.

Terry's hair is brown. Not mousy brown but a lush and polished hardwood brown. Cut short. Parted on the left. His eyes are a pleasant combination of blue-green which gives one shade predominance over the other, depending upon the lighting and what Terry wears at the time. In the sole light of the porch lamp, his eyes are blue. His mouth has a full and sexy lower lip. His upper lip is less full and less sexy. His jaw is square. His nose is disconcertingly small on a face that warrants something more bulbous or something knobbed from having been broken.

Jeffrey has known Terry for a long time. He's liked Terry for a long time. They've had sexual good times, at regularly scheduled circle-jerks, for a long time. But Terry hasn't been nearly the key figure in Jeffrey's high-school years that either Marky or Talbot has been.

"I must be thinking of finals," Jeffrey says, "and how I'm never any good at them. Enough to make anyone frown."

"That where your buddies are? Cramming for finals?"

"Marky memorizes lines. As soon as he graduates, he's off to Hawaii to shoot fill-in stuff they've obligingly filmed around him."

"And Talbot?"

Jeffrey shrugs. Hardly any of Terry's business that Talbot fucks around with some guy who works for Talbot's father.

"Graduated from something as mundane as standing around in a circle and whipping his dick with the likes of you and me?"

"So, where's Sam Nimms?" Jeffrey wants to change the subject.

"Sam is still on the fence," Terry says. "Although, he teeters more and more favorably in our direction."

"He'd better hurry in his fall. Come summer, a lot of us aren't going to be around to see it."

"Sam is hooked. Believe me. All he needs is for me to do a bit of fancy reeling-him-in. Until I do, come on in and join the others."

"How about you and I suck each other's cocks, out here on the porch, then go inside and fuck the others? Literally fuck them, in the ass."

Terry laughs. It goes well with watching a TV football game, back-slapping, farting.

"God, Jeffrey, but you're way too sexually adventuresome for me. Likely, you're too sexually adventuresome for everyone here."

"Have you never wanted to know what it's like having a guy swing on the end of your dick? Have you never wondered what it's like having your butt cock-stuffed, or having your hard dick strangled to ejaculation up some manhole?"

"Wondered? Sure. Wondered enough to give it a try? Not yet. However, when that time comes, I'll be sure to look you up to see if you're still interested."

They go inside.

"Okay, men, what say we get started?" Terry says.

The ensuing ritual pretty much is set in stone, especially since everyone present has participated on at least one previous occasion.

Furniture has been pushed back by Terry, before anyone arrived. The center of the room is spread with a king-size sheet to protect the carpet from cum stains that might have Terry's parents wondering. The sheet is dark blue, so anyone who pays attention (and Terry always does), can see where any hard-blast of cum sets down. Terry so far has judged Marky's cock-squirting abilities the best around. Some cock's don't have any real power behind their cum-shots, even the very first shot out. Some total loads merely ooze like slow-moving lava from the lips of a volcano.

"Gather round, gather round," Terry says "Make sure you're not so close across from someone that you're in his line of fire. Not that we have to worry too much without shoot-the-moon Marky in attendance."

"Where is Marky?" Denver asks. He has a mad crush on Marky. He looks puppy-dog disappointed his idol isn't here. Any time Marky cares to fuck Denver's ass, or swing Denver's dick, or vice versa, it'll happen. Marky, though, is occupied with other things.

"Alas, Marky cannot be with us this evening," Terry says. "Already the demands of his soon-to-be-stellar TV career have at him. In that, he has scripts to memorize. Although, he does send his best wishes that we enjoy ourselves without him."

They form the prerequisite rough circle.

Terry stands directly opposite Jeffrey, in open invitation for Jeffrey's cock to try and blast that far. Mallory stands to Jeffrey's right. Bob stands to Jeffrey's left. Gilbert stands on the other side of Mallory. Denver stands on the other side of Bob.

Mallory runs on the cross-country track team and, like Gerald McTalen (not present, never present), is downright skinny. Although Jeffrey has seen no one skinnier than Gerald.

Mallory's hand rubs its sweaty palm through his short-cropped blond hair. His nose is thin. His mouth is thin. His cheeks are gaunt. His Adam's apple, like one of those elevators on the outside of buildings, goes up and down, up and down — whenever he swallows.

Bob's hair is curly black. Not tight curls but loose ones that form girlish ringlets if grown too long. He hasn't let them grow too long since kindergarten. His eyes are brown. His eyebrows meet over the bridge of his pert nose. His mouth is cupid's-bow. He stands five-foot three. Not-so-tall makes him an excellent gymnast. Gymnastics make his body nicely sculptured. Coins can be bounced off his hard belly.

Gilbert's hair is ash-blond. His eyes are strikingly light-brown in an otherwise normal face. He does a lot of weight-training, but you'd never know by looking. His natural musculature is irreversibly long and lean. No chiseled effect but shallow definition that separates his muscle groups. Streamline and almost hairless, he's a champion swimmer.

Denver is cute, rather than handsome. His hair is fine, silky black; there's plenty of it, a lot of which bangs his forehead. His eyes are sky-blue. He has a button-nose. His mouth is full, sexy, seemingly capable of offering up delectably wet kisses. He stands five-feet-ten.

"Okay, boys, on my count, let's unzip," Terry says. "Three, two, one."

There are the combined sounds of zipper metal against zipper metal.

"On my count, let's go fishing. Three, two, one."

A hand, sometimes two, probe each open fly to locate hidden cock and balls.

"On my count, let's reel. Three, two, one."

Cocks appear in varying degrees of stiffness. Testicles spill round the lower lips of open flies.

Terry's cock, big when flaccid, gets bigger when stiff, but not much. Of the other cocks in the room, Mallory's cock is medium when flaccid but goes huge. Bob's dick is small when flaccid and stays small. Gilbert's prick starts out short and fat and ends up long and thin. Denver's penis begins seemingly nonexistent, within its bushing of dark black pubic hair, but pops out of that underbrush like a giraffe finished drinking water.

Terry's dick is hard and juts upward. Mallory's cock is swollen to its halfway point, between medium-softness and huge-hardness. Bob's pecker is hard but pokes less from his pants than his balls droop toward the floor. Gilbert's erection resembles one of those bun-size wienies sold in packages of eight at the local supermarket. It even has the same light-brown color and shiny casing. Denver's cock is medium but getting bigger. Jeffrey's almost nine-and-a-half inches are hard, but they can get harder.

"Okay, guys," Terry says. "Remember, this go-round isn't a race. It's not who gets off first that counts. It's who squirts the farthest. If you can do that by whipping off in two seconds, be my guest. If you need a little more time to prime the catapult for letting go a really wet-and-soupy wad, take all the time you need."

Jeffrey prefers his dick grasped within a firm and manly fist. His palm, as much as possible, contains the circumference of his prick. Firm and manly strokes move cockskin up and back over solid inner cockcore. Terry prefers that exact same kind of handhold. However, what's right for these two isn't necessarily right for the rest.

Mallory likes four fingers to his cock's belly, his thumb to his cock's back. The whole left side of his dick remains untouched. The uneven pressure exerted by his fingers and thumb flattens his dick slightly on each inward and outward masturbatory slide.

Bob tents his cockhead and first three inches of cockneck with his thumb and fingers. When his cock fucks inward, his cockhead collides with, and mashes against, his cupped palm.

Gilbert utilizes a one-finger one-thumb technique of whipping his pud, but varies that, as jack-off progresses, so that sometimes it's two fingers, sometimes three, sometimes even four, that ride the belly of his monster.

Denver's cock-stroking is always enthusiastic and never in any set manner. All the years he's masturbated, he's still uncertain which of the many stroking techniques is right for him, in that he finds pleasure in all of them and incorporates them all. At times, like this, the method he uses depends upon whose cock he watches being beaten at the time. If he looks at Jeffrey's cock or Terry's cock, each with a whole hand whacking it, he uses his whole hand to control of his pecker. If his attention shifts the beating of Bob's dick, by fingers and thumb tenting the head and first few inches of a dick, cockhead colliding with palm on each in-stroke, he does that. Any and all handholds are capable of bringing him to a quick, full, and satisfying blast-off.

"I'm coming!" Denver says in forewarning. It's necessary everyone announce his moment, so the distance of any and all cum-shots can be noted by the rest of the group.

Denver's bolt of steamy cream erupts, flies far, and splats blue sheet about a foot from where Mallory stands across from him.

"Jesus, kid!" Terry congratulates. "You must be thinking of Marky to shoot your goo that far."

"I'm coming!" Bob and Gilbert say in unison. Their creamy shots seem destined to collide, like asteroids on intercepting flight paths, but each falls short of the mark. Resulting splats face each other across the center of the sheet, neither having flown over the mid-point.

"Denver's wad still champ!" Terry says.

"I'm coming!" Mallory says.

No one, not even Mallory, figures he'll challenge Denver's present distance record. Mallory's cock always provides impressive volume but never gets any distance. This time is no exception. His thick and magmatic jism bubbles up and out the mouth of his dick and never gets airborne. Creamy, pearly slime frosts his thumb and fingertips and cum-ices his erupting dick.

Terry figures himself with a good chance to beat Denver's shot, if he can just keep from blasting a . . . little . . . while . . . longer. He practices a lot, by himself, and always gets better and better distance the longer and longer he's able to hold off. Problem is, it's always harder to hold off when in the presence of so much hard cock jutting from trousers. It's even more difficult to hold off once cream starts shooting in every which direction, and/or bubbles (as in the case of the spermal eruptions from Mallory's dick). At the moment, Terry has one helluva hard time keeping his ejaculation from happening. Nothing turns him on more than a circle-jerk. Which is why, unlike Jeffrey and Marky and Talbot, he never feels compelled to search out male-male sex in any different format.

"I'm coming!" Terry says. He doesn't want to come. Not yet. But his conscious will-power has absolutely nothing whatsoever to do with it. All of the cream already splattered on the sheet . . . as well as the cream going thick on Mallory's cock and still-stroking thumb and fingers . . . is just too-too exciting for Terry to hold out any longer than he's already miraculously managed. Actually, not too bad a lead-in, considering so few are able to hold off as long as Jeffrey always seems able to do.

Terry's dick ejaculates three consecutive squirts of heavy cream that cross the sheet's center line but don't match the distance Denver's cum-shots made before them.

"Denver, you cum-shooting sonofabitch!" Terry says, a graceful loser. "Even Jeffrey's fabled powerhouse dick is going to have trouble matching your cum's distance-traveled this time."

All attention focuses on the firm handhold Jeffrey maintains on his pecker. He's usually last to blast, and this evening no exception.

"I'm coming!" he says.

An impressive shot of wet exits the pursed mouth of his dick and tries for Earth-orbit. Had the ejaculate been aimed on a course straight across the sheet, it would have splattered Terry's shirt. As it is, however, most of the distance Jeffrey's spunk travels is vertical not horizontal. Two big splashes of his ejected jism touch down, one atop the other, just short of mid-sheet.

"Good, God, Jeffrey, if you'd only aimed it, I'd be cum-drowned by now," Terry says. He's disappointed it hasn't happened. His cock regains much of the hardness lost after eruption by his just thinking of how Jeffrey's cum might have ended up clinging to Terry's neck, face, even hair.

"Hey, Denver, congrats!" Jeffrey says as soon as his pleasure releases him from its spell enough so that he can say anything. Since there's no real way to measure the distance Jeffrey's cum traveled upward before splash-down, official victory for the evening goes to Denver who suspects Jeffrey's spunk the real winner.

"Shall we call it a tie, do you think?" Denver is more than willing to be magnanimous, because Jeffrey is a friend of Marky, and Denver would like to get friendlier with Marky. Before Marky graduates and heads off to Hawaii. Time already disconcertingly short.

"Jeffrey knows the rules," Terry says. "He wants the glory for the farthest shot, he gets his head out of his ass and takes proper aim."

"Terry is right," Jeffrey says. "You won fair and square."

Jeffrey is more convinced than ever that, graduation still on the horizon, official summer-go-your-own-ways not even upon them, things have already changed. Talbot has moved on to his security guard and to frequent sexual fantasies of sex with some young architect who works for his father's firm. Marky has, for the first time Jeffrey can remember, given something (memorizing lines), a higher priority than sex.

Jeffrey is determined he, too, must just accept that things aren't as they once were, and that they aren't likely ever to be that way again.

Suddenly, he's genuinely anxious to be off to Seattle, and to whatever those summer adventures that hopefully await him there.

CHAPTER SEVENTEEN

The rain takes Jason completely by surprise. It begins while the sky is still blue above him. Some atmospheric quirk blows the water in from the cloudy southwest. Still-existing sunlight reflects off the drops and makes the downpour all sparkly. It occurs within a stretch of barren, arid country that obviously hasn't seen rain in a very long time. Individual drops hit roadside dust and cause the same corona-like crater-effect seen on that television commercial that uses slo-mo footage of milk dropped into a saucer. From horizon to horizon, nothing grows green except the abundance of multi-arm cacti and low-growing sage.

There's no shelter. None. No house. None. No hut. None. No tree. None. No large rock. None. The cacti are too streamlined to afford protection, their arms spindly as well as spiky.

Within seconds, Jason is pretty much a nearly drowned rat. He's made more than a little uneasy by lightning that begins to blast away at the sky just to the southwest of him. Each new flash is accompanied by a clash of thunder.

At least the rain isn't cold. The day it intrudes upon is as unseasonably balmy as all the weather Jason has experienced since Florida. The wetness would even be a welcome relief from the heat if it wasn't so wet … if it didn't make Jason's clothes so sticky . . . if it didn't plaster Jason's hair to his head … if it didn't waterfall his forehead and pretty much blind him most of the time.

He wipes away as much of the water as he can. He surveys the long stretch of nearly straight highway ahead of him and to his rear. He wants to see an oncoming car. He wants in out of the rain before the rain washes him away. He has heard of just such desert storms causing flashfloods. More people drown in the deserts than ever die there of thirst or starvation. The road's adjoining gullies are awash with swiftly moving floods of water, many of which empty onto the roadway.

Gone is Jason's determination to barter with the next driver: sex for a ride AND for money. Cran had convinced him that no way should Jason sell himself short, out on the road, studs as good-looking as Jason few and far between. Few drivers, bored out of their gourds, likely, according to Cran, would object to paying a little something extra for the company of Jason and his cock. No one ever likely to be as generous as Cran, however . . .

Sex for a fee is now the last thing on Jason's mind. Hell, he'd be willing to pay to get in out of the deluge that falls more and more heartily by the second. Lightning strikes nearer. Thunder claps closer.

"Rain, rain, go away. Come again another day!" It hadn't worked for him when he was a child. It doesn't work for him now. "Thunder and lightning, bye-bye, too."

Is it his fate, then, to be washed away in this resulting wet-wash? To be struck by lightning or be blinded by it? To be made deaf by the thunder?

He should have realized his luck was bound to run out. Hitching couldn't be as easy as he initially found it, or the roadways would be crowded with guys, like Jason, thumbing rides. He'd had it good. Very good. He'd expected it to be good forever. Wasn't he fooled?!

His clothes are saturated with liquid. They're as heavy as chain mail. His pants legs are funnels that empty water into his shoes. His feet make squishy sounds, readily heard above the rain and only drowned out by the more and more frequent outbursts of lightning and thunder.

The sky gets bleaker. The patch of blue that was once immediately over-head is closed. Once white clouds are grey. Once grey clouds are black. Once black clouds are blacker, blackest.

Some kind of frightened small animal runs the road immediately in front of Jason. The animal is so fast, it's only a blur. A roadrunner? A fox? A feral house cat — no matter no house within miles? None. A rodent?

What about snakes? Jason doesn't like the idea of confronting any snake, washed from its hole, which may think there's some safety offered by the hard surface of the road. Forget the phallic fatness, roundness, and length of all ser-pents. Jason doesn't, nor has he ever, found them in the least bit of a turn-on. All they offer is one more probable obstacle to his survival on this stretch of highway, drenched by a rainstorm of Biblical proportions. He may well end up dead, his body undiscovered, his parents and friends (who believe him still in Florida), left to wonder what in the hell became of him.

The horn-honk and headlights-flash of a SUV, suddenly up behind him, scare the living shit out of him. He'd looked in that direction seemingly but seconds ago and spotted nothing. The splatter of rain on drenched blacktop, the roar of gully streams awash with forceful currents, the crack of lightning, the clap of thunder, proved more dynamic than any sounds the vehicle made during its swift approach.

The driver's handsome face is illuminated by another streak of lightning, closer, in the murky sky. The driver is bone-dry, even after he rolls down the SUV window and says something. Says what?

"What?" Jason is a drowning rat with no ship to desert. Cascading water metamorphoses him into a waterfall, right there on the spot. He's more skittish from imaginings of death by flashflood, by lightning, by snake-bite.

"Can I take your picture?"

Jason is sure he mishears. The expected, "Want a ride?" isn't anything near what the driver said. The guy probably doesn't want someone so wet inside his car. To damage and water-stain the car's upholstery. To entice a light-ning strike.

"Wait!" the guy says. Anyway, that's what Jason thinks he says.

The SUV moves on by. No ride there, then?! No dry refuge from the storm. No welcome heater. Unseasonably warm weather or not, unseasonably warm rain or not, Jason begins to chill.

The SUV pulls off onto the side of the road not far ahead from where Jason stands. Jason quickly closes the gap between him and the car. The driver, though, is out of the vehicle before Jason can ever get into it.

Jason is fascinated by how quickly the driver goes from dry to wet. Short-cut black hair plasters the guy's skull. Flannel shirt soaks to the point where it no longer hides the guy's pert nipples. The guy's crotch soaks to where his cock more readily bulges the now-drenched material.

"I need a lift," Jason states the obvious. He's joined the driver at the back panel of the SUV.

The guy opens the back. Is he offering an invite to the interior, via the rear? Does the man figure Jason's drenching of the storage space is likely to do less damage than wetting down the leather-seat upholstery? Except, the revealed space is cluttered with all sorts of photographic equipment and a western saddle. Is there a horse in there somewhere, too? Jason will willingly battle any animal for a dry spot of terrain.

"I need a photo," the driver says.

He flashes a camera before Jason's face. Everything is momentarily illuminated by a very brilliant arch of lightning. The follow-up crash of thunder is way too close for Jason's comfort.

"You need a photo?" Jason remains disbelieving, despite the props. He's forced to repeat. "You need a photo?"

The guy steps in closer. He's attractive, even when rain-soaked. (Have Jason's good-looks remained as much intact?). The guy's tan is enhanced by the water that clings in droplets to it. The poutiness of his coral-colored lips is magnified by water-slick. His long and lush black eyelashes are spillways for liquid. His eyes — lightning-illuminated — are crystal green.

"You're already wet, so what difference being wet for a few more minutes?" he says.

He stands so close to Jason that the steam from their bodies mingles into one fogbank around their legs. His breath has a pleasant minty smell.

His plastered flannel shirt now reveals evidence of the square pectorals that go with his pointy-tip nipples. Wet material, likewise, evidences scalloped abdominals, as if cloth were only wet Kleenex spread over large bumps in the landscape.

"I'm a photographer," he says. As if anyone else would request from Jason anything so bizarre, under the circumstances.

"And, I'm a drowned rat." Superfluous.

Only a madman would so willingly sacrifice the creature comforts of his dry automobile to join Jason in the rain.

"Glad to give you a lift," the photographer/madman says. "I'm headed all of the way to L.A. Glad to give you a change of clothes. Glad to give you a hot meal at the next available restaurant. All for just a few more minutes of your time spent in the rain."

Lightning strikes very close. Jason sees the resulting puff of short-lived smoke.

"We're going to be fried," Jason says.

"Stand over there, if you will?" The photographer points to a spot a little farther off the highway.

"And do what?"

"Just stand."

"You're kidding!"

"No. Just stand. Please. You're perfect. You're just what I've spent the last three weeks looking for."

"Right!"

"Won't take long. Promise."

Jason, so recently coaxed by Cran into believing the feasibility of requesting money before getting into any car, is now persuaded to pose for a picture in order to get into one. What a fucked-up world it becomes!

"Here?" Jason asks and assumes the spot.

"Perfect."

Jason disagrees. He's wet. He's cold. He's a posing monkey.

The guy snaps his camera. While standing. While leaning. While kneeling. From the left. From the right. Snap. Snap. Snap.

Jason thinks they're done. Gratefully, he follows the guy back to the open back of the SUV. Jason, even more, will welcome any dry spot, out of the rain, even if it's crowded somewhere among all the photographic equipment and the western saddle. The western saddle what the guy manhandles out into the rain.

"Hoist this over your right shoulder, will you?"

"I look like a horse?"

"You look like a cowboy."

"I'm here from Florida, for Christ's sake!"

"Maybe you are, but that's not what you look like. Illusion is the name of the game."

Game? The days are long gone when Jason enjoys playing in the mud.

"I look like shit!" Jason says.

"You're kidding, right?" the photographer says.

"Right!" Jason is in no-way kids.

The saddle is heavy. Jason doesn't envy any horse that has to carry the damn thing around all day. He has trouble getting it up and over his shoulder. That's the kind of "cowboy" he is.

"Take hold of the saddle horn, there," the guy says and gives a helping hand.

It's all so fucking unreal.

Maybe it's a dream. Maybe Jason is already knocked unconscious by lightning and hallucinates in his coma.

"Wait! Wait!"

As if Jason is going anywhere, weighed down by rain and the saddle.

The photographer produces a hat. A Stetson. Dry one moment. Wet the next. Downright droopy by the time it gets from the back of the car to Jason's head.

"Jesus!" Jason says. Never has he felt so much like an animal performing for its supper. He would feel less put upon if required to pull out his cock for a ride, for money, for a meal.

The guy snaps more photos. Lightning strikes more times, closer to home. The heat of it warms the backs of Jason's legs and his ass. If not for his being rain-soaked, he's sure he'd be on fire.

"Fucking great!" the guy says.

"You're fucking crazy!" Jason says. He's had enough. Of the butt-singeing lightning. Of the rain. Of the saddle. Of the cowboy hat. Of the kook with the camera.

"Here," the guy helps wrestle the saddle back into the SUV.

Jason dispenses with the hat by giving it a toss inside.

"Need a cock-suck?" the guy says. He's up close and very personal. His smile dimples ever-so-slightly his left cheek. His green eyes sparkle. His stiffening cock impressively extends downward along his left thigh.

"You're crazy!"

"Crazy. Horny. Cock-hungry."

Jason shakes his head, in disbelief.

The photographer doesn't take Jason's head-shake as a negative. Quite to the contrary, he goes to his knees in the water and the mud. His hands slide over Jason's slim hips. His thumbs hook round Jason's hipbones. His fingers curl back toward the crack of Jason's ass.

They can be lightning-fried on the spot. They can be swept away in the deluge already covering the road with over an inch of water. They can cause any passing motorist to veer off the road, seeing what he sees, and hit a cactus, die in a roar of soon-to-be-rain-doused flames.

So, why does Jason just stand there and let the guy unzip his pants? Cran would shake his head with disappointment at Jason's lack of business acumen. What better time to ask for cold cash than now? The photographer, obviously, is hooked.

Also hooked, though, is Jason. If he failed to recognize the lead-in as the turn-on it was, he doesn't mistake the turn-on of the here and now. His cock gets so hard, so fast, it's a miracle the photographer successfully wrestles the penile monster out of the tight-clad wet cranny into which it has ended up stuffed.

"You have a name?" Jason asks. His cock is out. His balls are out. The coolness of the rain-saturated air, outside the snugness of Jason's trousers, in no way makes the kid's cock less stiff, or makes his balls less likely to produce rich gallons of creamy cum.

"Danon (call-me-Dan) Wilcox." He's handsome as all hell, down on his knees, his face so close to Jason's released cock and balls that his peppermint breath sexily cools the cock's bulbous head.

"Jason (call-me-Jason) Summer."

"Hello, Jason. Hello Jason's big-head cock."

Jason has trouble deciding whether or not his hair stands up on the back of his neck because of Dan's mouth suddenly gobbling cock, or because of the electricity that saturates the air. The sudden reverberating boom, flash of light, and rush of heat can as well be the result of Dan's expert head-over-cock as of any natural phenomenon.

Jason leans back his head, his face to the blackness of the heavens. His mouth opens. The rain is sweet and refreshing on his lips. Overflowing rain-water cascades his cheeks, his throat, his shirt, his pants.

More lightning. More thunder. More pleasure radiates from his cock to his belly to his cum-filling nuts.

His hands are in Dan's black hair. The hair is so lush and so thick that it feels and looks lush and thick when wet. Few people have hair that looks as sexy when water-soaked.

Dan's sucking, which initially concentrates on the knob of Jason's pecker and on the first three inches of Jason's cockneck, now swallows the entire length of stiff pecker, from its head to Jason's balls. Cockhead and cockshaft plug Dan's throat. Suction tries to siphon, in and down, even more.

"Unbelievable," Jason says. All of it is so unworldly, the least of which is his dick getting so thoroughly polished in the middle of a Texas desert freak pre-summer rain, lightning, and thunderstorm. Jason remains drenched to the skin, although he's no longer as chilled by his drenching. Heat generates at his crotch and infuses the rest of his body to the point where his crotch literally steams, even more than before.

Thunder rumbles above and gives complementary sound to the pleasure running rampant inside Jason as Dan continues eating dick in pre-summer rain-fall. Lightning streaks the overhead sky, no real match for the electricity that suddenly sunbursts from cock-up-mouth-and-throat to all other parts of Jason's body. Jason dries from the inside-out.

"Sweet, sweet mouth, fucked by my big, big dick," Jason says. His hips commence automatic pumps to match perfectly the slide of Dan's mouth up and back . . . up and down . . . rise and fall . . . over the stiff cock. "So good. So very good. So very, very good!"

Dan's hand rolls Jason's nuts like marbles rolled in a bag. The rolling causes a dull ache more pleasurable for Jason than painful. Causes an accelera-tion of the rush Jason's body makes toward ejaculation of cream already too much for even his ample nuts to handle.

"I'm going to come," Jason forewarns. "Jesus . . . I'm . . . going . . . to . . . Jesus . . . oh . . . oh . . . come . . . sweet, sweet Jesus . . . come . . . oh . . . ahhhhhhhh . . . ahhhhhh . . ."

He takes hold of Dan's head, holds it in place, rams cock all of the way inside that head and leaves it slotted there. His dick swells larger and longer in final indication of . . .

"Come!" Jason squeals to the high heavens which respond with a loud flash of lightning and a simultaneous clap of thunder that shakes the landscape and everyone on it.

Once through pouted cockmouth, the creamy sex-cream enters the suction of Dan's face and speedily slides Dan's eagerly awaiting throat.

Jason is sure he dies and goes to some Norse Thor-hammer heaven.

CHAPTER EIGHTEEN

"I've a friend who lives there," is Jason's answer to Dan's question as to what Jason plans to do once in L.A. Jason figures it's best to seem to have a plan, rather than come off someone who started hitching one day, on a whim, and keeps on going. It's best Dan not think Jason will end up in L.A. at loose ends, without a pot to pee in, without anyone who really gives a damn.

Nor does Jason lie about the friend. He does have one who, at least the last Jason heard, now lives in L.A. The two had been really close when friend lived in Miami. They'd been getting closer, physically and emotionally, when the friend's father, had burst in and proceeded to shit bricks and deliver threats. After which, his friend's irate father ships errant son cross-country. Jason finally got a very short sorry-but-this-is-probably-for-the-best note to that effect, with a return L.A. address, 123 S. Caliente. Which Jason remembers, because 1, 2, 3 is easy enough, and *caliente* means hot in Spanish; Jason and friend having been in the midst of hot-getting-hotter sex when dear dad had appeared on the scene.

"You might think seriously about doing some modeling if my photos of you turn out the way I think they will," Dan says. Neither Jason nor he are going to have to wait long to find out if they're good or not. Dan has paid for adjoining rooms in a motel, and — eschewing digital cameras — he's converted the bathroom of the one into a darkroom. "I've friends in the modeling business. Definitely, I can get you an interview at the Rudolph Green Agency."

Jason Summer: model! Jason tries to see himself in some ad in some magazine, or on TV. It sounds good (too good to be true).

"Unless your friend already has you lined up for something."

Jason hopes his friend, feeling safe enough across the country from dear dad, might have Jason lined up for some hi-again-and-glad-you-came *caliente* fucking and sucking, once Jason appears on that 123 S Caliente doorstep.

"You freshen up," Dan says. "I really want to hurry those photos to see how they come out. Then, we'll go somewhere and eat, by way of celebration."

"Unless the pictures turn out looking like shit." Jason's impression of his photo session in the rain is still that of Dan clicking away in a downpour that left the two looking drowned-rats.

Whatever the photographic results, the hot shower feels good. His soak in that Texas downpour left him anything but refreshed. Especially as he'd waited for his clothes to dry in the blast of the car heater. The heater heat, combined with the mugginess outside, had left him with more of a headache than the …

"Jesus!" he says and turns toward the suddenly open shower door. He expects Norman Bates, from *Psycho,* but it's Dan. The photographer stands on the bathmat just outside the open door. He's naked as a jay. His looks, complete with stiff circumcised dick, are enough to take Jason's breath away, even without the benefit of surprise appearance.

"Pictures look great," Dan says. "Pictures look really great. Pictures look sexy-great, as you may well be able to tell by just how stiff my stiffy is."

"No denying your dick is stiff," Jason says. His own prick, semi-hard from the hearty and thorough soap-down he's given it, begins additional swelling.

No denying Dan and his hard cock provide a sexually inviting package. The photographer is everything out of clothes that Jason imagined in the clothes-plastering rainfall.

Dan's pectorals are square and hairless except for a fanning of hair across upper chest that funnels through deep pectoral cleavage and keeps on going, haloing flush-with-scalloped-abdominal navel, to mingle with the black strands of Dan's cock-sprouting pubic bush.

"I thought, maybe, we could celebrate by doing a bit of eating before we head off for eating. Or . . . ?" Dan says.

"Or?"

"Or, you could show me whether or not that big cock of yours feels even half as good up my asshole as it felt fucked to its balls up my sucking face in the rain."

"Didn't your mother tell you it's unsafe to be butt-fucked by a rubberless stranger?"

"'Always be sure the stranger's dick is rubberized, Dan,' is what the dear Mum always says." He produces a condom, already unwrapped, palmed in his right hand.

Jason is hotter than the temperature of the shower water warrants.

"Smart woman, your mother," Jason says. He turns more toward the spray so his rinsed-free-of-soap dick is free of run-off. He takes the condom and rolls it all the way down his erection.

"Good thing I bet on a long shot and brought along some extra-large," Dan says. "Your dick will stretch to bursting anything smaller."

He steps into the shower with Jason.

Jason doesn't move to make additional room. He wants the photographer really up close and personal. Nor is he disappointed. The hardness of Dan's muscles actually touches Jason on Dan's way in. Dan's pointy nipples brush Jason's chest. Dan's dick touches Jason's cock and stomach while temporarily jockeying with Jason's prick for what little space is available between them.

"I saved the lubricated condoms for later," Dan says. His hands are on Jason's shoulders. They slide the length of Jason's arms in petting caress. "I figure there's more than enough soap slick to be provided by even a tiny motel shower-room bar to get your dick plenty lubricated for its trip up my asshole. Tight as my asshole very well is."

"Why don't we find out?" Jason says. "Whether there is, indeed, enough soap on the bar. Whether your asshole is nearly as tight as you say it is."

"Oh, it's tight, all right. It only takes on the cream of the studliest cocks, like yours, my friend. Those cocks few and far between, even for a photographer, like I, who has access to some of the best-looking men around."

"Flattery will get you nine-and-a-half inches."

"Looks more like twelve."

"Who knows but that the sight of sexy you may have given my dick a few more inches."

No doubt of Dan's continued sexiness. No denial of how the very notion of cock-plugging the photographer's ass makes Jason dizzy.

All Jason's sex, on the road, up until now, has been beating his own meat for some driver's viewing pleasure, letting some driver beat Jason's prick, letting some driver eat Jason's erection.

Dan turns to the shower wall, opposite Jason and the spray. His hands splay atop the wet and water-dripping tile. His arms straighten. His hips arch back so the crack of his ass suddenly hot-dog-buns the uplifted shaft of Jason's wiener.

"Fuck me, stud," Dan says. "Put your soapy dick so deep inside me I won't be able to speak because of your cockhead poked into my vocal chords."

Jason's back blocks the shower water and splashes it fan-like from one side of the stall to the other. Soap in hand, he works up a bubbly froth, most of which manages to lather his hard prickshaft. More of the lather paints his balls. He rolls his slippery testicles. His pleasure is only increased by the pleasure-pain of hand-manipulated gonadal collisions.

He turns his attention to Dan's sexy asscrack. Dan's ass and crack seem hairless until Jason's fingers probe the depths of the slit where buttock meets buttock along their shared tight seam. A line of curly hair grows each muscled inner wall and encircles the dark wink of Dan's sexy, sexy pucker.

"If I cream prematurely, you hopefully have another rubber?" Jason says. He's in so close his belly mashes Dan's butt, his chest rides the slight forward curve of Dan's back.

"Eleven more of the original dozen."

"I like a guy who comes prepared."

"I like a guy who says my asshole is sexy and makes me fight off a premature come."

"Talk about premature come, it's going to take all of my concentration to keep from blast-off before I even shove in."

Jason isn't kidding, either.

What he does next — deliver a slap to one cheek of Dan's ass — is automatic.

"You've done this before, have you?" Dan says. (No, "What in the hell was that for?")

"A few times," Jason admits.

"You aren't doing anything to me, including hand-paddling my ass until it bleeds, to make me any the less needful of your cock up my shithole."

Relieved to find Dan adventuresome, Jason delivers another slap of wet hand to wet buttocks. The heat of hand-to-ass contact, the heat of the water, the heat of their bodies, contribute in making Dan's buttcheeks sexy pink.

"I want my dick gripped by your tight ass too much to hold off any longer," Jason says.

"My asshole is yours for the fucking," Dan says. "Come on in."

Jason's butt arches back, projected deeper into the shower spray. Water funnels his tight asscrack. Liquid spills the lower end of his butt seam and cascades the backs of his legs. Some of it defies gravity and flows between his legs, soaks his balls and only from there finally falls to the floor for final whirlpool down the drain.

His bar-of-soap-palmed hand pushes open the crack of Dan's ass. Jason's other hand wrestles Jason's cock from vertical to horizontal. Jason's bulbous cockhead slides the soapy crease from the small of Dan's back to the wrinkled eye of hair-encircled sphincter.

No denying Jason is in need of putting all of his cock all of the way up Dan's awaiting rectum.

At first, it doesn't seem possible Jason's cockhead can achieve entrance through and into a pucker so damned small. It's Dan, though, so turned on by the pulpy cockhead merely pressed to anal doorway, who proves the asshole up to the task. Dan's hips swing back and forcefully ride his sphincter up and over Jason's knock-knock cockhead.

"Sweet, sweet!" Jason says, his breath sucked away by the fiery pleasure lit by just his cockhead up the sexy photographer's ass.

"More cock, please!" Dan says and makes it so. His pucker, rubber-band-like beneath the coronal flaring of Jason's big dick, re-stretches as it begins its ride over the expanded cockshaft that begins immediately after the slight indent beneath Jason's sexily mounted mushroom cockcap.

"Yes," Jason agrees, a good two inches of his cock, plus his cockhead," suddenly disappeared up Dan's ass. Only a little over seven inches of Jason's dick left to go.

"More!" Dan says and takes an additional two inches which slide into place within the anal vise which has Jason dizzy with excitement.

"Yes! Yes!" Jason agrees. This time, though, he's beyond waiting for another back-up of Dan's actively participating ass. Jason's hips buck forward. One inch, another, another, and a bit more poke home.

"Agggrrunnngh!" Dan grunts pleasure as the lumpy head of Jason's dick collides, then passes by, the man's walnut-size prostate.

Jason's wet belly meets Dan's hard wet ass with a resounding sound louder than the hand-slap that preceded. Jason's scrotum, weighed by large nuts, and momentarily left stationary by the pull of gravity, begins its tardy follow-up to Jason's hip movement. It proceeds in an arc that whacks it into the hard strip between Dan's wide-spread legs. Had the balls flopped just a little farther through the breach of muscled thighs, the sex-sac would have knocked Dan's contracting scrotum that hangs the other side.

"I'm in!" Jason is amazed. Amazed he's in. Amazed he hasn't creamed along the way. Amazed he doesn't cream in the face of such a snug and complete penile penetration of vise-tight asshole.

"Tell me about it," Dan says. He's breathless.

Dan's mouth remains open. A deep breath sucks in heat, water-saturated air, and essence of writhing males in heat.

"Do I have all of your cock in me, stud?" he asks.

"All of me," Jason says. If Dan's voice is breathless, and it is, Jason's is decidedly reedy. Jason's mouth opens and shuts, opens and shuts, but says nothing.

"Give an extra push of your pecker, just to make sure."

Jason gives the requested extra push.

"Grind your prick in place."

Jason fucks his belly more tightly against Dan's ass.

"Ride this stallion, cowboy!" Dan says.

City-born-and-bred very-first-time-in-Texas Jason becomes the cowboy for whom Dan asks. He pulls his cock all of the way back to where sphincter-ring mouths cockhead, where corona flares. He pushes all of the inches right back in.

Intuition tells Dan who, after all, has been fucked before (if not countless times, at least several), that all previous screwings of his asshole dim in comparison to this one.

"Aggrrunngg . . . aggghrrung . . ." On its slide in, on its slide out, Jason's fist-size cockhead rams Dan's tender, getting more tender by the moment, prostate.

"Ride me!" Dan commands. "Ride me . . . all of the way . . . to fuck'n root'n-toot'n pistol-shoot'n let'n-loosen cream!"

Even while he continues to fuck, Jason runs his hands along Dan's extended arms, from forearms to biceps. His fingers slide round the arms to triceps. His hands glide underneath the arms. The bar of soap, still palmed, leaves its trail of slime.

Soap slick-paints Dan's right flank, his belly, his chest. Jason's other hand mirror-images but leaves only wet skin. Jason concentrates the bar over Dan's right nipple. The nipple goes hard against the small, getting-smaller, soapy rectangle. Dan's other nipple goes just as hard against Jason's unsoaped palm.

"Feels good," Dan says. "Feels fucking good."

For Jason, it feels good, too. Really good. His hard cock primes for blast-off up tight asshole. His fingers slowly dance the muscle definition of the handsome photographer's water- and soap-sheened torso.

In the end, Jason's hand, without soap, steals from the sudsy slick left in the aftermath of his other hand's exploratory feels. In a coordinated series of large and small whorls, Jason successfully soap-paints the whole front of Dan's torso. When both of Jason's hands slide into Dan's pubic hair, their knuckles sensuously contact the back of Dan's uplifted cock.

"Oh, yes . . . oh, yes," Dan says. His lower body begins a sequence of slow rolls that revolves his asshole around Jason's fucking cock. It's as if Jason's hard-on is a jump-rope turned from both ends.

Wondering how he's put off the temptation this far, and unable to resist any longer, Jason fists Dan's cock with both hands. The palm of his one hand still contains the motel soap which is now wafer thin and soft enough to mold that part of Dan's stiff prick to which it's firmly pressed.

Jason's fists ride the dick, and the soap leaves the same soapy residue on the penis that it's left elsewhere on Dan's body. Little of the soap washes away, because Jason's body continually shields Dan's body from the spray.

"Big cock," Jason says. He refers to Dan's impressive erection, not to his own.

"Mmmmmm." Dan can't manage any more of a response than that. It feels so good having this dick rammed home up his tight ass that speech is pretty much impossible. It's a bonus to have Jason's hands busy massaging the length of Dan's stiff pecker.

Everything goes perfectly. Coordination of photographer and pseudo-cowboy is so in-sync it's as if Jason fucking Dan is all old hat (Stetson?) for the both.

Dan's scrotum, as well as the corresponding bag that holds Jason's testicles, compact to basketball masses pulled tightly against the base of its accompanying stiff dick. Jason's one hand leaves Dan's erection and slides to soapy cupping of Dan's cum-bulged gonads. Jason rolls his handhold. The contained sack of goodies is so compact none of it, slippery as it is, escapes through any breaches between his fingers.

For Dan, Jason's three-prong attack — to asshole, to cock, too bull-like balls — is an exquisite composite of pleasure and pain, pleasure predominant. His hips take up wilder and more emphatic revolutions that stir his cock in Jason's hand, that tug his scrotum within Jason's grasp, that torque his asshole around the in-and-out movements of Jason's dick.

Jason assumes a lower bend over Dan's body. Jason's cock is full-stuck up butt. Jason's belly melds with the muscled mounds of Dan's buttocks. Jason's chest hugs the photographer's back. When Jason's cock pulls out, only his cockhead still in place, the move is smoothly accomplished.

The fuck moves into higher gear. The slaps of Jason's belly in collision with Dan's ass are louder than shower water splattering Jason's back and portions of shower-stall walls.

"You're fucking my butt . . . squeezing my nuts . . . playing my dick toward creamy cummy discharge," Dan says. He's between wanting his spunk to erupt, right then and there, and wanting it to stay put for a few more luscious moments of ecstatic build-up.

For Dan, well-known photographer, fucks of his ass by attractive studs, in and out of showers, are more easily come by than they would be by ordinary Joes on the street. Nevertheless, that doesn't mean every guy who fucks Dan does so as well as another. Some really stunning men, in the looks department, in the cock department, can't fuck butt for shit. Nor will they likely ever do so, no matter how many assholes they screw in their lifetimes. Then, there are the rare few, Jason among them, who take to screwing ass with the same consummate skill as a fish takes to water, as a bird takes to air, as an earthworm takes to ground.

"It doesn't get any better than this," Dan says.

Jason agrees. There's something magical about the wrap of Dan's asshole around Jason's entering and exiting pecker. There's something intimately exciting about Jason's hand on Dan's cock, Jason's hand on Dan's balls, Jason's body curved all the more tightly over Dan's back and ass.

Of all the sex Jason has had, this is the best.

Already, Jason's hyper-state tells him he's pumped this ass to the very brink of a deep and wondrous precipice. It's only going to take a few more slides of his stiff dick up Dan's snug behind to push Jason, once and for all, off the ledge and into welcoming oblivion.

"I'm going to shoot my wad any minute," Dan puts into words what Jason thinks and feels.

"Me, too, stud," Jason says. "Oh . . . me . . . too!"

One-and-the-same-time ejaculations, it has been Dan's experience, are the exceptions rather than the rule. Even in porn movies, of which he's seen more than a few on-location shoots, shared orgasms usually result more from skillful editing than from characters actually getting off at one and the same time.

Jason hasn't a clue whether or not he'll let loose his cum at the same time Dan manages a blow. He knows the remaining fuck-to-orgasm process is completely out of his control. He's on automatic pilot. No way he goes slower, should Dan make that request. No way he fucks faster. No way does he pause for a breather.

Jason's primed nuts are so far pulled toward the base of his dick that they're pretty much disappeared within his lower belly. His friction-heated cock, though, is swollen all the more impressively.

Dan's nuts contract into greater compactness. His cock gets friction-beaten bigger within Jason's constantly whipping hand.

"Oh, fuck, fuck!" Jason says.

"Cum! Sweet, sweet, thick-coming cum!" Dan says. His grunts are magnified by the special acoustics of the shower.

It's as if the cream Jason shoots up Dan's behind exits Dan's dick and cum-spatters the shower wall in front of the photographer's belly.

Still, Jason keeps fucking, hard and fast. Only later will he realize how lucky he is the deluge he feeds the rubber doesn't make his hard-on so slippery it exits the condom up Dan's fucked butt.

"Coming custardy cummy comety canon-shot of coagulating cream," Dan says.

Another spermal wad of his spunk joins the rest forming their spatter design on the shower-stall wall. After which, the cum that appears as merely an ooze pumped from still-stiff dick by Jason's gripping fingers.

Both fucker and fuckee strive to maintain balance on legs gone incredibly wobbly.

CHAPTER NINETEEN

"Tell me that's not one helluva photograph," Dan says. They're in the red-light lit motel bathroom-converted-to-darkroom. The photo in question rides the waves of its chemical bath.

"That's really me?" Jason is genuinely impressed and amazed. He certainly doesn't look anything like he thought he'd look, like he thought he'd felt, gone drowned-rat within that Texas deluge. Maybe, the difference has something to do with the never-a-part-of-his-real-life saddle hoisted over his shoulder. Or, maybe, it has something to do with the never-worn-before-or-since cowboy hat in its sexy tilt, and water-soaked lilt, on his head.

In the photograph, Jason stands in seemingly deep desert. Not a road, not a car, not a building, not a person, not an animal in sight. None. Within the deep blackness behind him is a multi-forked flash of lightning that cracks the sky and illuminates just enough existing sage and cacti to make their presence known. Jason, though, is surprisingly well-lit, although he's sure Dan's camera hadn't been equipped with a flash attachment. Jason's nipples are well-defined beneath rain-soaked shirt material that plasters his chest. His cock is readily evident beneath rain-soaked denim that hugs his crotch.

"I'll bet they're going to have you airbrush that bulge at my crotch," Jason says. He's still not sure who "they" are. He just knows Dan is in Texas on a shoot already thought finished when Jason had been stumbled upon in the rain.

Jason has to admit the results of that rainy bit of picture-taking emphasize how good at his job Dan is.

"Maybe they'll want the bulge toned down — just a bit," Dan says. "Maybe not. Your everyday person is surprisingly jaded, in this day and age, to pictures that would have sent his parents into apoplexy. We're talking media saturation of cock-ballooned underwear by Calvin Klein. We're talking C&A on *Sandbox*. We're talking anatomically correct dolls and mannequins, for Christ's sake! We'll just have to wait and see. Assuming, of course, I can get you to sign off on a model-release form."

Jason, who sure as hell never considered himself a model, and figures he still has about as much chance of ever becoming one as a snowball in hell, never considered he might have rights to any picture taken of him."

"I'll make it worth your while, of course," Dan says. He's afraid he'll lose out on the picture, and it's so perfectly what he wants. "I'll personally see the Rudolph Green Agency gets a copy. Hell, I'll shoot even more photographs of you, from here to sixty, between here and L.A., so you'll have a professional portfolio to knock Rudy's eyes out."

"What do you want the picture for?" Jason asks. It's not as if he's fearful of the picture, wet-crotch and all, ever coming back to haunt him. He knows art when he sees it, even if he's the subject matter. It's not as if his pants are down around his ankles, his dick playing lightning rod in the rainstorm. Anyone who can produce such a great picture from the catastrophe Jason thought it was at the time, deserves whatever legitimate use that can be made of it. He is merely curious.

"It's perfect for this several-page advertisement-insert for *Travel and Leisure* I've been working on for the state of Texas. The project has the work-title 'Texas Reigns'. Of all the states, Texas is the best, so come spend your tourist dollars here. Your picture an invitation to any guy or gal with a thing for cowboys. The extra advantages are the subconscious associations to be made between saddle and horse and 'reins' . . . between thunder and lightning and 'rain'. Reigns, reins, rain: goddamn fucking perfect subliminal triad!"

"So, where's this model-release form you want me to sign?" Jason can't believe he's reached this moment so soon after docking dicks with Jorge in that motel room. He wishes Dan a foreskin with which to dock. Although, with or without foreskin, Dan's cock can't be any sexier.

Jason is additionally turned on by just how good a photographer Dan is.

In evidence, Jason's hard cock pokes its bulbous head straight out from his completely naked body.

"Why does all of this picture stuff make me horny as hell?" he says.

"Turned on, are you, by the sight of that sexy young cowboy in the rain, nipples and cock showing through pants and shirt materials? That certainly does something for me. Just like it will do things for any potential tourist to the state of Texas."

Dan's completely naked body displays a cock that matches Jason's in hardness.

"You know what I'd like us to do with our hard cocks?" Dan says. "Prop mine, right along with my balls, up over the lip of the sink. Put yours to the opening of my asshole and fuck it right on in. So, we can watch our reflections in the mirror while you stick my butt and manhandle my prick. So, we can take an occasional glance in the direction of this photo of this very sexy cowboy in the rain."

"Sounds good."

"How's this sound? I put this condom over your dick for you."

The packet materializes and Dan's teeth rip it open.

"My dick is yours," Jason says.

"My ass soon to be yours," Dan says. "Do with it what you will."

He discards the empty packet into the wastepaper basket under the sink, puts the coiled rubber to his lips and tucks its nipple into his mouth. Suction helps hold it in place. He drops to his knees in front of Jason. He bows his face over Jason's stiff dick.

The condom, held by the purse of Dan's lips and by suction, kisses its open end to the head of Jason's dick. Dan's lips exert a downward pressure to roll the condom over Jason's cockhead. Rubber and Dan's mouth lock Jason's mushroom-corona.

"So, that's what's meant by, 'Look, mom, no hands!'?" Jason says.

Dan's mouth unrolls more condom and follows the rubber along that narrow bit of cockshaft that turns into the rounder and fatter cockneck that eventually connects to Jason's lower belly.

It's not a steady start-to-finish slide. Wet and sloppy pauses make sure whatever part of the cock is swallowed, at any one time, is sufficiently awash with spit. A froth of juicy saliva drenches the slowly entering dick as thoroughly as any Texas downpour ever drenched Dan and Jason in the desert. In the end, Dan's mouth wraps the very base of Jason's erection. Dan's spit oozes small liquid strings that catch within the thick matting of black pubic hair that makes a V at Jason's crotch.

The slippery lubricating of Jason's cock isn't devoid of pleasure for either participant. Dan, as always, is turned on by cock, in general, shoved into his face, by Jason's cock, in particular, shoved in there. Jason is turned on by Dan's sucking and munching and chewing and gobbling and . . .

"Mmmmmm," Dan hums over his mouthful.

Vibrations turn Jason's cock into a resonating tuning-fork. Sound waves provide sympathetic vibrations of Jason's cum-filling nuts.

"You want my cock up your ass, we better put it there," Jason says. There's a difference between Dan's mouth and his asshole, but it's not such a difference that Jason's cock can't shoot cum into the first as well as into the second.

Dan prefers his butt fucked to his mouth screwed. Even with Jason on the delivering end. Jason's cock is so damned perfect when up Dan's rectum. Dan can't remember another time all his senses told him a more perfect pecker was jammed into place. Jason's cock up Dan's asshole is a prodigal son returned. It's a missing piece of jig-saw no longer missing. It's a yin having found its one true yang.

Dan leaves Jason's stiff dick glossy with spit, but he does leave it. He stands. A slight turn to the right, a step in that same direction, and Dan's naked lower belly pretty much aligns with the leading lip of the porcelain sink. A slight raise on his toes, a slight lean forward, and Dan pools his scrotum on the rim of the cool ceramic bowl. His skin-and-hair-draped nuts are like large boulders left behind by some swiftly moving river or sliding glacial ice. His impressive cock sprouts from his balls and scrotum, like some exotically erotic long-stem phallic plant.

"Fuck me," Dan says to Jason's reflection in the mirror. Jason moves up close behind him. A slight forward thrust of Jason's lower body all that will be necessary to position his cockshaft within the crack of the ass.

"I do want to fuck you," Jason says.

He fists his cock. He arches back his hips. He pushes down on his cockshaft. His cockhead ends up aimed through the breach of Dan's slightly open thighs.

Jason releases the downward pressure on the length of his dick. His cockshaft raises, like a drawbridge on well-oiled sprockets. The pulpy tip and back of his cockhead make contact with the lowest part of Dan's ass, where butt curves to its meeting with balls. Some of the spit on the head of Jason's dick attaches to the hair growing the back of Dan's scrotum.

"I want your hard dick inside me," Dan says. There's pleasure in the delay, but it doesn't make his need for his sticking any the less desperate.

Pressure from Jason's guiding hand still prevents his cock from flipping completely upward and leaving a spitty trail all of the way through Dan's asscrack. Jason's cockhead proceeds slowly into and along the seam of Dan's joined buttcheeks. Jason counts upon the man announcing when cockhead hits target area, and he isn't disappointed.

"Right there. There!" Dan says. "Shove it on in, or are you going to make me beg for it?"

"Will you beg for it?"

"Sure. If that's what it takes. Please, give me your prick hard and deep up my butt. Pretty please, run all of your stiff inches all of the way up my entire rectum. Pretty-pretty please, stuff your hard and gigantic dick up my tight asshole."

"Before all the slip-and-slide spit evaporates?"

"Yeah, before all the slip-and-slide spit evaporates."

"Certainly wouldn't want that, now, would we?"

Jason's hips buck. Momentarily, he thinks he's not got his pecker as perfectly aligned as Dan has led him to believe. It seems his condom-nipple cockhead blunts against solid flesh and bone, not against likely-to-yield anal entranceway.

"Harder!" Dan thrusts his ass back.

The photographer's asshole — finally — opens, like a camera lens, around the fat head of Jason's cock. The sphincter pauses slightly, in its yawn, as it hugs that narrow portion of slippery cockneck just beneath the cockhead. Finally, though, the anus recommences its yawn and widens for the remaining inch after increasingly thick inch of still to be butt-swallowed pecker.

"Oh, yes!" Dan says. His prostate renews its acquaintance with the pleasurable boxing-glove punch of Jason's cockhead.

"Your butt, my cock, your prostate, made for each other," Jason says. His hard belly grinds Dan's hard ass. His pubic hair entwines with the sweatier strands that line the asscrease and halo the cock-speared pucker.

Quite aside from his buried-to-his-balls dick up Dan's ass, Jason enjoys the view. Over Dan's shoulder. The mirror reflects the front of Dan's torso. The man's square pectorals. His dime-size nipples. His scalloped abdominals. His lovely big and startlingly erect cock. His strong neck. His handsome face. Jason's head over Dan's right shoulder.

Flushed faces. Bite-swollen lips. Tousled hair. Dilated eyes.

Jason's arms slide beneath Dan's arms. Hug. Jason's hands slide over Dan's nipples. Nipples go tack-like sexy. Dan's muscles sculptured, delineated. The photographer's flesh velvety soft.

Jason's chin rests on Dan's shoulder. Jason's tongue licks Dan's cheek. Tastes salt. Tastes musk. Tastes studly.

Aphrodisiacal tastes! Aphrodisiacal smells! Aphrodisiacal slides of flesh against flesh.

Jason's cock is on the move up Dan's asshole. Out . . . in . . . out . . . in. Way in. Balls flap against butt. Way out. Sphincter rubber-bands cockneck just below the flare of cockcorona. Tight.

Jason's fingers tent Dan's nipples. Pinch.

"Ohhhhhh," Dan moans.

Dan's butt revolves. His asshole stirs around the in-coming . . . out-going . . . pumping . . . fucking . . . cock. Jason's cockneck torques against Dan's prostate.

Dan is at a loss as to why this cock, Jason's cock, is so-so good, so-so much better than any cock before it, likely so-so much better than most, if not all, the cock to come after it. This cock just the right length . . . just the right circumference . . . just the right peculiar (big-head) shape . . . just the right penile key for Dan's anal lock.

Although Dan has Jason's cock (all of it) Roto-rootering his ass, non-stop, he wants . . . needs . . . craves . . . more . . . more . . . more.

"More cock," he says. "More fuck."

Jason complies. Not that he could stop, even if he wanted. This asshole does wonderful things . . . for him . . . for his dick. It conjures pleasures few, if any assholes, have ever conjured. It milks him as few, if any assholes, have ever milked him.

And Dan loves what Jason's stiff dick does inside him. He loves being speared on it as securely as any pig stuck on a lance. He loves the movement of it, the friction of it tugging his asshole lining slightly, this way and that, before and after each slide-through.

Could Dan come to love Jason who has this lovely cock Dan so loves? It would be easy to do. Except, love isn't something Dan schedules for this particular time in his life. His career has just gotten on the fast track. Love of one specific cock can be detrimental to his long-range plans. It would be best to be rid of this cock before it becomes addictive. If it hasn't already become addictive, in that Dan has no intention of immediately evicting it from his asshole.

"Love your cock," Dan says. As if saying it makes it less so.

What happens is, he loves Jason's cock all the more. He loves the way its bulbous cockhead continually battles his prostate. Bump . . . bump . . . bumpedy-bump. He loves the resulting jolts of pleasure. He loves the genuine sunbursts of heat that scald him from the inside-out. He loves the heat that causes his tanned flesh to gloss with perspiration.

Jason fists Dan's dick. He pumps it. He pulls its loose skin up to provide it with a fake prepuce. He slides loose skin down the cockshaft to put the heel of his cock-gripping fist into hard compression against Dan's nuts aligned atop the washbasin's lip.

"Oh . . . oh . . . oh." Dan's grunts accompany the spasms his asshole makes around its cock-plug and the pulsations his prick makes within Jason's hard-fisted hand.

"Tight ass," Jason says. "Big cock."

"Hmmmm," Dan says. His head drops back on his neck. His Adam's apple thrusts into high relief toward the ceiling. His hair caresses Jason's neck and cheek. The red light of the makeshift darkroom adds an unworldly quality.

Movements of cock up butt, hand on dick, make the chemical bath tremble, tiny ripples riding the photo of the sexy, handsome, soaking-wet cowboy. Jason still can't recognize the cowboy in the ripples as the same person presently reflected by the mirror.

Dan leans harder against the sink. Pressure of the porcelain rim against the top of his thighs, beneath his balls, makes his dick stand taller. Not that it isn't already so stiff it can easily be broken off at its roots should Jason manhandle it in a violent and less uncaring way.

Dan's scrotum, already contracted, contracts more. His balls, already rolled in on the base of his cock, tuck in closer.

Jason fucks ass. Dan fucks hand. Hard . . . harder. Fast . . . faster. A dance. Well-choreographed. Few mistakes. Smooth-gliding. A pas de deux toward climax.

The sink creaks under the strain of Dan fucked and jacked off against it. The wall behind the sink creaks in sympathy.

"I come!" Dan says. "Sweet Jesus, I come!"

His cock is a geyser in eruption. Great frothy spurts of hot cum jettison. Wet and soupy dollops of goo splatter the mirror above and behind the sink, the sink sideboard and faucets, the sink basin.

Jason's cock doesn't stop pumping as it, too, shoots. Its cadence is automatically timed so each explosion of gunk occurs on the finale of an in-stroke, cock buried as far up Dan's butt as Jason's cock-length lets it go.

Waves of chemical bath become tsunami and slap up and over the container.

Dan's pleasure on ebb, he's still addicted to Jason's cock. He never does drugs, just because he wants to avoid this very feeling of dependency.

Something has to be done to extract him from his predicament. Not now, though. Jesus, not now.

"How about we spend the rest of the night, you fucking my ass?" Dan says. "Pausing only so long as it'll take my sucking face to resurrect your orgasm-softened dick."

"Thought you'd never ask."

CHAPTER TWENTY

Jason stretches, long and sensuously. His arms lift above his head. His toes point. A couple of vertebrae pop along the length of his spine and relieve pressure points. Except for a few remaining cricks, he feels great. Surprisingly great, considering his raucous night of hot and heavy ass- and mouth-fucking of Dan, indulged non-stop until earlier that morning.

His eyes still shut. He's not sure what time it is. He tells its daylight by the sunshine that paints his closed eyelids through the blinds of the motel window.

He stretches again to relieve the last of his muscle tension. All that remains is a pleasant residual ache.

He fondles his big cock-gone-bigger-and-puffier after its night of hard use for other than pissing. There's a fine dusting of his dried cum on his crotch. There's as fine dusting of Dan's dried cum on the sheets.

He rolls in Dan's direction. He wants to give the handsome stud a morning hug. A kiss. If Jason's overworked cock can get hard, it wants to give Dan a little something, too.

Dan's side of the bed is empty.

Jason's eyes, gummy with sleep, open wider. The bedside clock says nine a.m. Except for Jason, the bedroom is empty. The bathroom door is open, no sounds of anyone in there.

Jason throws back the sheet that covers him. Dried cum floats in snowy showy display. He sits, his legs over the side of the bed. His erection, begun in anticipation of its morning greeting to and by Dan, pauses en route to complete stiffness. His dick no longer juts, having become a fallen log on the white landscape of sheet between his thighs. His scrotum is a pool of dark hairy flesh.

He gets up too fast and pauses while his resulting dizziness dispels. The door that connects his room with the one adjoining is slightly ajar. He walks over and pushes through to the other side.

In a robe, Dan sits at a small desk. His hair is wet from a shower.

"Morning." Dan's smile is wide and welcoming.

Jason crosses to the desk. He moves in behind Dan. He puts his hands to Dan's shoulders and begins to knead.

"Oh, yes," Dan says appreciatively.

Jason can't keep his hands off the guy.

There are three piles on the desk's marred surface. One includes all of the photos Dan has hand-picked for inclusion in the "Texas Reigns" advertising layout scheduled for *Travel and Leisure*. The photo of Jason-in-the-rain is on top. Another pile consists of a photo of Jason-in-the-rain and a manila envelope addressed to the Rudolph Green Agency, Los Angeles. The third pile is another copy of the Jason-in-the-rain photo, this time with an accompanying manila envelope not yet addressed.

It's the third pile Dan taps with a forefinger, when he says, "What do you think about masturbation?"

"Mine? Yours? Anybody's?" Jason isn't sure where the question comes from, but he's delighted their morning conversation turns sexual. "I'm all for it."

"I know a guy," Dan says. His eyes are shut. He rolls his neck while Jason's fingers continue expertly to massage. "He helps a lot of attractive guys in their careers. He helps me in mine. He helps several big names in show business that you'd recognize right away from movies and/or from television."

"Oh?" Jason says into the pause. He doesn't know where Dan goes with this, or what — if anything — it has to do with masturbation.

"He likes to watch guys jack-off," Dan says and makes the connection. "Occasionally, I run across someone I think he'll enjoy watching. I think he'll enjoy watching you. I'd like to send him your picture. If . . ."

Jason is ready to accept the reality that good sex with this guy, any guy, doesn't necessarily mean life-time commitment.

"What are your thoughts on the matter?" Dan says.

"What else does this certain someone expect besides watching? You left off with that mighty big 'If . . .'"

"Promise, he only watches. Doesn't even pull out his dick and whack-off. Not that I've ever seen, or had reported, anyway. Maybe his jollies are just mental, and the kind only he can understand. All I know, he can be really generous with people he likes and with people who aren't above beating off their meat while talking about it. The last bit is where the 'If . . .' comes in."

"The 'talking about it'?"

"He likes a guy to keep up a running commentary, from start to finish."

"Like?: 'My cock is beginning to swell. My God, it's getting big! Will I even be able to fist it? Let's see. Oh, yes, I've my fingers around most of it. Not around all of it, though, because it's such a fat cock, wouldn't you agree? All the more hot and horny when it's hard.'"

"Believe it, or not, some guys can't do that. Some get so self-conscious they even lose their erections. Get all tongue-tied. Get all embarrassed. Can do the fuck and suck, days and nights on end, but talk about it? No way!"

"Can't imagine my ever being struck completely dumb."

"Would you mind giving me a demonstration?"

"I'd prefer doing other things for, to, and with you than polish my dolphin."

"The feeling is mutual. But, if I send your picture to this guy, and he is interested, and how can he not be interested, I don't want his hopes raised for nothing. He's a good friend. He's an influential friend. He can be a good friend to you and open all kinds of doors to a world of which you can now only dream."

"You want me to jack-off for you, right now, talking all the while, just to prove I can do it?"

"Unless, after all the workout my ass and mouth gave your pecker last night, you figure you need a bit more recovery time."

"I've had more than sufficient time for my quick-recovery cock to recover, thank you very much. By now, my cock even has a reserve stiffness that'll easily see it through one hands-on jack-off. My balls have another ocean of cum that'll provide remainders for whatever sloppy seconds and thirds you may decide are of interest."

"I see sloppy seconds and thirds as providing me with plenty of interest."

Jason stops rubbing Dan's neck.

"So, when exactly would you like me to convene this little show-and-tell beat-my-meat and let-me-tell-you-how-I-do-it?"

"How about right now?"

"Okay."

Jason walks his sexy nakedness on over to the bed, and he sits down on it.

"Well, as you can readily see, my cock, in expectation of seeing you again, is even now completing the reaction it began in the other room. It's a tad puffy from last-night's workout, but that'll only provide additional bulk — see there! — when it reaches it's final stand-at-attention."

Jason has a good view of Dan at the desk. He can see underneath the desk to where Dan's hard cock juts free of the man's breached robe. Dan's stiff dick makes Jason's cock harder, faster.

"It's quite a handful," Jason says. "I can't remember a time my fist actually got all of the way around it, except for where it narrows, here, just beneath the flare of my bulbous peckerhead. See how my cockshaft indents, so that if I put my forefinger just so, like this, around the right side and belly of my prick . . . if I curl my thumb, like this, around the back of my dick . . . if I squeeze really hard, like this . . . I can just make fingertip and thumb-tip meet up here, like this, on the other side."

Unlike his mysterious friend, Dan can't keep his hand off his own cock. His fist drops to the neck of his erection, where his prick juts through the flaps of his robe. It takes hold. It starts pumping his studly cockshaft before Jason's fingers even start any massage of Jason's penis.

"May I momentarily focus your attention on my genuinely sizable balls?" Jason says. "Notice how they pool, here on the bed, between my legs, encased in a scrotum of skin-almost-liquid. See how the whole lake of hair and skin and testicles moves on its very own, without my even touching it? Actually, it's undergoing a change that'll see the whole of it contract into one big fat ball at the base of my erection."

"Don't I know it!" Dan says. He's unable to help himself from making comment. If he were a settling-down kind of guy, he wouldn't share Jason's picture, or Jason, with anyone. He'd keep Jason for himself. He'd selfishly indulge in night after night after night of the same kind of intense and heated Jason fucking ass and Jason fucking mouth that had filled their previous evening. Maybe Dan should shuck whatever bennies he can derive by passing Jason along! Isn't Dan's reputation as a photographer well-enough established, as it is? Does Dan really want or need to be as famous as his friend's influence can make him?"

"Sometimes, I start right out cupping my sex sac and its contents, like this …" One hand scoops beneath Jason's pooled mass of hair, skin, and balls. "… and keep up an ongoing massage of my balls and scrotum all the while I caress my pecker. I don't know why, but the combination of nut-rolling and dick-beating makes a jack-off so much better for me than if I just leave my gonads on their own."

"Sexy, handsome, big-dicked, but-nutted stud!" Dan says.

"Several ways to whip the old pud, spank the monkey, strangle the snake. A full and firm handhold is always a great way to go. I mean, if I want to move a lot of loose skin back and forth … back and forth … along a lot of solid inner cockcore, tight fist is the best way to do it. See how just such a grip, yanked upward along the shaft of my penis, travels enough skin up and over the head of my dick to give a hint of just how big this already big cock of mine looked before some doctor got to its foreskin with a pair of snippers."

"Sexy, sexy," Dan says.

But, jerking off that way, my hand conceals a good deal of my stiff pecker. Something tells me you prefer seeing as much of my dick as you can see. So, maybe if I just hold to it with four fingers and a thumb? Three fingers and a thumb? Two fingers and a thumb? One finger and a thumb? You possibly think that just one finger and one thumb can't possibly provide enough friction for a prick as big as mine to get all the way to spermal spitting. Wrong! My ejaculations don't require massive movement of skin over stiff inner dick. It's more a matter of concentrating just the right kind and right amount of pressure to just the right spot on the neck of my big dick. I'm talking this spot, right here. See? On my cockbelly. Just beneath the flare of my cockhead. On this little bit of skinny cockneck. I concentrate pressure here, each and every time my lone finger glides up, then down … each time my thumb pushes down, then up … and hearty gushes of creamy cum will come on out in finale to say hello. Here, let me show you."

"I've seen enough," Dan says. More than enough to know Dan's friend and Jason are made for each other. Dan has no doubts Jason would still be talking at the very end. Jason's cock squirting its cum like a six-shooter emptying its bullets. Dan's friend enjoying it all.

Dan, though, wants more than just to watch until inevitable jack-off finale.

"I can start over again, if that doesn't do it for you," Jason says.

"Doesn't do it for me, you sexy shit! It does it for me so well there's no way I sit here and let all that luscious cum of yours end up wasted on you and your stroking fingers."

"In that case, consider my dick all yours." Jason open hands form a wide parenthesis in the air to either side of his up-jutting pecker. His prick weaves slightly, left, right, left. There's an accompanying slight but obvious up-down bounce.

"And, don't I want to have at it," Dan says. He's down on his knees, bedside, in no time. His hands clamp Jason's thighs and push them wide as he scoots in between.

He bows his head.

Jason's cock, visible one second, is completely disappeared the next. Gone and swallowed, all of the way into Dan's hard-sucking face. Cock slid through lips, along tongue, into and down . . . down . . . down . . . hugging throat. Locked there. Clamped there. Imprisoned there. Except, jail time for any real inmate as enjoyable as it is for Jason and Jason's cock, and there will be people clamoring for incarceration.

Greedily, Dan eats Jason's pecker. He's amazed, having so satisfied himself only last night, how morning sex with Jason is as aphrodisiacal as ever. He can't seem to get enough of it, or get enough of Jason's body.

Speaking of places he hasn't been . . .

Dan spits out the length of hard cock. The prick, spit-coated and slimy, recommences its back and forth, forward and back, weave.

"I want to lick out that sexy asshole of yours," Dan says. "I want you on your back, your legs in fillet, your butt poked up so far into my face that my head gets lost up your anus."

Jason prepares for the tongue-licking of his ass. He can't wait for the feel of Dan's hot tongue turned loose on the winked and waiting rectum. Nothing like a good tongue-wipe to get this morning's sex, get any morning's sex, jump-started.

Dan's hands grip the up-jutted asscheeks of Jason's offered ass. Forgotten, for the moment, is the hard shaft, anchored to Dan's lower belly, with a weightiness that tugs downward to plump out the hair-covered V of his crotch.

Dan's fingers push Jason's asscheeks all the more outward from their shared crease. The asscrack opens to its hair-lined valley. The puckered anus is a mere wink of a doorway.

Dan's tongue touches down so far south it achieves wet contact with Jason's waterfalling scrotum. After doing that, however, it's a quick tongue-slide, along the hair-line, to a slippery lap of Jason's awaiting pucker. Tongue rolls its tip and penetrates the asshole-opening.

Dan's swabbing tongue thoroughly washes the area. The licking and accompanying spit rob the area of each and every funky taste and smell that has accumulated during the night. Nothing matches what there would be had Jason taken a morning shit, but what's there does Dan nicely, thank you very much. It's sexy and subtle ambrosia of sweat and animal muskiness.

Dan does what he does until even the faintest of tangy butt-tastes and smells are gone. When he's finished, the asscrack and first inch inside the butthole have become downright bland eating.

The head of Jason's hard cock pokes the kid's navel.

Like a starving man presented with a multi-course feast, Dan is temporarily unable to move because of the sheer, unadulterated wonder of all else that's being offered.

"Now, a thorough wet-down of your big prick, one more time," Dan manages finally. "From its bulbous cockhead to its bulbous cockballs. Then, I sit down over it and play horse-on-the-merry-go-round."

"Or, you could fuck my ass?" Jason says. "I'd really like you to fuck my ass."

If Dan hasn't gotten around to fucking Jason's butt, it isn't because he consciously makes it a point to keep the ass out of the fun and games. He has simply been too content with Jason's cock up butt and mouth to bother. There's something so miraculous about the way Jason's big cockhead, topped by its big mushroom of a cockhead atop the slight taper of immediately supporting cockneck, battles the photographer's prostate.

In no time, though, Dan's cock is rubber-draped, lube-slicked, and ready for fucking. Actually, it's more than ready. It trembles within its opaque casing. It gives little jerks, some of which slap its head back hard against Dan's hard belly.

"You want me like this?" Jason lifts both legs, his knees up and out to either side. His hands grab his buttcheeks and pull out. His asscrack, asspucker, and asshair remain slick from Dan's tongue-licking.

"Damn, I don't think I've ever been quite this horny," Dan says.

The jut of Dan's sizable dick leads him closer.

Dan falls forward and pushes his chest in tightly against the backs of Jason's lifted thighs. Ideally, Dan's cock would automatically align with the offered asspucker and shove right on it. Dan's cock, though, doesn't align properly. It bends painfully against an unyielding dot of buttocks.

"Fuck me," Jason says. "Fuck my tight ass."

Dan's hand reaches between his belly and Jason's ass. Dan grabs his dick and manhandles his cockhead to Jason's a-hole.

"Oh, sweet Mother of God, no!" Dan bellows frustration. His dick does something it hasn't done since his balls dropped upon onset of puberty. Prematurely, it creams his load. Without even getting inside Jason's asshole.

Dan's nuts let go reservoirs of creamy goo and flood the whole mess into the rubber nipple at the tip of the fuck-only-thin-air dick. Dan holds his exploding pecker, unable to let go. He desperately tries to poke his dick, even as it explodes, up Jason's so-sexy butt, but to no avail. His explosions of spunk go nowhere except to bubble the condom over his cockhead.

"Shit!" Dan is disappointed and disgusted.

He pulls back to the same standing position he had before he'd fallen on Jason's waiting body-on-the-bed. The weight of the magmatic cream that cocoons his cock is so heavy, and so susceptible to gravity, it lowers his prick, like deadweight, between him and the bed. Dan is at a complete loss as to what to do or say next.

"I feel like a fucking novice," he says finally.

Jason's legs are still uplifted. Jason looks at Dan through the space between open and fuck-me-please thighs.

"Did I so exhaust you last night that you're only good for the one come this morning?" Jason says.

Dan laughs. His situation isn't as bad as he's assumed. Aside, that is, from having just come off as someone who has never fucked a butt in his life.

Dan's dick, blast-off or not, isn't going soft. Take off its weighty cum-filled rubber, and his cock stands almost as tall as before creaming. Certainly tall enough, hard enough, to take up where it just left off.

"Or, have we already used the last available rubber?" Jason says.

"In which case, I'm prepared to go stark-raving mad with my need to have you inside me."

Dan ties off the rubber's open end and drops the result on the rug with a soupy splat. He pulls a couple tissues from a carton by the side of the bed, and he wipes away the residue wetness that rides his cockshaft. The tissue is flimsy, single-ply, and cum-soaked sections tear off and stick to his dick. He picks the bits of tissue off, as if he removes lint from an arm-filled sleeve. Then, he starts again: fresh rubber, fresh lube.

The photographer crawls up onto the bed, up and onto Jason. Slowly, he gets his dick to the exact position he had when the beginning of his last eruption occurred. He's afraid he's destined for another premature ejaculation. How frustrating, even the possibility of come after come, to cock-softness, without ever managing a penetration of Jason's inviting butt!

"My asshole isn't going anywhere," Jason says. Actually, he's made all the more excited by Dan's premature ejaculation and continuing hard dick. If only Dan can now slip his giant of a pecker up Jason's anxious-too-have-cock butt! Dear God, Jason wants this to happen!

"Cock headed in," Dan says. His hips exert pressure that smashes condom-nipple between Dan's cockhead and Jason's still-closed pucker.

As soon as the pressure exerted by the man's cockshaft to cockhead is just enough, Jason's sphincter succumbs to all the knocking on its door and rolls on open.

"Mmmmmm," Jason says, definitely feeling his butt-filling.

No way can Dan stop now. He pushes his dick farther into and through Jason's snug anal doorway. He follows with even more inches of very large blood-glutted cockshaft.

"Ohhhh, yes . . . yes," Jason says. His asshole eagerly swallows another big gulp of stiff meat.

"I want shoved up you . . . down you . . . in you . . . all of the way through you," Dan says. He's still in control, still able to pause before feeding asshole more dick, but it's control that threatens to desert him in the face of all the pleasure his already submerged inches of cock churn to life within him.

"Ugh!" Jason grunts when more cock up his butt punches cockhead into his prostate. The punch emits a jolt of pleasure-pain into the surrounding anal canal.

Undeniably, there's something about the push of cock into this particular butt that intuitively tells Dan the ass is truly one of a kind.

It's the sudden reach of Jason's arms, a clamp-down of his hands to Dan's asscheeks, a grinding upward of his hips, that put the rest of Dan's cock into the asshole in one massive final swallow of hard erection.

"Jesus!" Dan sounds as if he's in pain. The whole length of his swollen pecker is so securely vised by Jason's asshole that the cock actually gains an inch in length to compensate for what it has lost in circumference due to hearty compression.

Jason's mouth opens. His lips bubble spit. His eyes shut tight. His whole conscious being suddenly centers along that section of his asshole presently plugged with Dan's hard dick. His brain frantically computes the pleasure within the multiple spasms of goodness that shake his body.

"Feels so good!" Jason shifts his ass, this way and that, beneath the pressure of Dan's pressing-cock-home belly.

Dan feels more than good, more than so good. Dan can't remember ever feeling quite this good after nothing more than having placed the entire length of his cock up a tight asshole. Some kind of magic is at work.

It takes all of his concentration not to undergo another premature ejaculation. So much fucking pleasure!

Jason's anxiousness for Dan to continue is an almost tangible "something" in the air. Dan wants to provide this ass a series of meaningful and enjoyable pumps. He wants this butt to know, from the onset, his cock is capable of showing this ass the kind of good time this ass deserves.

Jason's cock, not Dan's, lets go its load, this time around. Jason, who hasn't even touched his pecker, or had it touched, since cock started up his butt, is taken completely unaware by his steely dick suddenly spurting great gobs of spunk to cum-paint his belly, his chest, and his neck.

"Ugh . . . ugh . . . ugh!" Jason says. Each grunt heralds yet another expulsion of creamy goo from his testicles, through his dick, to touch-down somewhere along his sex-hyped body.

His eyes shut, Jason doesn't see the strained expression on Dan's face as he attempts to maintain control, as he swiftly progresses toward ejaculation. Dan's efforts are made less and less successful by the way Jason's asshole spasms and gropes the whole length of the boner inside it.

Dan rides Jason's upturned ass, like a sinking ship rides rugged sea. His cock is wrung senseless up Jason's behind. His strangled dick radiates pleasure . . . more pleasure . . . too much pleasure.

Dan's balls let go in eruptions of spunk made all the more pleasurable by the attendance of his wish-I-could-have-held-off frustration.

"I'm coming!" Dan's announcement is superfluous, in that he knows he creams.

Jason is too caught up in his own orgasmic shudders to know or care what Dan or Dan's cock may or may not be up to.

Dan has no choice except to hold on for dear life, afraid the vacuum up Jason's butt that so forcefully gulps Dan's cum will succeed in sucking his guts free, on the tail of exiting jism. Dan is already in the process of being turned inside-out where his cock pulses deep and forcefully inside Jason's sex-racked body.

CHAPTER TWENTY-ONE

Talbot thinks of Kane. His thoughts are accompanied by the boner swollen within the crotch of his trousers. Surely, one of his jerk-off fellow classmates, shoving and pushing past him in the school hallway, can't help but notice the third leg, forever stiff, Talbot sprouts continually, these days, and carries around with him.

"What's up with Sam?" Terry says, catching Talbot on the way out the front door.

Talbot has a six o'clock with Gerald's old man and with Gerald's cousin. He would dump the whole lot for an immediate go at Kane. God, does Talbot wish the security guard wasn't so goddamned paranoid about fucking and sucking in the work place. Peter isn't nearly as cautious, when it comes to fucking his tricks in the old Spa.

"Sam?" Talbot responds vaguely to Terry's question. He's back to wondering what he would have to do, by way of seduction, to get Peter in bed — or on a Spa locker-room bench.

"What do you mean, 'Sam?'?" says Terry. "Sam Nimms, you shit for brains. Please, get your head out of your asshole. You think I mean Sam Whitts?"

Sam Whitts is a genuinely nerdy guy, transferred from Glover High, over in Gloversville. He's so much the stereotypical "brain", it's downright scary.

"There's something wrong with Sam Nimms?" Talbot says.

"Isn't that what I just asked you? Speaking of Sam . . . I asked him to join in one of our little jack-off sessions. Thought he was coming right around to the idea, too, but now he seems to have some kind of a hair up his ass and heads in the opposite direction every time he sees me."

"You sometimes come off a bit aggressive," Talbot says. "I remember thinking just that the first time you approached me. Sam is probably just trying to figure out what there is about him that has you red-flag him as likely to enjoy flogging hog in group sessions."

"You're kidding, right?" Terry is genuinely disbelieving. "Anyway, I've this sixth sense, and I've never been wrong about a recruit."

"Wasn't it Barry who threatened to break your right arm if you ever brought up the subject again?"

"Barry is a deep-down closet queer, if ever I saw one."

"If you say so."

"Tell Sam, when next you see him, that I'm suggesting only a bit of harmless fun."

"Like we spend a lot of time together." Actually, they had a physics lab together, that very day, but Talbot skipped it.

"He's been asking around for you."

"So people keep saying. Now, if you'll excuse me, Gerald has arranged for me to meet his cousin who's a sophomore at Princeton."

"Ask the cousin if he'd like to pull his pud with some very interested of-legal-age high-school guys."

Talbot shakes his head to show just exactly what he thinks of that suggestion.

"How about you ask Gerald to join us?" Terry tries a different angle. "Tell me you haven't noticed just how well-hung he is?"

There's no way Talbot comes as far as from junior-high school with Gerald and hasn't, at some time, seen his naked dick in a school locker room.

"You don't like 'em as skinny as Gerald, though, do you?" Terry says. "Someone else, then, accounting for that boner in your pants, good buddy?"

That Terry so easily spots Talbot's hard dick makes Talbot suspect others are equally as observant.

"I've really got to go."

"Better whack that hard dick of yours to less visibility," Terry calls after. "Gerald's cousin might get the wrong idea — or the right one."

Talbot flips Terry the bird without bothering to turn back toward him.

Not that the perpetual hardness of Talbot's cock, these days, doesn't have him inclined to take Terry's advice, about whacking it to less visibility, or at least to a degree of softness that won't make it so obvious in his pants.

The eventual distraction, though, of Gerald, Gerald's old man, and Gerald's cousin, as Talbot expects, sees the recalcitrant dick finally under control. After all, Talbot isn't sexually interested in Gerald, or in Gerald's dad. Although, Gerald's cousin, Matt . . .

"You'll fit right in at Princeton," Matt says. The two are out on the balcony that overlooks a garden so extensive that it's hard to imagine the city on all sides. Gerald is off somewhere. Gerald's father has a conference call in the library.

"I'm not in yet," Talbot reminds.

"Uncle Paul may not be a Princeton alumnus, having preferred Yale, but he's got connections there. You and I are lucky Gerald heads for his old man's stomping grounds. Who wants cousin Gerald's kind of competition, right? Although, maybe you can clue me in on how anybody so skinny can turn on so many guys."

Talbot is uneasy by how Matt automatically assumes Talbot is clued in to Gerald's sexual proclivities. Luckily, Matt doesn't wait for Talbot to chime on in. He has a tendency to monopolize their conversation, often even going so far as to answer his own questions.

Talbot does like Matt's preppy good looks. Short blond hair, pert nose, cupid's-bow mouth. What looks like a damned nice body beneath a crisp button-down shirt. All evidence of a nice cock within the crotch of neatly pressed and creased slacks.

"I think Gerald subconsciously sprained his fucking ankle just for you," Matt says. "What do you think?"

"Huh?" That's what Talbot thinks.

"He says you think he's too skinny. I think he thinks what you say is important. Only way he could start to fatten himself up was to find some excuse to stop all that marathon shit."

"I don't think Gerald and I are nearly close enough for him to drop out of marathon running because of anything I think, or don't think."

"You've been together since junior-high school, haven't you?"

"We moved into the area at about one and the same time, yes."

"Think he'd line up his family clout behind just anyone headed for Princeton? Nope! I don't think so. He's buttering you up for something, you can bet on it. Probably simultaneously buttering up his asshole as well."

For not the first time, Talbot tries to remember Gerald with a bit more meat on his bones. All he comes up with is Kane's hunky and naked body Kane's impressive security-guard physique. Them, he thinks of Peter's naked ass dimpling as the architect's cock pokes Gerald's ass. Kane and Peter on the one hand, Gerald on the other: no way they balance, by way of Talbot's interest.

"Jesus!" says Matt. "I've just been assuming you're gay. You are, aren't you? Gerald said you were, but maybe I've given too much credit to what's just that skinny shit's wishful thinking."

"Oh, I'm gay all right."

Matt is visibly relieved.

"Gerald says you and some of your classmates like regularly getting off by yourselves for fun and games. Lucky you.

"Gerald knows about my attending circle jerks, does he?" Talbot doesn't mean to say it aloud. It slips out. Not that Terry, in his quest to recruit one and all, has ever been all that discreet.

"I'm a tad surprised Gerald isn't right in there with you, dick pulled out of his pants, his fist whipping his meat to climax? On second thought, he tends to be a tad snobby."

Talbot wonders where Gerald has presently gotten off to.

"Think we should head inside?" Talbot says.

"Nope," Matt says. "Uncle Paul's conference calls last for hours. Gerald is probably off somewhere whacking off that big dick of his."

Talbot tries to remember the last time he paid all that much attention to the exact shape and size of Gerald's prick. All he comes up with is a very vague recollection of something impressively large.

"Always wished my dick was bigger," Matt says with a shrug. "Even tried hanging weights on it, and on my balls, when I was younger. Lucky I didn't pull everything right off. You a size-queen, Talbot?"

Food for thought! Kane has a big cock. Architect Peter has a big dick. Jeffrey and Marky are hung like horses.

"It's not the size but what you do with it," Talbot says magnanimously, because it's likely true, not to mention appropriate after Matt's candid admission.

"I'd hate to yank out my dick and have you take one look and tell me to stuff something so small back in my pants," Matt says.

"You plan to pull out your dick for my look-see?" Talbot is definitely interested.

"Well, Gerald did tell me he thinks you've the hots for some security guard at this place where Gerald's architect friend is working."

So much for keeping anything a secret! Talbot's mind's-eye flashes skinny Gerald laid out on that Spa locker-room bench. Actually, it's more a vivid recollection of Peter, naked and fucking up a storm, poking cock in and out . . . in and out . . . in and out . . .

"Gerald says you're the only guy he knows who can arrive at school, in the morning, sprouting a hard-on, and exit every evening with your dick still as stiff as steel." Matt is acutely aware of the movements in Talbot's pants which, even now, herald yet another boner on the rise.

Why in the hell can't Talbot remember Gerald paying as much attention as Matt insinuates?

"Come on," Matt says. He heads off the balcony and onto a path that leads into the garden. "Let's see if we can't take care of what you've got there, in your pants, so you won't have to turn away from my uncle every time he heads in your direction, the rest of the evening."

Talbot follows Matt down the garden path. Talbot's hard cock chafes his pants.

Matt locates a bench, among some hedges. It's concealed from the house and under-lit by ground lights. Matt sits and pulls Talbot, still standing, to where Talbot's cock-bulged crotch is at Matt's face.

Matt reaches for and finds the zipper of Talbot's fly. Talbot catches Matt's exploring hand and stops it for just a moment.

"You see my dick, I see yours; that's the deal," he says. He doesn't care if Matt's dick is pinkie-finger small and thin as a pencil.

"Let's not make this too complicated," Matt says. "We're not exactly in circumstances that allow a whole lot of time and leeway. Gerald sees we've disappeared into the underbrush and, despite all his promises to be good and keep out of the way, he'll be on us like a dog licking his own asshole. So, how about your dick pulled out, you seated on the bench, my pants dropped, my asshole seated over your erection, me bouncing up and down, before I take hold of my dick and start beating it in keep-time cadence?"

"Thought you'd never ask. Except, how about I beat your cock for you?" Talbot says.

What Matt ends up showing, in the cock department, is a helluva lot more than he's led Talbot to expect. Granted, it's not as big a cock as Talbot's cock. Granted, it's not as big a cock as Peter's cock. Granted, it's not as big a cock as Kane's cock, or Jeffrey's cock, or Marky's cock. Nonetheless . . .

Talbot likes the overall look of Matt's erection. It's perfectly circumcised. It's perfectly round. No visible veins. No moles. No discoloration from its overall copper shade. Its bushing V of pubic hair confirms its owner is a natural blond. Matt's scrotum, more drooped when he's less excited, is a perfect complement.

The rubber fits Talbot's dick like a glove and is lubricated enough — hopefully — to ease the slide of pecker into Matt's asshole.

Talbot is sure there's a whole world of loose-ass people out there, but Matt isn't one. No matter how much stretching his ass regularly receives beneath the onslaught of all those hard ivy-league preppy Princeton dicks.

Matt takes his own sweet time descending his ass over Talbot's erect pole. Continuously, he performs little back and forth, up and down, round and round movements.

There's very little required of Talbot, except presenting his pole for Matt's sliding. His hands go around, up and under, Matt's still very button-down shirt. Matt's chest and belly are more hairy than Talbot imagined. Talbot's fingers comb a forest of blond strands to pinpoint an obviously indented navel, pointy nipples, and enough rippled abdominals to prove Matt spends a good deal of time in some gym.

Talbot tweaks the hell out of Matt's nipples. He pinches their nubby centers to additional rock hardness.

Matt's ass reaches cockroots. Talbot's attention diverts to Matt's cock and balls. The dick makes a nice, comfortable handful. Backed up on Talbot, as Matt is, the preppy's muscled butt nestles Talbot's lap. Talbot's arms wrap Matt's midsection. One hand couches Matt's dick. The other cups Matt's testicles. The illusion is that Talbot labors over his own prick and balls.

"Eeeeee . . . eeeoweeee," Matt says. "Where have you been all my life, Mr. Studly?"

Talbot is infinitely pleased his dick's fuck of Matt's butt holds its own in any comparison Matt makes with any dick there before. If Matt is merely feeding him a line of complimentary bullshit, that's okay, too. Talbot is more and more inclined to think himself a sucker for flattery.

Matt is pretty much in control. He doesn't waste time and provides the giddy-up that gets him into a series of slow up-and-down shifts along pretty much the entire length of Talbot's pecker. Talbot's masturbatory movements drag Matt's velvety outer cockflesh up and down Matt's steely inner cockcore. He holds his hand in place and lets Matt's bouncing fuck Matt's cock . . . up and down . . . through stationary fist. Talbot's other hand keeps masterful possession of Matt's balls. Matt's nuts swell larger and larger with more and more spunk.

"Nice," says Matt. His head drops back slightly so his short blond hair brushes Talbot's face.

It isn't all that long before there's that tingly something in Talbot's nuts, accompanied by his scrotum's elevation from where it has hung to where it almost disappears into his lower belly.

"You have me so hot and horny," Matt says, "I don't know how long I can hold off my blast."

"You nearly blasting?" Talbot asks. If Matt doesn't squirt soon, Talbot is going to beat him to the punch.

"You know just how damned sexy you and that big boner of yours are? Let Matty tell you. *Muy* sexy. *Mucho* sexy. My balls about ready to pop their heavy load."

Matt bounces on Talbot's dick a helluva lot harder and faster than he did but seconds before.

"Jesus, I'm going to come!" Talbot warns and bites Matt's sexy neck.

Talbot beats Matt's dick fast and furious. His fingers work nuts as if gonads are marbles in a wash machine.

"It's now!" Talbot says.

"Ditto!" Matt screams.

"Boo!" says Gerald who jumps from the shadows.

Talk about your sweet-Jesus lift-off of space shuttle from Cape Kennedy! Matt's ass would be airborne if Talbot's cock didn't ride up, right along with it. When Talbot's butt slams back onto the seat, Matt's ass drops by sheer force of gravity one final time to an ultimate squashing of lap beneath muscled butt. Hard dick is thrust so deeply inside asshole that Talbot wonders if cockhead is seen when Matt opens his mouth.

After which, Talbot knows that getting scared shitless can be aphrodisiacal. All those rides, in all those amusement parks, are designed purely for one thing, and one thing only, and that's to get a guy's rocks off. All those scary movies are purely to stimulate the libido. Because Gerald's sudden appearance and accompanying sound affects conjure, from somewhere deep inside Talbot, an extra jolt of sexual electricity that keeps his spermal floodgates wide open and pulsing prime ecstasy for far longer than Talbot ever expects possible.

"Gerald, you shit!" says Matt down from his sexual high before Talbot. "If I'd been sucking his cock when you did that, I could have bitten it off."

"Cousin Matty's asshole do you any damage, Talbot?" Gerald is all innocent smiles.

It's only then Talbot is genuinely aware his fist, over Matt's cock, is sticky with Matt's exploded goo.

"I'm supposed to find you two and head your asses back for dessert," Gerald says with a wide-wide smile. "Dad is so delighted I've once again started eating he's special-ordered one of those double-chocolate cakes from Forbidden Desserts. Better make it a snappy clean-up, because I won't be able to cover for you for too long. And should dear daddy stumble across the two of you, in your present state of disarray, well . . ."

With a wave, he heads off.

Matt eases off Talbot's cock still planted firmly up his butt. His fingers hold Talbot's rubber in place with the expertise of someone who has performed the ritual dismount more than once.

Talbot, though, rolls the used rubber off his puffy dick, all of its sizable ocean of semen safely contained.

"Why don't you let me have that for a souvenir?" Matt says, his hand out for the used rubber.

He ties off the rubber Talbot gives him and slides it, with some difficulty, into his front pants pocket.

CHAPTER TWENTY-TWO

All this time, even with some major fucking with Kane, and a bit on the side with Matt the preppy from Princeton, Talbot never completely forgets how turned on he was by Peter's fucking of Gerald's skinny ass in that Spa locker room. And, since he's already broken his own rule of never to trick with an employee of his father, by fucking and sucking up a storm with Kane, he more and more obviously tries to catch Peter's eye — in just such a way that will let the architect know Talbot is just as available for fun and games as Gerald is. Talbot can't help but figure Peter will come around. For Christ's sake, Peter has bedded skin-and-bones Gerald! Peter has to see Talbot as more of a catch than Mr. Count-My-Ribs.

Talbot manages to maneuver Peter to one side, the two of them alone, at the job site Talbot just happens to visit "to see Talbot's father" (although, Talbot knows his father is elsewhere at the time). Talbot's dick is erect, like a drawbridge before a castle moat. Talbot allows Peter a good look-see at his bulged crotch, in order for the architect to know for sure that Talbot comes nearly as well-equipped, in the penis department, as does Gerald the-big-dick-skeleton.

For whatever his reasons, Peter continues to play hard to get.

"Mr. Crane," Peter says, in seemingly the strictest confidence, "there is a solution for the problem you seem to have a good deal of lately. And, despite what you may have heard to the contrary, you'll not end up with hair on the palm of your hand, or gone blind, should you choose to avail yourself of it."

Talbot plays and replays this brief encounter over and over in his mind. Peter having managed to say, without having actually said it, that he much prefers Talbot take care of whatever Talbot's acute hard-cock condition.

Headed home from school the next day, Talbot again mulls over his latest apparent failure with the architect, when Sam falls into step beside him.

"I've decided to let you do it," Sam says, no preamble.

"Do it?" Talbot hasn't a clue: damned strange, considering most of his waking, and sleeping, hours, these days, concerns nothing but sex, sex, sex.

"Fuck my ass," Sam says and stops Talbot dead in his tracks no less quickly than had a ton of bricks dumped out of the sky directly atop him. I've thought about what you said, long and hard, and it's what I want. My parents are conveniently in Vegas for three days. The housekeeper has this afternoon off. Or, don't you find me attractive?"

"You fishing for compliments, Sammy? That's what it sounds like to me. You more than able to walk up to any mirror and recognize Mr. Studly when you see him."

"How about we do all of it?"

"All of 'it'?"

"Cock-sucking, ass-licking, ass- and face-fucking, and . . ."

"You've given me a boner. Are you happy?"

"From what I hear that's not all that hard to do these days."

Talbot has to find some way to make his erections less obvious. Maybe if he ties his prick to his leg.

"So, your parents are in Vegas?"

"Right."

"And the housekeeper will be gone by the time you get home?"

"I told her to fix enough supper to warm up for two."

"You knew I'd say yes?"

"I'm an optimist."

"Well, optimist, what say I call my dear mom and dad and tell them about this overdue lab project you and I will be working on for most of this evening?"

"You can use my cell-phone."

After which, they're soon at Sam's place, Talbot suggests they skinny-dip in the pool.

Casually, Talbot drops his pants and puts on full display his boner which has been there all along. He dives into the water. The weight of his dick takes most of the grace out of his move and threatens to sink him directly to the bottom. He comes up spitting.

"Hope you play with dick better than you dive with it," Sam says.

Sam is stripped and looking mighty fine. His body is that of a swimmer who does a lot of weight training. His muscles are long and lean, with just enough bulk to provide impressive definition. A slight line of blond hair dives the center of his chest and belly to arrive, after a slight detour around his innie navel, at his blond pubic bush.

Sam's penis isn't overly long, but it's bulky. Its weightiness never allows it to get much higher into erection than its presently askew leftward jut from his belly. His uncut foreskin adds to the sense of velvet-covered steely preponderance, although his cockhead thrusts completely free of the available cowl. His balls are elevated, one to each side of his dick, like boosters along the shaft of the main rocket.

"It's going to be damned hard playing with your dick if you keep it up there," Talbot says.

Sam enters the water in a near perfect slicing of liquid made no less impressive by the cumbersome erection he brings with him. Talbot is backed against one side of the pool when Sam comes up for air. Sam spots Talbot and swims over. As soon as Sam's feet touch bottom, in front of Talbot, Talbot puts his hands on his schoolmate's waist.

"Goddamn, you're handsome," Sam says.

It's the same words Talbot was about to use to describe Sam. If Talbot was beaten to the punch, it's not because he fails to marvel at just how good-looking Sam is.

How many times has Talbot looked at Sam in the past and not seen what he sees now? The genuinely exquisite way blond eyebrows and lush eyelashes frame blue-blue eyes. Rainbows of color flash the watery prisms of splashed water speckling smooth-smooth tanned skin. Pink lips. Mouth open for a long, extended and breathy, "Ahhhhhh," as Talbot takes hold of Sam's dick beneath the water.

Talbot cups Sam's billowing balls. Cock-occupied fingers provide an upward stroke of dick that makes foreskin flow up and over the head of Sam's erection.

"Ohhhhh," Sam says softly. The fondling of Sam's cock and balls is a bona fide pleasure.

It's only when Sam's expression turns to abject embarrassment that Talbot checks the water sloshing between them and recognizes the pearly streamers of cum blossoming the surface. Several strands of Sam's cum net Talbot's pubic hair.

"Not the end of the world, fuck-buddy," Talbot says. It's not all that long ago that Talbot was creaming his load with nothing more needed to pull his hair-trigger but Kane's touch. "Not when you've the stamina we do. Your cock hardly any softer now than before it spit all this pool-drowned cream."

Talbot gives Sam's cock a squeeze to confirm the pecker is no deader, after one go-round, than Talbot's after Kane's first go at it. Albeit reluctantly, he then releases his handful of cock and balls. He taps the edge of the pool.

"Sit up here."

Sam comes up and out of the water with the skill and grace of an otter. Exactly as Talbot imagines and plans, Sam's weighty cock extends along, and is supported by, the pavement between Sam's legs. The thick and stiff rope of a dick aims in Talbot's direction.

"Just scoot a little closer to the edge," Talbot says.

The cock, with its dirigible fuselage, slides nearer.

Talbot puts his pursed lips to the head of the dick. He gives a hearty suck.

He expects Sam's natural reflexes to make Sam, at least momentarily, pull away. Silly-ass Talbot! Horny Sam instinctively fucks his dick unceremoniously all the farther into Talbot's mouth and throat. He doesn't give Talbot even a passing chance of gagging on the sudden mouthful before Sam pops his cock completely free.

"That's what we're here for," Talbot says. He holds to Sam's legs. "It's called eating dick, yes?"

"I want to eat your dick," Sam says. "You sit up here, and let me in the water."

"It's not as we have an either/or situation here. We don't have to crowd every single thing into the next couple of seconds. Unless, of course, you figure your mom and dad might show up, sometime this evening, after all."

"Even if they did, we'd hear the garage door."

Patiently, Talbot sucks Sam's dick to climax, poolside. This time, Sam holds off blast-off far longer than Talbot ever managed with Kane's experienced mouth wrapped about Talbot's dick in a similar manner.

Sam's cream tastes walnutty. Definitely stronger in flavor, but no less delicious than Kane's cum

When Talbot sucks the dick bone- (boner-?) dry, for this go-round, he comes out of the pool. Sam and he rustle up chaise-longue cushions to make flagstones of the pool's apron more comfortable.

"Now, my turn with your big cock, yes?" Sam says eagerly.

Talbot presents his cock in a side-by-side sixty-nine position, so as to give himself a second go at Sam's prick.

Sam sucks Talbot's dick with amazing skill. If he doesn't swallow the substantial cock all of the way to the bottom, there's no faulting his technique in sucking the first couple of inches while coordinating masturbatory hand-strokes along the unswallowed length of Talbot's erection.

Surprisingly quickly, at least as far as Talbot is concerned, Sam has Talbot squealing like a stuck pig. The quickness of Talbot's orgasm is reminiscent of how it was for him with Kane's hungry face cock-diving between his muscled legs. Somehow, he'd mistakenly expected this to last far longer, with Sam doing the sucking.

"Mmmmm, mmmmmm good," Sam says and comes up for air. He licks his cocksucker lips free of Talbot's steamy cum, as if he has discovered the joys of sticky cotton candy. "It's now two to one and counting."

The sucking bastard literally takes Talbot's breath away by, in one massive deliberate gulp, swallowing each and every last inch of Talbot's available erection. Doesn't choke. Doesn't gag. Doesn't flop around like a harpooned whale. Just burrows in, as if there's still a bit more dick, somewhere, that he's not yet managed to swallow.

Belatedly, Talbot does the same for Sam's cock. A quick swallow can be good, very good, especially when it's least expected and takes a guy completely off-guard. But, there's as much, if not more, to be said for a long, slow slide, from cockhead to cockroots, suction just so, tongue doing this, then that, throat muscles providing a kind of vibratory flutter.

Sam's eating of Talbot's dick is put on hold by the sensuous and slow dive of Talbot's head over Sam's twice cum-ejaculated erection. It doesn't take Sam long, though, to identify the nuances Talbot uses and make every attempt to make them his very own, even elaborate on them, as he renews his suck on his companion's pecker.

CHAPTER TWENTY-THREE

Talbot taps on the glass of the locked Spa door. Inside the lobby, behind the desk, Kane looks up and frowns. Talbot taps a little harder. Kane frowns all the more. Talbot knocks loudly on the glass. Kane looks this way and that, as if he's not certain from where the resulting racket comes.

"Come to the goddamned door!" Talbot says.

"Go away!" Kane says.

Talbot bangs genuinely hard on the glass. Window glass, on all sides, vibrates sympathetically.

Kane gets up, comes to the door, unlocks it.

"Hi!" Talbot says.

"Jesus, Talbot! I thought we'd agreed that you'd stay clear of here."

"Actually, we didn't actually agree. And, since I happened to be in the neighborhood . . ." Talbot's boner, as usual, bulges the crotch of his pants and states the obvious.

"Are you fucking-A crazy?" Kane says. "Didn't I tell you my old man may very well have me watched? Didn't I tell you we have to be careful?"

"I'm hot and horny and tired of being careful. Even if someone is watching, how are they going to know what we do inside one of these closed-door rooms?"

"If you get me any more fucked up with my father than I've already managed on my own . . ."

"I'm not going anywhere until you pull out your cock and let me suck it off while I beat off my erection to climax," Talbot says.

Kane's arms still fold defensively across his chest but Talbot's hand tents his hand over the bulge at Kane's crotch. Talbot is reassured when Kane doesn't pull away. No way Talbot is convinced the security guard's cock is hard for any other reason than the prospect of hot and heavy sex, here and now.

"Find us a hole to hide in," Talbot says.

"Kane lets Talbot squeeze by, and locks the door behind them.

It's dark where Kane leads. There's a lot of junk. Talbot thinks Kane is purposely out to lose him: Theseus in a labyrinth deserted by a having-second-thoughts Ariadne.

It's only when Talbot literally bumps Kane's sexy behind, Kane turning to take firm hold and tug Talbot to him with a tightness that forces their cocks, momentarily, to do battle for whatever very little space remains between them, that Talbot knows Kane is truly hooked.

"We are crazy, crazy bastards!" Kane says, turns lose, and sloughs his crisply pressed uniform.

Talbot, excited by Kane's emerging nakedness, drops fully clothed to his knees. Kane manhandles his freed dick and slaps it back and forth across Talbot's face. The slaps spot Talbot's cheeks with sticky preseminal goo. Talbot's mouth would have to be a heat-seeking missile to lock on to so fast a moving target. Not that Talbot complains. He's more than just a little excited.

"Jesus, take my dick!" Kane says. His hand cups the back of Talbot's head. His hand aims his dick haphazardly toward Talbot's face. The first thrust of Kane's hips almost cock-spears Talbot's left eye. A second thrust, no more successful, punches a juicy dot of preseminal ooze to Talbot's left cheek.

"You prefer fucking my nose," Talbot says, when that's where the pulpy head of the dick lands next. "Or . . . ugghhhh . . . ugh!"

Clever Kane has homed in on the sound of Talbot's voice and has poked dick halfway down Talbot's throat. A quick follow-up plants the rest of the gristly meat, hard and fast. Just as quickly, though, Kane drags his penis out to where Talbot sucks in badly needed air.

Then, Kane pops his dick right back in. He smears even more preseminal juice along the slide way of Talbot's tongue and throat. This time, Talbot is better prepared. He knows he'll survive until Kane next lets him up for a breath.

"Jesus, Jesus," Kane says. His cock is on the move — out, in, out. After which, he grunts and groans.

His hands are on Talbot's head. His hips fuck his cock deep, then withdraw the same cock almost all of the way.

Talbot has little to do or say about any of it. He holds on for the ride, one of his hands clasped to the back of each of Kane's muscled thighs.

"Fuck . . . suck . . . fuck . . . suck," Kane says. There's something decidedly erotic in the way his dick bangs away at Talbot's throat; the way his lower belly slams Talbot's face on each in-stroke and pugs Talbot's nose at one and the same time; the way his scrotum, initially balls-suspended to where it had enough flop to slap Talbot's chin, now is more and more a compact pillow.

Talbot doesn't need sixth sense to know when Kane is on the verge of blast-off. Talbot has had enough sex with Kane to recognize his handsome partner's distinctive little sounds just prior to climax. Talbot knows how Kane's swollen cock swells larger, as flooding cum balloons testicles to bursting.

Kane's cock makes one deeply probing final in-stroke and stays put. Kane's belly grinds Talbot's face. Kane's compact scrotum deeply indents beneath the pressure exerted by Talbot's chin.

Talbot smells and feels the dark pubic hair that grows on the thick roots of Kane's cockshaft.

"Sweeeeet Jeeeeesus!" Kane hisses. He spews a mess of jism that can as easily be gasoline for the intensity of the holocaust it causes.

Simultaneously, Talbot's body is beset by a corresponding wing-ding, hot-damn, what-the-hell-is-happening-to-me?, gut-melting, Jesus-fucking Christ, "Now!", explosion. His dick ejects thick and sticky goo into which his cock slumps into softness.

Kane's softening cock comes free of Talbot's mouth with a resounding "Plop!" It leaves behind even its tardiest sperm which Talbot's sucking has siphoned from the penile straw.

"Must say, I'm unprepared for the mess I've made in my pants," Talbot says and gets to his feet. "Which tells us both just how much of a turn-on I find eating your big sausage."

He steps, sockless, out of his loafers. Quickly and deftly, he unbuckles his belt, unzips his fly, and peels his pants down around his slim hips and nice ass. No way does he want the crotch of his trousers visibly cum-soaked with the juices presently contained within the protective cupping of his underpants.

He pulls back the elastic band of his briefs and takes a look at his cock nestled inside.

"Talk about a flood of Biblical proportions," he says. His dick is as drowned in its self-made goo as was any disbeliever, deprived of the sanctuary of Noah's Ark, drowned in those reputed forty days and nights of rainfall.

He drops his shorts. Which, despite all his attempts at prevention, butters his legs with goo. He steps out of his underpants. He folds unsoiled cotton forward over soiled. He uses whatever bits of dry material remain to mop up some of the mess on his cock, on his balls, on his legs. Most difficult to retrieve is the slime that entwines the hair of his pubic bush.

"Here, try this," Kane says. He's produced a clean handkerchief. It's the linen kind Talbot hasn't seen anyone blow their nose on in ages.

Talbot takes advantage of the offer, as well as the unspoken one that provides Kane the cum-messed shorts by way of exchange.

"Who would believe one pair of balls and one cock could provide such a deluge without even being grabbed, fondled, beaten, or even touched?" Talbot says. He's still amazed and fascinated by how he's managed a climax while doing nothing more than suck Kane's sexy erection.

When Talbot is finished with the hanky, he folds it over and over on itself to provide a damp square. Only then does Talbot fully realize what Kane has been up to in the meantime.

Kane has rolled Talbot's soiled underwear into a sausage-like tube, the majority of slick cum contained on its inside, like cream within a Twinkie. He's fully inserted his once-again stiff cock into the breach at one end of the material.

"My dick is again slick," Kane says. He torques the cotton tube around his hard-getting-harder meat and gives a tug that drags the rolled material upward along his again-sticky pecker.

Riding the inches of Kane's emerging prick is the lubricant robbed from the underpants that previously claimed it.

"Feels good," Kane says and re-inserts his prick into the tunnel just exited. His fist grips harder and squeezes more cum to a mating with the already slippery length of his resurrected boner. "And it'll feel even better if you can find a rubber, find a hard-on somewhere within that softened length of penile meat drooped from your belly, and find it in yourself to plunge your rubberized dick far and wide up my waiting asshole."

Which is all the verbal stimulus needed to begin putting the starch right back into Talbot's pecker. By the time he has located a prophylactic packet in his dropped trousers, freed the rubber from inside, and overcoated his dick, it is standing tall and — once again — ready to go.

"God, I do love a stud as quick on the recovery as I am," Kane says. He's proceeded, in the interim, into a heartier fuck of the tubular roll of cum-messy undershorts. His prick makes wet noises each time it churns the friction-warmed goo on insertion, and each time it breaks the vacuum and retreats back outside. The curly pubic hair at the base of his belly is frosted with streamers fucked free of the pseudo asshole.

"I think I'll detour a moment or two to suck your balls while they're still flaccid enough for sucking," Talbot says. He goes back to his recently abandoned suck-cock kneel-position. This time, he sucks up first one, then the other, of Kane's fat nuts. He pushes his pursed lips right up against the base of Kane's dick. His lips clamp off the upper-most droop of the ball-sac. He rolls the nuts from one cheek to the other. He soaks scrotum and scrotal hair with wet-warm saliva. His cheeks concave against what's held between them.

The testicles come together, one side of each flattening against one side of the other. The resulting dull but pleasurable ache oozes upward and outward, first to Kane's crotch and then to the rest of his body.

Talbot has a good view of the continual motions of Kane's cock in and out of the roll of underwear. A halo of creamy build-up forms at the opening of the material with each total insertion of Kane's prick. Each time Kane's cock pulls out, the halo disintegrates into a slick that rides the circumference of Kane's dick all of the way to where only his cockhead remains unsheathed.

The continued flaccidness of mouthed scrotum tells Talbot that he still has time before Kane's growing pleasure peaks in another eruption. Kane's little mewls and grunts and groans aren't nearly the intensity of those he'll voice when tipped on the very brink of orgasm.

As for Talbot's nearness to his next orgasm, that's bound to take a longer lead-in than the last time. The last time was a definite surprise, not likely soon to be repeated.

Though, even with time to spare, Talbot doesn't linger overly long where he is. Once his saliva fully dissolves whatever the delicious flavors that cling to the scrotal hair and the scrotum, the resulting ambrosia swallowed to do its aphrodisiacal "thing" in his belly, Talbot lets the gonads, one at a time, pop free. The released sac-contained globes do their little dance, like dew-wet exotic hair-covered drupes slightly windblown and suspended from the sizable limb of some tree.

Still on his knees, Talbot comes at the underwear-fucking Kane from the rear. Kane's asshole is tight. Talbot has every intention of providing all the natural lubricant needed, at the opening of Kane's butt, and just on its inside, for at least easy beginning of the upcoming long and forceful slide of hard dick he plans to see performed there.

His hands go, one to each buttocks. His thumbs angle inward along the curves that meet to form the anal crease. He pries outward. The crease becomes a crevice. The crevice grows sweaty strands of butthair. The bottom provides the telltale indentations of puckered asshole.

Talbot's face presses into the crease. Asscheeks part farther. Talbot's nose slides down the crease. Nostrils smell asshole but pass it by. Talbot's tongue sticks out and flicks the back of Kane's balls. On its return, his tongue drags along the line of flesh that connects Kane's nuts to his asscrack.

Talbot's face moves back up the crevice. Once again, his nose detects the funky smells of Kane's butt but moves on by. Talbot's mouth, though, stops at the winked anal eye. Talbot's tongue-dabs the circle of puckered skin, rolls to put its slippery tip to the deepest part of the puckered indent. Talbot's tongue plays miniature prick and slides inward through the door.

"Oh, Jesus, yes, rim my fucking asshole!" Kane says. His handful of cum-soaked underwear performs an even heartier pump along the length of his straining erection. "Tongue-fuck my butt until you French-kiss my tonsils from the inside-out."

"Talbot comes up a tad short of Kane's passion-inspired request, but he does all he can do to get Kane's ass ready for a good cock-fuck. He feeds spit through the funnel of his butt-fucking tongue, in order to smear the first couple of inches of asshole with lubricant. When his tongue slips out, and the sphincter closes behind it, a lens of thick spit squeezes from the asshole to monocle the visible eye of the pucker. The magnifying qualities of the saliva make the asshole seem larger than it really is.

"Time for that butt-fuck," Talbot says. He comes to a standing position directly behind Kane. His hands reach around to begin an exploratory slide down Kane's muscled chest and belly to hairy crotch in order, once again, to measure the flaccidness of Kane's scrotum. His discovery of a sac definitely shrunk since the last check tells him Kane's pleasure continues on the rise.

Talbot doesn't waste any time. He goes up on his toes and aims his cock straight between Kane's thighs, just beneath the hang of Kane's buttocks. His hips hump forward and his cockhead fucks empty air until it taps the back of Kane's balls, like Talbot's tongue likewise tapped that very spot not all that long before.

The back of Talbot's cockhead and his cockback withdraw along the fleshy pathway between Kane's nuts and his asscrack. The cockhead slides up and into the crack. Asscheeks close in on the cockhead and in on an accompanying two inches of stiff cockshaft.

As Talbot's mouth before it, Talbot's cock locates Kane's pucker.

Kane feels the correct positioning of Talbot's prick at his butthole.

"Shove it in, stud," he says. "Shove it in fast. Shove it in deep. Make me know I've got your stiff prick up my yin-yang."

Talbot laces his arms upward beneath Kane's arms. Talbot's hands slide up Kane's chest. His fingers curl over Kane's shoulders in Talbot's direction. Talbot uses his anchorage on Kane to exert the force necessary to provide lift for Talbot's whole body. Talbot's chest slides upward along Kane's back. Talbot's feet almost come completely off the floor. Talbot's cock shoves full-depth up Kane's asshole.

"Eeeeee!" Kane squeals his pleasure. And, no doubt, the filling he feels is pleasurable. It doesn't have him bemoaning any threatened damage to his asshole. It has him begging for continuation of the same. "Fuck me … fuck me … yes, for Jesus's sake … fuck me till I can do nothing more than squeal!"

Talbot certainly has a good time. The insertion of his cock up the asshole, in one speedy thrust, caused his scrotum noticeably to compact in mid-swing forward. By the time Talbot's nuts go as far forward as they can, in the wake of the companion cock's anal-sticking, there's not enough looseness in their sac to do anything but hang firm.

Talbot's cock withdraws to its pulpy corona and shoves right back in again.

"Ohhhhhh, yes," Kane agrees with everything Talbot does.

The fuck progresses full-speed from there. As does the masturbation of Kane's hard forward-and-upward thrusting dick within the tube of cummy underwear that Kane's pumping fist keeps constantly in motion.

The intensity of the dual assault on his person — from the rear and from Kane's expertise in escalating self-abuse — keeps the building pleasure in a constantly upward spiraling momentum.

The hardness of the cock, the bulges of cum-replenished nuts, the vigor of the participants, would fool any Johnny-come-lately voyeur into thinking the upcoming ejaculations are — Jesus, have to be! — the very first of the evening.

The two assume a familiar and well-tested rhythm — a coordination that makes everything work (cock up butt, and cock up rolled cummy underpants). So well-performed is the *pas de deux,* there's no lost effort. Each and every scintilla of energy is successfully focused on achieving orgasm … orgasm. Cock up butt … cock up tubular cream-lined cotton … ejaculations.

Even most of their grunts, pants, groans, moans, and conversations fade away, needless accoutrements to bodies so attuned to the moment that each knows, via osmosis, what the other feels, needs, wants, demands.

"Lovely," Kane finally says, as his balls jettison their gallons of newly manufactured sperm.

"Oh, yes," Talbot says, his syllabic hiss, in finale, somehow suitable accompaniment for the long and luxurious emissions of his heavy cream that commence their explosion from his filled-to-capacity testicles.

CHAPTER TWENTY-FOUR

They're about to walk on by.

Talbot comes up short. Kane, as if part of the same chain gang, stops, too. "What?" Kane says.

They're en route to several showers that Kane says have been made operational for the work crews that will be involved in renovations of the Spa over the next few months.

Kane and Talbot can use a good wash after the sex just completed. Talbot's dual-cummed dirty underpants can be washed in the process. Each also harbors expectations that he has just enough libido left to engage in one more heated sexual go-round, once the hot water of the showers surrounds and invigorates the two of them.

Talbot walks over and straddles the bench. It's the very same bench on which he's seen Peter fuck Gerald's skinny ass. It, and what happened on it, are the catalysts that got Kane and Talbot together. Not that they possibly wouldn't have managed, without the bench, and without the seed event that occurred right there atop it, but that wasn't the way things had progressed.

"I want you to fuck me right here," Talbot says. He lies his back on the bench. He drops a leg over each side.

His imaginings, for not the first time, of the sex he's witnessed between Peter and Gerald, cause his already overworked pecker to stretch longer. Although his cock isn't yet swollen to official stiffness, it's going through all of the motions to indicate boner-status isn't all that far behind.

Kane is a little less certain he's up to the fuck that Talbot requests of him. He has figured to rely upon the sensuousness of the enveloping shower water and the massage of his — or Talbot's — soak-bubbled fingers, to coax his sex-softened dick into a renewed able-to-stick-ass condition.

"You want to fuck here?" Kane says. He stalls to see if, as his gut-feeling indicates, his viewing of Talbot's stiffening dick is going to be enough to coax his own pecker into suitable resurrection. "Now?"

"I want to fuck here," Talbot says. He lifts his splayed legs and pulls open his asscrack to present his winked anal pucker. "Now. You, down on the bench between my legs; your dick fucking my asshole like sixty."

Just like Peter's big cock had fucked Gerald's skinny ass like sixty.

"Well ..." Kane says. Languidly, he manhandles his soft dick and flaccid balls, as another man might contemplate a suggestion by rubbing his chin. No denying, as always, Kane finds Talbot a sexual turn-on, especially the way Talbot's cock seems to have no qualms about performing the miracle of rebirth even as Kane stands watching it. He finds it more and more likely his dick will match Talbot's, boner for boner. Definitely, he's reassured by the spasms of penile-rejuvenation his hand detects as it continues to fondle his genitalia. And even if, in the end, his cock does fail him, what's to prevent him from spreading out on the bench and inviting Talbot's obviously up-for-it dick to come on inside?

"My asshole wants your pecker, stud," Talbot says. He's more and more anxious to have the feel of Kane's dick inside of him as his own cock gets more and more stiff. Already he formulates how, during the fuck, he'll fantasize himself as Gerald, fantasize Kane as Peter, and recreate the total turn-on package they had presented.

"Well, if that's what your asshole wants," Kane says. How amazing that his dick isn't failing him, is actually swelling fatter and fatter, faster and faster, within the increasingly speedy massage delivered by his kneading fingers!

Some guys — Talbot and Kane, it would seem — are just faster on the road to hard-dick recovery than other guys. If it, admittedly, doesn't happen for Kane with everybody, it certainly seems to manage whenever the prospect of sex with Talbot rears its head. He only remembers one other guy who could get Kane's pecker hard and keep it there for so long, or so swiftly have it pumping back from softness, and Kane's old man had ruined it by shipping Kane here to L.A. How long will it take Kane's father to find out about Talbot and begin calculations as to how many female orifices are, as a result, being deprived of Clydesdale seed? As if sperm, like female's eggs, were a finite commodity.

When he's between Talbot's legs on the bench, his dick is able to stand quite well on its own, although not quite as upstanding as it would be were this his first sex of the evening. It certainly has regained enough boner-quality to manage the penetration of asshole that Talbot is so anxious to have it achieve, here and now.

Kane dons a rubber and goes belly-down into the saddle formed by Talbot's awaiting body. The bench is damned hard against his knees, and against the palms of his hands, but he doesn't give a damn. What's a little pre-fuck pain and discomfort when he knows the pleasure that awaits him? Even his worst sex with Talbot is better than his best sex with some of the others he's fucked around with (don't know about those, do you, Dad?). Besides, a little pain, it's his experience, can intensify the pleasure that accompanies or follows.

"Jesus, your horniness makes me horny," Kane says. No denying it. It takes a miracle-worker sex-machine to bring out Kane's sex-machine attributes. Thank you very much, Talbot!

"And, I'm horny only because I can't get enough of your cock," Talbot says. True. This time, though, his horniness is, likewise, related to his mental projections of Peter fucking Gerald's ass.

"Cock preparing to come on in," Kane says. His hips arch to downward align his dickhead to the pucker presented by Talbot's lifted legs.

"Now!" Talbot says. "In ... in ... yes, just like that ... only deeper ... deeper yet ... yes ... until your hairy balls ... yes, yes ... slap the small of my ... yes, just like that ... back!"

The squeeze of Talbot's tight ass around and over all of Kane's inches is almost — but not quite — too painfully pleasurable to endure.

Had the witnessed-by-Talbot fuck-of-Gerald been those two's first fuck of that evening? By the time Talbot had stumbled across Peter and Gerald, there had possibly been time enough for progression to sloppy seconds. First screws weren't usually known for being all that horribly long and drawn out.

Kane's cock comes out of Talbot's ass as far as the groove that encircles the flare of Kane's cockhead. His cock goes in, and his pubic hair presses indentations into Talbot's lifted butt.

"Faster! Jeez, harder! Please!" Talbot says, breathless. It's what Gerald said, speared on Peter's cock, Gerald breathless on this bench, Peter's studly body laid out between Gerald's open thighs, Peter's dick up Gerald's skinny ass.

What had Peter said? Could Talbot make Kane say the same?

"Tell me how slow and easy is better than fast and hard," Talbot says.

"Slow and easy is better than fast and hard," Kane says. Not that he can manage slow-and-easy. Fast-and-hard is just too damned inviting. No matter, what with his entire dick has already been through this evening, commonsense should demand Kane be ready for slow-and-easy.

Gerald's hands had been around Peter's neck. Talbot put his hands around Kane's neck.

Gerald's legs had lifted only as far as anchorage over Peter's ankles and calves. Talbot lowers his legs into similar placement atop Kane's legs.

Gerald's head had lolled this way land that. Talbot's head lolls.

"Ah ... ah," Gerald had said.

"Ah ... ah," Talbot says.

And, Peter had said what? Now, requiring Kane to say what?

"Tell me what a butt-fucker you are," Talbot says.

"You've never had a butt-fucker as expert as I am," Kane says. Not exactly an echo of Peter's words, but it does nicely.

"Ahhhhhh," Talbot says. It's spontaneous and not something Gerald had sighed. "Yes ... fuck me ... yes ... yes."

Hadn't Gerald's cock squirted cream on his skinny belly before Peter's cock had let go?

No way Talbot's dick provides a second spontaneous ejaculation in one evening. If it's going to squirt, it needs help. Talbot fists it, pumps it, beats it, whips it, twists it, demands it run the race to beat Kane's cock to explosion.

"Tell me I'm not going to come before you do," Talbot says.

"Right," Kane says. He's truly amazed by how passions, mere seconds before thought nearly tamped to nonexistence, rekindle and stoke to firestorm intensity inside him.

"Goddamn sonofabitch!" Talbot says. Although, it was Peter who said that during the Peter-Gerald fuck, wasn't it? It's getting harder and harder for Talbot to remember exactly what happened or what exactly was said, what with the present upsurge of pleasure inside him caused by the way Kane's cock not only batters Talbot's prostate but slides back and forth across it.

"Hot damn, I'm going to cream!" Kane says. His hips slot his cock completely up Talbot's asshole. His balls pull so far up into his lower belly that there's no visible evidence they exist.

So quick. So fast. As if Kane's body hasn't been drained … drained … drained … by all that's come before.

If there's pitifully little spunk released up Talbot's butt by this explosion of Kane's pulsing erection, everything else is unmistakably, gigantically, orgasmic. Genuinely … truly … soul-shakingly — gigantically orgasmic.

Tremors shake Kane senseless as he rides the saddle provided by Talbot's parenthesizing legs.

Talbot's spewing cum splatters their chests and bellies.

It takes them almost as much time to recuperate as it took for them to proceed through build-up and experience ejaculations. For the longest time, they just stay where they are, still united, cock still up butt, both their dicks still pulsing, cum long-gone.

"So, this Peter whose name you called out when you started creaming…?" Kane says. "He's the architect who works for your father?"

"I called out his name?" Talbot is amazed and a little embarrassed.

"You don't remember?"

"I saw Peter fuck someone on this very bench the night you and I first got together. Remember, I told you?"

"So you did."

For a moment, Talbot thinks Kane is ticked Talbot's fantasy has intruded. Kane's wide smile, though, alleviates any such concern.

"I wonder if it's the same guy Peter fucked on the high-dive in the natatorium the day I spotted them at it," Kane says.

"On the high-board?"

"Looked like two sibling eagles battling to see which one tossed the other out of the aerie first. The pool being empty and far below, it scared the shit out of me to see them up there. I figured screaming would do little more than disorient them and send them over the edge. In the end, both survived, although it looked damned hairy to me. So, don't even suggest we try that as the very next item on our sexual itinerary."

Neither Talbot nor Kane is disconcerted or surprised when neither of their pricks thickens beneath the stimulus of their shared shower. A shower that includes hot and sensuous water, slick and bubbly soap, and Talbot washed by Kane and vice versa. Sexual-rejuvenation miracles are hardly miraculous if they're too commonplace.

Once Talbot is dressed and out the front door, the lock clicked behind him, Kane heads to his desk in the front lobby. The phone rings. Kane is relieved no green light blinks to indicate someone called while he and Talbot were occupied.

He answers the phone. "Security," he says.

"Talbot Crane getting his dick shitty up your butt, or vice versa?" comes the reply.

"Dad?"

"What the hell were the two of you doing so long away from the front desk?"

"Are you here in L.A.?"

"Only my eyes are there in L.A."

"You're having me watched?!"

"Does that answer my question?"

"Talbot's father's firm is renovating this place, as I can't believe you don't know. Talbot is learning the ropes and stops by quite often merely to take a look before the renovation crews make things start to happen."

"Nothing to tie you down in L.A., then?"

"You're letting me come back home?"

"I'm letting you go to Denver. We're setting up a branch office there. I've Glen Winchester on site with instructions to walk you through the procedures. You do well there, and we'll see about you coming home. Your mother misses you. I could use someone to cover the business end while I get in a helluva lot more golf."

"About time!"

"Except, don't come home expecting any quick reunions with your friend whose fucking-around-with-you ended you up in L.A. in the first place. He seems to have dropped out of sight."

Kane doesn't say, "Oh!", though that's what he thinks. Having had such good sex before being exiled to L.A., and after having had such good sex with Talbot while in L.A., the chances of having good sex in Denver aren't all that good. So, by the time he gets back home, Talbot expects he'll be horny as hell. The prospect of cruising for someone new, even if his father has mellowed a bit on Talbot's homosexuality — which hasn't been confirmed, by any means, quite yet — isn't something to which he looks forward.

"Talbot, you still there? Bemoaning the sudden difficulties of starting up here where you left off, are you?"

"You think he's ever going to want to see me again, knowing what a homophobe my old man proves to be?"

"There'll be a car there any minute. The local office is sending over someone called Stuart to take over your shift. You have about two hours to make your flight. Your ticket is already at Delta's main counter."

"You want me to fly out tonight? In two hours?"

"No ties to hold you in L.A., isn't that what you said?"

"That's what you said. I've things to pack."

"Leave your apartment and car keys with Stuart. I'll have your things shipped by professionals. Whatever you need for the moment is already in Denver." Kane doubts that.

He doesn't doubt, though, how right he'd been never to have had Talbot over to the apartment to leave hard proof as to what they've been up to.

A limo pulls up outside. Daley Stuart gets out of the back, looking more like a chauffeur, in his security uniform, than the driver who opens the door for him. Stuart is in his fifties, has the makings of a causes-his-pants-waistline-to-roll-over paunch, has thinning grey-to-white hair, has a wife, has three kids, has about as much sex appeal, in Kane's opinion, as the Pillsbury Dough Boy.

Kane unlocks the front door.

"Guess you're headed off to greener pastures," Stuart says as he comes on in.

"You need a briefing on this place?"

"Naw, I've filled in for Raleigh on days."

"Okay, then," Kane says and hands over the keys to the building. He can't think of anything else to say, so he turns to leave.

"Something about a couple of additional keys?" Stuart calls after.

Kane finds his apartment and car keys and hands them over.

The limousine door makes a quiet swoosh as the driver closes Kane inside the auto. Kane settles back in the luxurious seat and stretches amid the smell of almost-new leather. He's glad he's closer to a permanent return to the home office, but he would prefer word of his departure to be more personal for Talbot than hearing about it from Daley (Dough Boy) Stuart, or even from Paul Raleigh. Does he, though, dare risk a phone call from the airport, assuming he has time? Obviously, his father has him watched. Kane doesn't want to blow this chance if, as his father insinuates, this move takes Kane closer to assuming at last some of the reins of company management. What is there for Kane if not the family security business?

He burrows his hard ass deeper into the cushioning leather. He undoes the top right button of his uniform blouse. He pulls out the tightly folded piece of white linen. He puts it to his nose.

He sniffs. He smells the essence of Talbot as relayed by the still-not-dried cum Talbot had wiped from his dick onto the hanky.

Inside his trousers, Kane's cock snakes toward new life.

CHAPTER TWENTY-FIVE

Drake Stone, actor (AKA Bob Smith, son of a Pocatello, Idaho, farmer Larry Smith), loves the Hawaiian heat. He especially loves it, after all of those cold Inland Empire winters of his childhood. And, he can't wait for the slightly higher temperatures of official Hawaiian summer. Some people say, what with Hawaii's balmy all-year temperatures, they can't tell the seasons, but Drake can tell.

Drake is completely naked. No big deal, since he's used to being almost naked for most of every day. If Hawaii is a land of handsome guys in swimming suits on sandy beaches, most of them are there on vacation, it's Drake's job — the bit role of Kyle, on the popular TV series *SandBox* — that has him strip down to a bit of Spandex and walk, run, jump, and/or swim there.

There are no cameras now, though, as Drake jacks-off. Not that he couldn't do what he does before a camera. Christ, he's flogged his hog for years. Sex was never much of a mystery for the son of a farmer. Drake grew up with animals rutting all of the time in pens, in fields, in pastures, in stables, in barns. He genuinely likes his big stiff dick in his curled fingers. He enjoys the rhythmic up-and-down pump of his fist over his dork. He loves the warm, then wet, sensations that come from a good masturbatory lead-in and a hearty cumblasting orgasm.

So, he enjoys stroking his dick, within the heat of this decidedly warm, although still officially springtime, Hawaiian evening, even though he does what he does, this time around, as much for Ronnie Williamstaad's benefit as for his own.

Brown-haired, brown-eyed, five-foot-six wunderkind Ronnie, is the "in" TV producer of the moment. To the surprise of everyone but him, he came directly to that august position from college film classes. All he'd arrived with, in TinselTown, was the expensive clothes on his back and in his Louis Vuitton luggage, the very expensive BMW he'd received as a graduation gift from daddy, some of his father's extra money in-pocket as collateral, and, of course, the all-important idea.

Single-handedly, Ronnie Williamstaad brought the genre tits-and-ass television drama (albeit with a twist), back into the American living room, at a time when everyone else said T&A, for the sake of T&A, was definitely in the decline.

Ronnie accomplished his retrograde miracle, or so reasoned pundits in retrospect, by unabashedly adding cock and balls to the T&A prime-time mix. Thereby tapping into the whole gay audience — closet and otherwise — who were tired of having to go to pay-TV in order to get their daily dosage of C&A. Even straight guys turned out to be eager tuners-in, in order to compare what they had to offer up on their local beaches, by way of filling snug-fitting swimwear, with what was offered up, weekly, by television actors; a phenomenon that should have been predicted, if just because of the universal big-dick/little-dick comparisons going on in all the supposedly straight and he-man locker rooms.

Before *SandBox,* every T&A show regularly put its male actors in the background and/or in baggy swim suits neither flattered nor flaunted sizable genitalia. Ronnie made no bones about putting big cock and big balls up there with big tits. As far as the display of tight buns, Ronnie gave male and female ass equal airtime. That a lot of people missed the boat, on that one, meant a lot of television people got the ax because of it, after Ronnie came along to point the way.

Drake's cock is big, his balls are big, and his ass is photographic-tight. His big cock is what he now beats all the faster.

"I'm getting there," he says. The nearer he gets to orgasm, the better he feels. A damn pity Ronnie, always the voyeur, refuses to join in. "My balls are really cum-ballooned and about ready to go. My cock is swelling all the bigger in my hand. Can you see my cum-filled balls better if I shift in this direction? See how my cock has increased in girth so much my fingers no longer are able to close around it? It won't be long, now."

He pumps. Jesus, he pumps. He wants to cream, but both Drake and Ronnie prefer he prolong orgasm, during these sessions, for as long as humanly possible. So, Drake does his best to hold on a bit longer before shooting his streamers of gooey cum.

Drake got his job on *SandBox* just because he was so good at beat . . . beat . . . beating . . . his dick and keeping up a running commentary all of the way to cream-splattering finish. If he keeps on doing it, and doing it well, he's promised a bigger *SandBox* role. Hell, it's rumored both of the show's main stars (one of them female) got where they are today by masturbating for Ronnie.

Drake would be willing to do a helluva lot more than just whack his wienie in order to keep from going back to boring farm-life in Idaho. And since Drake would be masturbating, anyway, with or without Ronnie for company, he's more than happy to provide a few moments of viewing pleasure, every few days, for his show's attractive producer.

"Just a few more pumps, I'm afraid," Drake says. "I've that on-the-very-brink feeling. See how my scrotum is all yanked up against the very base of my stiff dick? We know that's the position it always assumes when my cock starts squirting, don't we? You ready to see my cum?"

Ronnie never answers. He always just sits there. His cock never makes an appearance in or out of his pants. There's never any evidence of wet spots at his crotch, no matter how often Drake's cockblasts web Drake's fingers with sticky goo. If Drake finds it strange, he figures everyone has "his own" thing. Who is Drake to criticize, especially when he's having such a good time?

"Ready? Set?" Drake says.

Drake's piston-like fist goes into overdrive. He wants to prolong it a little longer but — sorry, Ronnie! — holding out any longer just isn't in the cards.

"Yes . . . yes . . . yes!" he says.

Just a few more beats of his fist. Just . . . one . . . or two . . .

The orgasmic balloon is about to pop inside him.

"I'm about to shoot."

His cock is about to let go.

"My never-been-sawed-off shotgun is about to fire."

His hips dance in hand-fuck accompaniment.

"Ohhhhh . . . ohhhhh . . . here it . . . fuck, shit . . . comes . . . comes . . . Jesus H. Christ, comes!"

And, it does. Oodles of it. Gallons of the stuff. Far-and-wide shots that end up cum-speckling the hardwood floor. Medium-range shots that drool Drake's chest and belly. Final oozes that frost his fingers like icing frosts a cake.

Ronnie gets up and leaves, pulling the door shut behind him.

Drake is left, cum-spatter all around him, his hand soaked in sperm.

"So . . . so . . . much . . . goo," he says. He's always amazed by how much cum his balls produce for these sessions. It confirms just how much pleasure he gets from jacking off for the watching Ronnie. There's never as much jism when he whips his dick solo.

He showers. Long. Sensuously hot water glosses his skin and emphasizes his deep tan and exquisite muscle-definition.

He dresses and goes to Jules. Of course, he shouldn't. Drake has an early-morning shoot. Except, it's not as if he hasn't already memorized most of his lines.

Jules is delighted to see him and Drake's big dick.

Jules Brange (AKA Benjamin Tajgmini from Chicago, Illinois), plays Lenny Mason in *SandBox*. His is a slightly meatier role than the one Drake plays, but it isn't so much meatier that it puts him on a different social tier.

Jules is six-feet tall. He's richly chocolate-colored, except for his dick which is so brown it appears black. He has close-cropped curly black hair, black eyes, black lips that are more thin than thick. He has a square jaw on a pleasantly square face. His body looks athletic, more the result of sessions with a special trainer, at the local gym, than from any play-ball sports activity. For Jules and Drake, going to the gym is mandatory, because of their deep-seated desire — their need — to look good in the swimsuits the TV series regularly requires them to wear.

The rumor is that Jules was hired by Ronnie to be the token black guy on *SandBox*. Jules doesn't give a damn why he was hired. He's just delighted to play a Harvard-grad stockbroker instead of one more movie character who's a drug-taking, jive-talking, hip-hopping, gang-banging shit-head punk. No way does he have any second thoughts about having jettisoned his burgeoning B-movie career in favor of small-box TV.

In fact, Jules *was* hired by Ronnie to be the token Afro-American. He was, also, chosen because of his cock. Not because Ronnie has this thing for big cock. He doesn't. Ronnie's bag is merely watching guys and gals get them-selves off with a bit of hand-movement and finger-play. Cock-size has nothing to do with any of that. Jules's cock is not big at all. Not small. Merely average: five inches soft, six-and-a-half inches hard. Just the right size, in accompaniment with Jules's balls, to present, in any revealing swimsuit, just the right package (according to all the demographics available as to the *SandBox* viewing audience), not to threaten white male viewers, and to please Afro-American viewers who are sick and tired of the stereotypical big-dicked black-man stud.

Certainly, Drake doesn't hold Jules's average-size cock against him. Figuratively speaking, in that, literally — ha, ha — he has had the cock up against him, and inside him, plenty of times. Drake, who has been around the sexual block a time or two, since leaving the farm in Idaho, prefers taking on an average-size penis. That preference is indicated by just how quickly he drops, naked on all fours, into dog-style position, and presents his ass to Jules, as if Drake were a dog who presents his ass to another dog for sniffing.

"How about we integrate your black cock with my white ass?" Drake says. "Nothing but nothing can return whatever starch has been drained out of my pecker by my session with Ronnie, other than your cock making its rounds up my tight asshole."

"One genuine example of a bona fide successful integration coming up," Jules says. He dons a rubber with the ease of some old-timer donning a hat, and he comes down to join Drake on the floor. "How's that big white dick of yours doing, by the way, my Idaho-farmer friend?"

"Nothing broke that you can't fix," Drake says.

"Even though, I'm sure, Ronnie had you strangling your snake silly."

"Even my well-strangled snake easily revives once your snake goes slithering up my ass."

"Let's see just how right you are."

Jules holds his cockshaft and guides its head into the upper part of Drake's asscrack.

"You will tell me 'when', won't you?" Jules says.

"When," Drake says as soon as the pulpy cockhead makes contact with his awaiting pucker.

"One touchdown achieved. One how-are-you-in-there? and a may-I-come-inside? about to commence."

Drake kowtows to some far corner of the room, his forehead, his hands, and his forearms against the floor.

Jules officially starts the butt-fuck with an insertion of his cock, neither slow nor speedy. He follows, without seeming pause, with a slide on out, almost to cocktip. After which, his dick immediately plows right back in. Each in and out makes contact with Drake's prostate and causes all sorts of good things to happen inside Drake's belly.

Beneath his stomach, Drake's scrotum begins to elevate at the same time his cock, still drooped, begins its first jerks toward half-mast.

Jules holds Drake's hips, fingers curled forward and around hipbones.

Each in-fuck of the cock through the funky corridor of Drake's butt causes chocolate belly to bang against white ass. Chocolate ball-sac swings forward at the end of each insertion and, for awhile, keeps on swinging until Jules's scrotal fuzz entwines momentarily, each time, with the longer hair that grows on the bag that contains Drake's testicles.

"Don't you have an early shoot in the morning?" Jules says and punctuates with a grunt. He isn't scheduled for anything until late tomorrow afternoon.

"Nothing to keep me from some major shoots with you this evening," Drake says.

"No one ever says you aren't a prime example of endurance personified," Jules says. His cock, once again, is out to its crown, just before it heads back on in through Drake's awaiting sphincter. "I just wish I knew how you do it."

As good as Jules always finds his sex with Drake, there's no way he'd have cock up this guy's butt if he had an early morning on the set. He tried that do-both regimen once, and it hadn't worked out for him. Making movies, TV or otherwise, is tiring business, and he doesn't care what some know-nothings say to the contrary.

"I just can't seem to get enough of your cock," Drake says. It has nothing to do with inches. It has everything to do with how Drake would like those inches to just keep on fucking him silly ... forever and ever ... amen.

They have fucking each other down to a science. Or, since they are actors, they have it down to an art. They have been with each other enough, have become familiar enough with the script of what they do, to have long-since perfected their roles to Emmy-Award-winning performances. There are hardly ever any glitches in the action.

Jules's cock just keeps pumping away, having assumed a steady rhythm of in and out ... in and out. Drake just stays where he is, his butt accepting, then releasing ... accepting, then releasing ... Jules's fucking inches.

The more readily visible result of their success, in conjunction with the verbal profusion of their increasingly helpless-to-control grunts and groans, is the returning stiffness of Drake's dick. Where, upon his first going dog-style on the floor, his prick had hung, head down, his cockhead is now suspended straight out on stiff cockneck. Pouty cockmouth paints sticky goo to the over-hang muscles of Drake's belly.

Chocolate belly whacks white ass. Again. Again. Again. Whack sounds get louder as flesh-to-flesh collisions produce more and more sweat on the ass and on the belly; the resulting wetness somehow magnifies the acoustics of the screw.

"Oh, you do fuck white ass well," Drake says. He reaches the point where he wants to fist his dick — better yet, have Jules reach a hand under and fist it — but he needs his dick hard for what Jules and he so look forward to after this mere prelude to their fuck-and-suck evening.

More than Drake, Jules feels the orgasmic build-up of their butt-fuck. He hasn't just come from a cumming with Ronnie. His last such session was last week, his next not scheduled until next week. He had just been contemplating a good fuck of his hand when Drake showed upon his doorstep. And, hadn't Jules been glad to see him.

An outsider might think Jules had a virtual smorgasbord of *SandBox* hot ass and horny cocks from which to choose, nightly, but a rigid pecking (pecker?) order keeps certain people in the cast and crew from screwing around with certain other people in the cast and crew. Some guys on the same rungs of the hierarchy are only into fucking cunt. Which leaves Jules, not counting his regular use of his hand, having sex with Drake, or with Gordon Sills, or with Timothy Preen — when Tim isn't too occupied brown-nosing every male and/or female ass on the rungs above him.

No way Jules pumps Drake's tight asshole for as long as Drake wants, nor for as long as Jules wants. It's just way too pleasurable to last.

"Cream in the cacao pods," Jules says. He refers to the cum in his chocolate balls. "Your ass about to get a good squirt."

"Just a little longer, stud," Drake says. He always says the same thing. Although by the time Jules has promised a buttful of cum, no way can he reverse the screw's already out-of-control forward-momentum, and Drake doesn't really want or expect him to. More fucking by Jules's cock would merely see Drake grab his own dick and helplessly jerk it off to climax. Which, at least for a while, would deprive them of the much anticipated follow-up.

"Sorry," Jules says. He's not sorry at all. Either he squirts the load in his testicles, or his nuts explode.

Whack: chocolate belly against white ass.

"Sweet shit!" Jules says and leans on over Drake's ass and back.

Jules's balls erupt their steamy, creamy contents. Jules's hips keep time with the expulsion of sperm by providing rabbity little butt-humps in accompaniment.

Jules drools on Drake's back, and he pants like a dog long without water.

"Yes ... yes ... fucking yes," Drake says. His pleasure is so goodness-gracious, he can almost — almost — come without taking hold of his dick.

Jules doesn't speak again until he's long finished.

"Hot damn," he says. "Hot, hot damn."

He still takes a good minute to unglue his sweaty cheek, chest, and belly from Drake's sweaty back and ass.

He pinches off the open end of the condom where it grips the base of his butt-stuck cock. He holds the cum-filled rubber in place and pulls it, and his dick, from Drake's asshole.

"I feel like you take a piece of me with you," Drake says as Jules's cock and cum pop free.

Jules removes his condom and wipes his dick dry with a convenient tissue. Drake overcoats his own boner with latex. Jules goes down on the floor and onto one side. He turns away from Drake, but it's not his I'm-done-and-now-want-to-nap posture. It's his let's-spoon-and-you-fuck-my-butt-at-one-and-the-same-time invitation.

Drake slides up right in behind him. He scoots in even closer. His head is against Jules's shoulder. His chest is against Jules's back. His belly is against Jules's ass. His cock ...

Jules lifts a leg. Drake's prick pokes through the breach between chocolate thighs. Drake's cockhead butts the rear of Jules's gone-flaccid scrotum.

With one hand, Drake tugs his dick so its back rides up and into Jules's asscrack as far as the awaiting pucker.

"That something knocking to come in?" Jules says.

"Knock … knock."

Drake's cock shoves up the ass to Drake's balls before Jules even starts to say, "Come on in."

* * * *

The wake-up alarm goes off early the next morning, while Drake's cock pumps an umpteenth soupy load up Jules's tight asshole.

So what if Drake isn't in tip-top shape as he walks the cordoned-off section of beach later that morning? How much sleep does he need to strut, look handsome and studly, glance seaward, spot the shark fin, order everyone out of the water, and run to the rescue of the big-busted *SandBox* babe swamped by panicked swimmers?

"Out of the water!" he yells.

He runs for the water.

The water is like glue around his legs. It's so fucking hard to push on through. But — see there! — he has the broad by her arms and he helps her ashore.

Except, something about the shoot isn't quite right, and they have to do it again … and again … and again.

By the fifth re-shoot, Drake wishes he hadn't shown Jules such a fucking good time. The sand has become quicksand, the water has become cement.

"Out of the water!" he yells.

The water seems a million miles away. His legs ache. Sweat and salt and sea and sand blind him. The broad isn't pulling her own weight, and she makes him work especially hard to get her sorry ass back to shore!

He trips. Hits hard. The pain shoots from his right ankle all of the way up his leg to his groin. The broad complains he's pulled her down. The surf momentarily recedes to leave Drake and the bitching babe, her tits almost out of her skimpy bra, beached like unwitting sea-slugs.

Drake tries to stand. Jesus, the pain! His ankle is unable to take his weight. He goes down.

"Medic!" someone yells.

Nowhere is that in the day's shooting script.

CHAPTER TWENTY-SIX

"Talbot!" his mother calls up the stairs. "The phone. Gerald McTalen."

Talbot picks up and says, "Gerald?!"

Gerald waits for the click that tells him Talbot's mom is off the line. Not that she would listen, even with the prospect of her son's helped-along acceptance into Princeton. Talbot's mom and his dad are pretty good about respecting his privacy.

"My dad wants you for supper," Gerald says.

"I'm a pig, apple in mouth, on a platter?"

"Can't say no to this invite," Gerald says. "I'll tell the old man you'll be here by six o'clock tonight."

At six-of-six, Talbot is at the MacTalen residence. At seven-of-seven, Gerald's father says, "Oh, by the way, Talbot, you're definitely in Princeton."

They're eating chocolate, in cake-form, from Forbidden Desserts. Gerald shows signs of having achieved some much-needed weight gain.

"In?" Obviously, Talbot's mind wanders.

"Damned right!" Gerald's father says.

"Gee!" Talbot says.

"Congratulations," says Gerald's father says. He stands and shakes Talbot's hand.

"Gee!" Talbot repeats, like some Polly-want-a-cracker parrot. Somehow, he manages, "Thanks!" and makes it sound as sincere as it deserves. "I mean, thanks a heap!"

"I've some business to take care of for a few minutes," says Gerald's father says, "but we'll meet up again before you leave, Talbot. I've some names of people you should talk to, locally. Getting into any school is only the half of it, if you expect to get everything out of the experience that you can."

Gerald's father turns to his son.

"Think you can keep Talbot entertained for an hour or so?"

"I think so," says Gerald.

"Feel free to use one of our telephones, Talbot," says Gerald's father says on his way to his study. "We've several private lines, and one should never forget parents at a time like this."

Talbot calls and gives his mom the good news. No disguising his father's delight. Which makes worthwhile whatever Gerald expects from Talbot in return.

"Let's walk," Gerald says as soon as Talbot hangs up.

"You've gained some weight," Talbot says, following along. He means his comment as the compliment.

"My father is as delighted as you are that I'm off my marathoner's diet."

A few seconds later, Gerald stops in front of a familiar garden bench.

"Know why we're here?" Gerald says.

Pay-back time, Talbot thinks. Nobody gets anything for nothing.

"You're thinking it's pay-back time," Gerald uncannily hits the nail on the head. "No one gets a free ride, right? You have it wrong. Your acceptance by Princeton is a done deal, whether you fuck my ass or not. I've pulled in too many markers with the old man to change my mind now. Dad has pulled in way too many markers to change his mind now. Gumming up the works for you, at this point, would cause a major loss of face. So, you're off to Princeton. Congrats! No strings attached."

Is Talbot disappointed that Gerald isn't insisting on sex? Despite Gerald's obvious weight gain, which makes him more attractive, he's still as unattractively skinny as a bean.

All along the line, though, Talbot has expected to fuck and/or suck Gerald, or let Gerald fuck and/or suck him. Part of the reason Talbot let Matt squat over his dick is because of all the strings the Princeton student can pull in Talbot's favor. That Talbot somehow finds Matt a genuine turn-on is mere icing on that cake.

Talbot knows Gerald knows Talbot's cock has been fucked up Matt's ass. Talbot has come this evening convinced Gerald expects no less, from Talbot's cock, by way of recompense. Hell, Talbot is prepared to do more than that, if it's required.

Gerald laughs and sounds genuinely delighted. "Don't worry, buddy, you're not going to have to fuck my hot ass for my getting my dad to give you a helping hand into Princeton." He sits on the convenient bench and pats the place directly beside him.

Talbot sits. Up close, Gerald smells pleasantly of lime.

" I came into this knowing you see me as a sexless and skinny freak," Gerald says.

"I never said that." No matter, Gerald is right on the mark.

"You think I don't see where your preferences lie?" Gerald says. "So, I say to myself: 'Self, what do you do to get Talbot's cock out of his pants and up your ass, whether he finds you attractive or not? He wants into Princeton. Hell, I can help him manage that.' Not that either my father or I could have helped you if you hadn't already come with adequate academic and extracurricular credentials, but you'd already have those in place, don't you? And there's no denying your father's money and contacts had you on the fast track."

That fast track, without benefit of the ivy-league good-old-boy system, could have been a fast track to nowhere, and Talbot knows it. So does Gerald.

"If you were to fuck me," Gerald says, "and stick your big cock up my skinny ass, it would only be so you could shut your eyes and fantasize my skinny butt as the butt of someone more studly, like, say, Peter Flanner or Kane Clydesdale."

Well, he hit that nail right on the head, but Talbot doesn't think Gerald needs the humiliating embarrassment of Talbot admitting to it.

"Rustled up a bit of self respect and self worth in the end, I guess, is what I did," Gerald says, with a shake of his head. "Decided I enjoy helping you just for the pure pleasure of the helping. After all, we go back a few years together, don't we? You always a nice, friendly, polite, guy, too. Never once nasty or snotty. Giving me every reason to like you, quite aside from your having a face and body to die for."

It's warm out. The slightest trickle of perspiration runs Gerald's face. He has good bone structure. Off his runner's diet for just a few more weeks, and he'll likely — maybe — be genuinely good looking — again.

"Maybe, someday, if you ever decide you want to fuck me, the person, just not see me as some kind of fill-in for someone else . . . . Or, maybe, when I'm really old and ugly, genuinely vindictive and unusually mean and cranky, I'll call you in and scream, 'Look at all I did for you. The least you can do for me is fuck me in the ass.'"

Talbot is embarrassed he comes through such a winner, with so little effort. He's been a real shit, through it all, thinking of little else but himself, his pleasure, his needs, his desires, what people can and should do for him . . . him . . . him. Begrudgingly, he'd decided, but only if pressed, to provide the minimum recompense to Gerald for favors due. Except Gerald has realized just how much Talbot is prepared to short-change him, and he has decided not to bother, making Talbot come off, even by his own estimation, a pretty superficial, selfish jerk, and all-round heel.

"Just enjoy," Gerald says. "On the whole, you are, and I suspect will remain, a pretty decent guy."

He kisses Talbot on the cheek, and Talbot lets him. Talbot puts his hand to the back of Gerald's head and shifts to touch lips to lips.

Go figure what happens next.

The kiss is a catalyst. Anyway, Talbot guesses it's a catalyst, based on how his lab teacher once described one.

Never have two guys shed their clothes faster than they do. Like, one moment they're dressed and about to part friends . . . they kiss . . . and, the next moment, they're naked as jays, Talbot's cock rubberized with a condom.

Talbot is on this roller-coaster ride, and there's no way in hell he's getting off the fast track. So . . . .

Gerald goes to his back, pretty much like he'd done for his fucked in the Spa by Peter. Something about the time . . . or maybe the place . . . or maybe the lead-in . . . makes Gerald come off less skinny kid and more sexy-as-hell.

Seeing Gerald's cock, Talbot remembers just how large it has always been. It's the only part of Gerald that seems to have genuine bulk. That's because his thinness makes his dick seem all the larger in comparison. Big at its bulbous and circumcised tip, the largest part of the cock anchors thick roots into the V of Gerald's lower belly.

Talbot positions himself so his stomach falls atop Gerald's cock once his own cock plugs up Gerald's eagerly positioned asshole. Talbot's hard prick is up Gerald's behind, all of the way to Talbot's cum-bulged balls. So fast was the shove inside, assisted by Gerald's up-thrusting buttocks, the asshole initially seems fucked by Peter (and others?) to the looseness of a barn. Except what follows is the clamping down of all looseness, with a vengeance, on and around Talbot's stiff pecker. Talbot groans as much out of fear for his cock being squashed to nothingness as from the admitted surge of up-tight-asshole pleasure.

The concave of Gerald's belly, between his prominent hipbones, provides a natural saddle for Talbot's stomach which grinds strangled dick to a halt. No way Talbot pulls out without turning Gerald inside out.

"So, it seems you fuck me after all," Gerald says.

No one is more amazed than Talbot. He not only fucks Gerald, but he enjoys it.

"Yeah, it looks that way," Talbot says. If Gerald's asshole doesn't soon turn loose its death grip on Talbot's stuffing erection, the two are destined to be permanent Siamese twins.

Gerald crawls his legs even higher up Talbot's body, the backs of his thighs finally supported by his fucker's shoulders.

Two things happen in quick succession. Gerald's asshole becomes less form-fitting, but not much. Somewhere inside Talbot, a switch turns on that converts him into a genuine, all-around, root'n-toot'n fuck machine that pretty well screws Gerald's asshole without any conscious say-so in the matter. Like, the automatic pilot he'd become while fucking Kane's ass.

He screws himself into a hyper-state that leaves him without a clue as to how he got there.

How he almost passed this up, dissuaded by some stuff and nonsense about what constitutes good sex, skinny equaling a blah sexual encounter, leaves him all the more excited by how he has somehow had the good sense to cast aside previous prejudice to jump right in.

Gerald manhandles his own dick. Talbot flies higher and higher with each successive stroke of his cock up the asshole. His eyes squeeze shut. It's an unconscious reflex that allows him more concentration in making this a good time for both.

"Open your eyes, stud!" Gerald says. He provides another tensing of anal muscles that collapses his asshole so securely, along the whole length of Talbot's dick, that all Talbot's fucking grinds to a complete halt. Any success in getting cock started again will likely do physical damage to both.

Talbot opens his eyes, as instructed. Gerald looks right up at him. Talbot wonders if his own eyes are nearly as dilated and glassy as those he sees.

"Who are you fucking?" Gerald says.

"Fucking you," Talbot says, glad as hell he's given the right answer that relaxes Gerald's asshole around submerged cock. "I'm fucking the living shit out of your sexy asshole."

"The sexy asshole of skin-and-bones me," Gerald says. His hands are on Talbot's ass for resumption of the bumpy ride.

"Sure as hell! Fucking . . . fuck . . . fucking . . . skinny . . . sexy . . . asshole."

"And loving every fucking second," Gerald says.

"Loving . . . every . . . fucking . . . second," Talbot echoes in his particular pleasure-induced staccato.

Which sees asshole initiate its fluttering — no other word for it. Damned anal vibrations dance the entire length of Talbot's dick, each and every time his cock plugs to his balls. The continuing sensations are so lusciously intense that Talbot prefers them, his cock deep-sixed, over any continuation of in-and-out strokes.

"Fucking Gerald's skinny . . . sexy . . . fluttering . . . butt," Talbot says.

Which is just about all he manages, about to go down for the count. No way does his cock, encased in that tight tube of rubbery shuddering butthole, survive much longer.

"Fuck skinny Gerald's skinny ... fluttering ... ugh ... Jesus-sexy ... tight ... ass!" Talbot grunts as he drains so much of his creamy cum up the eagerly vacuuming rectum that anyone would think the whole Amazon watershed lets go a year's supply in a few massive bursts.

All of which leaves Talbot one cum- and energy-drained dude.

*   *   *   *

Jesus, what a stroke of amazing good luck! Unbelievable! That one of the best fuck of Gerald's senior year comes by way of his seduction of Talbot. Something only planned, spur of the moment, once Gerald decided any longer-lasting relationship with Peter wasn't worth the continued effort of diet and marathon running.

It had been Gerald's cousin, Toby Cornwall, university long-distance runner who, after having been fucked by Peter at Yale, convinced Gerald there was no more sublime sex than being stuck on Peter's big cock. Toby had insisted the more skeletal a guy got, the more hot and horny Peter got to have at him. Which had turned out to be true.

Gerald's seduction of Talbot was a helluva lot easier than all of the effort put into landing Peter, and it had only come about because Gerald tired earlier than expected of diet and marathon ... and Peter, thereby, lost interest in the weight-gaining Gerald ... and Gerald, thereby, suddenly needed something, after Peter's peter but before all the hard ivy0league dick of his freshman year at Yale.

CHAPTER TWENTY-SEVEN

His name tag says D.Stuart.

"You're Mr. Crane's son, right?" D. Stuart says. He sounds as tired as he looks.

"Sorry, sir," Talbot says. "My dad thinks he may have left some papers in one of the back rooms, and he asked me to stop by to take a look."

D. Stuart looks like someone few people call sir. Therefore, he might better be sucked up to (figuratively, not literally) if Talbot uses the title.

"Sure, go ahead," D. Stuart says. It's highly unlikely the chief architect's son is up to anything but what he says he is.

"I thought Kane Clydesdale was on night duty," Talbot says as an apparent afterthought. Somehow, he must have confused Kane's night off.

"He was shipped off to more easily climb the corporate ladder, wasn't he?" D. Stuart says, and sounds I-should-be-so-lucky. "His old man who, you probably know, owns the company, had him transferred to the Denver office."

Kane gone!? Goddamn!

"When?"

"Just last night. His old man sent a limo to deliver him to the airport."

Of course, it's possible Kane's old man found out about Kane and Talbot. But surely Kane needs at least a couple of days to clear out his things? Kane was always too paranoid (a well-found paranoia, it would seem) about the prospect of being watched by his father's goons to invite Talbot anywhere near Kane's apartment, but that doesn't mean he hasn't driven by a couple of times.

"Actually, I think my father left those papers he's after on a Xerox machine back at the office," Talbot says and turns to leave.

"You sure you don't want to take a look, just to be sure?"

"Nah, it's okay, but thanks."

Kane's apartment, actually a small one-bedroom bungalow, is one of six accessed by a walkway that connects Palm Avenue to Aroilla Boulevard.

Talbot spots someone (not Kane, but maybe one of the other tenants), headed in his direction, from an adjacent bungalow, as Talbot turns in at Kane's place.

The building Talbot confronts is dark, except for the lone porch light. It looks vacant. It even smells vacant. Certainly, it exudes an aura of vacancy.

He rings the doorbell. Nothing in response, except for bell reverberations within obviously empty space.

"You looking for Kane Clydesdale?"

Talbot turns. The guy Talbot had figure on his way out has backtracked and stands at the pathway to Kane's bungalow.

Where Talbot had previously been so focused on reaching Kane's place that he'd only had a vague inclination that the guy he passed was genuinely handsome, even in the dim lighting, he confirms that handsomeness now, complete with its dark hair and superb build.

"Yeah, but he doesn't seem to be home," Talbot says.

"I just talked to the neighbor who says Kane's things were moved out this morning. Mistakenly, too, was picked up a couch and chair that belongs to the landlord. Everything, including Kane, off to Denver. Looks like we both missed him."

"Did you know he was leaving?"

"Me? Hell, no I just got in from Miami. Thought I'd look him up, because he and I used to be really close until his old man shipped him here to L.A."

"You the one who got Kane's old man so concerned that ...?" Talbot leaves the question open-ended. Just by looking, he knows he would have been worried, too, had he been Kane's homophobic father and found his son fucking around with this genuine hunk of tan and muscle.

Mr. Just-in-from-Miami laughs. He has a nice laugh. By some miracle of lighting (or absence thereof), his eyes (blue? black? blue-black?) actually sparkle.

"You the one who got Kane's old man so concerned that he's shipped him off to Denver?" Mr. Miami says.

It's Talbot's turn to laugh. If Kane is gone, and every indication points to that being the case, what Talbot has here at least holds out the prospect of being a damned nice consolation prize.

"Name is Talbot Crane, by the way," Talbot says ands comes down off the porch, hand extended. Fuck Kane for allowing himself to be jerked this way and that by his jerk of an old man!

"In case Kane never named names, mine is Jason Summer." His hand-shake is firm and warm and sexy as all hell.

"And, here we stand, two victims of interfering-father-produced *coitus interruptus*."

"Kane really should take the old goat back for a better model," Jason says. He still doesn't let go of Talbot's hand. If he's arrived not knowing whether or not Kane will be happy to see him, he divines Talbot as delighted to have him just where he is, Jason still squeezing gently on Talbot's fingers and vice versa.

Talbot doesn't have to be hit over the head to feel the vibes of sexual interest emanating in his direction.

"You carrying around that obvious boner in your pants as a kind of glad-to-see-you-again-Kane hello?" Talbot says.

"Speaking of boners carried around in pants," Jason says. His head inclines just slightly in Talbot's direction.

Talbot's bulged pants are such a Seventh Wonder of the Modern World, these days, even can-care-less-about-it Peter noticed and made comment.

Jason releases Talbot's hand in order to rearrange the stiffness presented in his own pants. The invitation is obvious.

"There's a park just down the road," Talbot says. "Kane and I go there, because he's too paranoid to have me show up here."

"Lots of trees? Lots of underbrush?" Jason's fingers remain at his crotch. His kneading brings his erection into even higher bas-relief. Not that Talbot needs any additional enticement.

"Lots of trees," Talbot says. "Lots of underbrush."

They reach the park in no time. They don't proceed through the gauntlet of brambles and brush to that hard-to-reach spot where Kane always insists Talbot and he link up. The park is dark enough to provide more than a few spots which, unsuitable in daylight hours, won't give any unauthorized someone any look-see in the dark without benefit of a powerful floodlight. Talbot leads the way into one such bit of gloom.

"Well, this certainly turns out to be my lucky night," Jason says. "Let's hope you can soon say the same."

"Well, this certainly turns out to be my lucky night," Talbot says. "That soon enough for you?"

No way they stay dressed. A continuing high pressure area, one of but many marching, seemingly unendingly, across the southern United States, continues the warm summer-like weather. When summer does arrive, it'll be hard-pressed to duplicate the balmy good weather that precedes it.

Neither Talbot nor Jason's expert eye misjudges how the other will look naked. Each emerges from his clothes just as tanned all over and well-muscled as expected. Both cocks are as big and as hard as previously presented within crotch-cupping trousers.

"I have rubbers," they say in unison. They laugh in unison. They present condom packets in unison.

"Do we flip to see who goes belly-down first?" Talbot says. Should he fish through the pockets of his discarded pants for a quarter?

"Nah," Jason says. "I get first dibs on belly-down honors."

He uses his clothes as cushions between him and the ground. He lies down and rests one cheek on his folded-beneath-his-head arms. His hard cock burrows and fucks the clothes and ground beneath him.

Talbot is intensely desirous to poke Jason's asshole. Kane, at least for the moment, is pretty much forgotten. Go figure! Easy come, easy go? Talbot's not to reason why?!

Talbot doesn't waste time but pries open Jason's asscrack and locates the inviting pucker. Small pucker. Tiny-little wink within its black-hair parenthesis. Inner curves of the anal seam are slightly damp with sweat from their walk from the bungalow.

"Are you as ready as I am?" Talbot says.

"Couldn't be any more ready, unless you'd like to give my cock your fist to fuck."

Talbot gives Jason's cock his fist. He can't imagine Jason being any more turned on by the wrap of fingers around hard meat than he himself is turned on by it.

"More than ready," Jason says. "And, please don't have any hang-ups as regards how you have to go slow and easy, this being our first time."

Talbot would like to go slow and easy. However, the truth be known, he's deprived, by inner forces quite beyond his conscious control, of any ability to go slow and easy. Actually, he has been deprived of that option ever since his first glimpse of studly Jason completely naked.

Talbot's cockhead has long since leaked its first bit of preseminal goo. It's as if that ooze, not the industrial slick on the condom, is what provides the slide way for his cock to enter the butt in one forceful push, from cockhead to balls. The resulting hug of the being-entered asshole, and the accompanying friction-caused heat of sliding cock against anal walls, leaves Talbot breathless and burning.

"Jesus, I'm in," Talbot says, wondrous slide complete.

"Tell me about it," Jason says. It's as if Talbot's cock thrusts all of the way into the base of Jason's throat. Jason, stuffed to his gills, is in Seventh Heaven.

"You okay?" Talbot says.

"I'm fine, buddy."

"I'm fine, too."

Jason's belly shifts against the cushion of folded clothes. His asshole provides a sensuous shift round Talbot's plugging dick. Anal mortar and penile pestle grind more excruciating pleasure into reality

"Ohhhhh, my!" Talbot appreciates, even more so, the tightness of the fucked asshole. His hand gives Jason's cock an equally intense squeeze.

"Now, really fuck my butt," Jason says. "Can you do that for me, stud? Can you screw me silly and leave me begging for more?"

Actually, Talbot wishes he were the one belly-down. As good as his cock feels, buried to his balls, up this asshole, there's something about the genuinely sensuous knobbiness of Jason's cockhead, confirmed by the movement of Jason's cock within Talbot's hand, which promises special things when inserted up any guy's butt.

Not that Talbot is prepared to pull out and change places. He's come too far for that. As he begins actual butt-fucking motions, he proceeds farther down the irreversible pathway he'll travel until climax.

"Tight ass," Talbot says. "Sure it's not virgin?" a complimentary but likely superfluous question, considering the lead-in.

"Virgin-like is about as close as it gets, buddy," Jason says and gives his butt a quick rotation that turns his asshole around the length of sticking dick.

Whack! Talbot's nuts hit Jason's fucked ass for the very last time. Continuing scrotal elevation simply tugs Talbot's testicles too close to their eventual complete compaction, against the base of Talbot's stiff dick, for any additional swings.

On each inward fuck of Jason's cock through Talbot's curled fingers, Jason's scrotum does some compacting of its own.

The fuck proceeds faster … faster … faster. Cock up asshole … cock up fist. Pure bliss! Visions blur. Eyes dilate. Sweat runs down chests and bellies and backs and asscracks and soaks black pubic hair and red.

Wet sounds. Loud sounds. Birds-disturbed-in-their-tree sounds.

"Aggrrahhhhh!" Talbot sounds.

"Aghr … aghr … aghrrhhhhung!" Jason sounds.

A dual atomic blast. Two marvelously simultaneous detonations. Tree-shaking. Earth-shaking. Sky-shaking. Solar-system shaking. Universe shaking. Quantum-physics shaking. Soul-and-body shaking.

"Jesus!" Talbot's spunk gushes uninterrupted.

"Fuck!" Jason's sperm squirts ands cream-paints Talbot's fingers and the space between his belly and the clothes-covered ground.

Cocks continue to release cream, coordinated. Each blast into butt matches a blast through the vise-like confines of Talbot's quickly sliming fist.

CHAPTER TWENTY-EIGHT

This isn't the way Jeffrey imagines spending his time during his last few days before high-school graduation. He tries to get involved in all the school "things" that have most everyone else all excited and giddy, but none of it does much for him. Not without Marky and/or Talbot. Marky and Talbot are Jeffrey's best friends, his mates, his fuck-buddies. At least they had been. They had been the Three Musketeers who did everything together. So, what happens?

Jeffrey is piqued that the "togetherness" of Marky, Talbot, and him has fallen apart, during what should be their most glorious days of school. Especially, he blames Talbot. At least, Marky has the excuse of this television thing, the show shooting scenes around him. If he arrives in Hawaii unprepared, all shit hits the fan, and probably Marky's acting career right along with it. Talbot, though . . . who would have guessed he would end up spending so much time, before Princeton, with a security guard (for Christ's sake!), with skinny-ass Gerald McTalen, or wanting to spend sexual time with Peter-the-architect-who-works-for-Talbot's father?

When the modeling agency calls and asks if he wants to come in for an interview, for a possible local shoot, to take place over one weekend, what does Jeffrey have to lose? He's encouraged by the person on the phone who says the "client" specifically picked Jeffrey's picture as someone "right" for the product being sold. The product being some kind of see-through plastic cell phone aimed at the have-to-have-one-of-everything market. By the looks of the full room that awaits Jeffrey at the agency, however, the client's "pick of potential" didn't stop with Jeffrey's picture.

Jeffrey, who comes looking for relief from the boredom, is bored. Whoever thinks modeling is an exciting job should look again. It's more like going to the office of a dentist. In that the first interview of the morning has Jeffrey feel as if he's having a tooth pulled. He's asked to dance. Solo. In front of some fat broad, a camera, a cameraman, some piss-poor music playing in the background. When he asks what dancing has to do with a see-through plastic cell phone, neither the cameraman, nor the fat woman conducting the "interview", is all that forthcoming. After which, Jeffrey expects to be told to get lost. They ask him to wait.

Wait for what, for Christ's sake?! Damn Talbot! Damn Marky! Damn the sescurity guard and the architect!! Damn *SandBox*!

If anyone asks him to sing, he'll tell them to take their locally shot-over-the-weekend photo shoot and stuff it up their and the agency's collective ass. Decorating for the prom can't possibly be more ridiculous.

He came expecting his companions to be interesting. Most everyone, though, is too damned picture-perfect. Too much well-cut and well-coifed hair. Too many square jaw lines, dimples, cleft chins, tanned and well-turned-out physiques. Too much forest to see a tree.

Ah, now! Jeffrey's attention is on the guy just through the door. Black hair. Dark-complexion. Great physique. Definitely not one of the look-alike mannequins. Looks downright fresh. Probably new to the game. A kindred spirit?: He looks as if he finds all of this as silly as Jeffrey does.

However, if the guy is new to the business, his portfolio is definitely done by a pro. Jeffrey gets a glimpse of the kid's pictures flipped through by the woman at reception. Jeffrey knows good pictures when he sees them, because the photographer Jeffrey produced a batch of genuine shit.

The receptionist puts through a call to someone in another room. That someone (or someone sent by that someone) comes out front and takes charge of the new guy's portfolio. The guy is directed to an empty chair almost directly across from Jeffrey.

Mr. Studly sits. There's eye-contact. Mr. Studly smiles. Sweet smile. Sweet guy. Probably, soon to be chewed up and spit out by the dog-eat-dog modeling business. Not like Jeffrey who refuses to be chewed up and spit out. Jeffrey has a firm resolve to succeed. What will he do, where will he go, if he doesn't?

Jeffrey waits. He provides the guy with a do-you-believe-this-shit-? roll of the eyes.

The guy obliges with another sweet smile. During which, he's personally escorted to one of the back rooms. To dance solo? Jeffrey would like to take the guy in his arms and, big-dick to big-dick, dance him around the room. Jeffrey has every confidence the kid's dick is a big one. The kid's basket is obviously bulged as it flashes Jeffrey in passing.

Jeffrey's name is called. No one to escort him; he has to walk on his own. To where he talks to another "someone", this time male, who tries small-talk while Jeffrey turns this way and that to mug for a video camera.

"What was all the dancing stuff?" Jeffrey says.

His latest interviewer looks confused . . . besides looking incredibly ugly with his thinning hair, his large sloping forehead, his large nose, his large and jutting jaw. So many trolls behind the scenes of a business renown for its physical perfection!

"Oh!" The interviewer has an epiphany. "One of the proposed shots calls for a disco."

After which, Jeffrey is again assigned a chair in reception, as is the escorted-to-his-seat Mr. Studly. Jeffrey or Mr. Studly keep disappearing, separately, into one or the other of the back rooms. Each time one of the other, they exchange (meaningful?) smiles and/or give-me-a-break-from-all-this-shit glances.

Jeffrey's last interviewer comes close to asking him to sing. What the woman says is, "Can you sing?"

"Like a frog," Jeffrey says.

"You look like someone we can use in an upcoming commercial for a top client," she says. ""Dancing, singing, trying to make everyone out there feel 'in' wearing khaki or poplin. I'll look at the tape of you dancing and get back to you."

"Right." No way Jeffrey holds his breath.

"By the way, you've a part in the shoot over this weekend if you want it."

"Really?"

"Background only, I'm afraid, but it'll look okay on your résumé."

Jeffrey can't believe all of this bullshit actually lands him a job.

"A car picks you up outside our offices, here, at seven o'clock tomorrow morning, and please don't be late. Don't worry about wardrobe. Just wear something comfortable that you'd wear out for a night on the town. If the look isn't right, one of our staff will do corrections on-site. Questions?"

Jeffrey's only question comes to him on his way out through reception: "What happened to Mr. Studly?"

Answer: He awaits Jason just outside the door.

"So, do you get to hold a see-through plastic cell phone and shake your bootie like the rest of us?" Jeffrey says.

The kid looks handsome-confused.

"The photo shoot behind this cattle-call," Jeffrey reminds. Although, technically, it probably wasn't a cattle-call in that Jeffrey hadn't gone in cold, the client supposedly having pre-screened his photo.

"Oh," Mr. Studly says. "I was just introducing myself around and showing my portfolio. By way of introduction to you, by the way, I'm Jason Summer."

Jeffrey provides his name, in exchange, and then asks if Jason's portfolio is so good the agency has decided to keep it.

"I don't know about the 'so good' part, although the guy who did the photos is a real pro. The head of the agency is out of the office until later tonight. They say they'll give him a look and courier the portfolio back to me in the morning."

"You been in the business long, then?"

"Just starting. Wouldn't be here, now, if the guy who shot my photos didn't think I have a chance and push it."

"You waiting for this guy now?"

"Merely trying to figure if I've time to make it back to my place before I pee my pants."

"There's a bathroom in the agency. There's another just down this hall. Come on."

The most enjoyable part of Jeffrey's day, job-landed or otherwise, is going to be standing beside this kid at a public urinal.

Except, as luck would have it, both urinals are in use. Jason hightails it to the nearest stall. A frustrated Jeffrey takes the one next to him.

Luck-on-the-rebound provides a connecting glory-hole.

While Jason is hopefully distracted in making pee sounds in the water of his toilet bowl, Jeffrey sits on the toilet seat and leans for a hopefully clandestine peek through the glory-hole.

Jason's still-in-progress hearty river of piss is a joy to behold! Sexily, he pisses . . . and pisses . . . and pisses . . . he makes Jeffrey's cock go so stiff that Jeffrey couldn't piss if he badly needed to.

What's genuinely exciting for Jeffrey is how, once Jason's cock finally stops pissing, it isn't reeled in and/or tucked away. Jason turns slightly in Jeffrey's direction and provides an even better view of a cock made all the more exciting by it bulbous head, its narrowed cockneck (just below the coronal flare), the quick swelling from narrowness to downright thickness at belly-sprouted cockroots.

What genuinely excites is Jason's cock elongation, even as Jeffrey watches it. Big gets bigger . . . bigger gets even bigger.

Jason's cock no longer hangs over the lip of his open fly, but juts, as his balls are scooped out to accompany it. One of his nuts droops lower than the other, but only for a quick fraction of a second. Then, both nuts begin a subtle up-and-down juggling act until, finally, they're perfectly aligned.

The outside door of the restroom opens and shuts . . . opens and shuts. Jeffrey and Jason are now alone.

"Come on," Jeffrey says. He wants Jason's cock. He's hungry for it. "Stick it through, and I'll show it a good time that it and you won't soon forget."

Jeffrey fucks his mouth up real close and personal to the mouth-like glory-hole. He French kisses it. His tongue, long and slippery, flicks snake-like out the other side. Jeffrey is a python out to swallow its prey whole.

Like a sizable animal hypnotized by the snake out to have at it, Jason's cock gets closer and closer to the fed-through tongue at the glory-hole.

Jason pushes down on his cockneck and aims his cockhead directly at the hole. The next flick of Jeffrey's incoming tongue makes contact. It sends electric shocks through Jason's entire body. It leaves nutty tastes on Jeffrey's taste buds and makes Jeffrey hungry for more ... more ... more.

"Come on . . . come on," Jeffrey says. Momentarily, his tongue is back to his side of the glory-hole. He fumbles with his fly and wrestles his stiff dick into the open. His fist encircles his meaty erection and begins whipping.

The temptation to fuck the glory-hole and the hot-wet mouth beyond is too much for Jason to resist. Once again, Jeffrey's tongue does its in-and-out dance in open invitation. Jason puts his cockhead to the tongue tip. The tongue is solidly smooth and slippery. Its resulting hearty lap leaves the bulbous tip of Jason's cock spit-glossed.

Jason sticks his cock to the hole and partially through it. If Jeffrey's tongue retreats, there's pleasure for Jason and his dick within the wet-warm cocoon offered by Jeffrey's ovaled lips on the other side.

Once Jason and his cock have the sampling of Jeffrey's hot-and-hungry chewing, there's no way the rest of Jason's cock is missing out on the follow-through.

Jeffrey is ready and willing to suck up each and every inch Jason offers. The quick slide of hard cock into Jeffrey's face, along the slightly curled slide way of his tongue, into his throat, down . . . down . . . down . . . is accomplished with nary a gag.

Jason's belly bangs the stall partition and strives to feed Jeffrey the last fraction of dick left unavailable within the surrounding ply that separates one stud from the other. Jason's balls slap the partition, just below where his cock stuffs the hole, and the slapping leaves a splotchy blot of sweat.

Jason's hands clamp the top of the partition and hold there. Jason's weight suspends from his fingers. His legs are weakened by the pleasure of Jeffrey's sucking on Jason's thick and lengthy sexual poker. His cheek presses the partition and leaves a sweat-mark.

"Jesus . . . oh, Jesus," Jason says.

There's something uniquely pleasurable for Jeffrey in the bulbous tip of Jason's dick, the slight indent of cockshaft that supports that tip, the hefty enlargement of the cockshaft, thereafter, all of the way down to where the last bit of hard dick affixes to Jason's hair-grown crotch.

Jeffrey's face pulls back, and bits of Jason's slippery cock again come into view. So sexy and unique: the bump of the kid's cockhead through Jeffrey's throat and mouth. Jeffrey pauses in his suck, only Jason's fist-like cockhead contained. Talbot's lips rubber-band the slight indent of cockneck that supports the bulbous crown. Jeffrey's tongue-tip fucks the tiny mouth of Jason's erection.

Pleasure jerks Jason's hang-by-his-hands body. Reflexively, his hips pull back. His inches of released dick return to his side of the partition. His cockhead, though, is still locked on the other side, inside Jeffrey's sucking mouth.

Jason's hips return to the wall with a loud bang and feed his recently released inches right back through. Jeffrey's face, which followed the retreated cockshaft and saved it from complete disappearance by keeping control of its cockhead, remains stationary as Jason's cock returns into the humid depths of Jeffrey's eating face.

The tastes of the thickly stiff dong dissolve within Jeffrey's spit and are swallowed down. They are a powerful stimulant that has Jeffrey crave all the more. If such aphrodisiac can't survive too much salival washing, it provides sufficient appetizer to make Jeffrey work all the harder for the creamier meal being prepared within Jason's balls.

Jeffrey's cock isn't forgotten. Jeffrey's fist whips harder ... harder ... to keep pace with the spiraling enjoyment he derives from eating Jason's wondrous pecker.

Jason climbs the wall, literally. His handholds tighten. His body rises. Then he slides against the wall. His handholds loosen. His body sags.

United by Jason's hard cock, separated only by a thin layer of ply, the two achieve a coordinated rhythm that leaves them less concerned with the mechanics of what they do than with merely appreciating the pure pleasure of it. Jeffrey's back-and-forth bounces of face, along the length of Jason's cock, are matched by the ram-rod to-and-fro swings of Jason's lower body.

The bathroom door opens. Someone comes in. the door closes.

Jason and Jeffrey are too far gone, in what they do, to care if they have company, one or many, beyond the sensual little world cocooned around them.

The newcomer unzips at an unoccupied urinal. He hangs his medium-size dick over the porcelain bowl. He lets go a stream of pale yellow piss that aims at the circular bar of disinfectant soap on a small square of metal screen. Finished, the man winds in his dick. He zips up. He washes his hands. He leaves.

The bathroom door opens and closes.

"I'm about to fuck your mouth full of cream," Jason says.

He had almost said it when the guy was at the sink. Jason's pleasure so great, at the time, he'd thought for sure he'd announce his eruption to the world with such garbled intensity that his noises would bring the guy running to save whomever strangled to death in the toilet stall.

"And, by God, is it ... going ... to ... be ... a pearly mouthful!" Jason's hips bounce into higher gear.

Jeffrey is ready. Jesus, is he ready. He's over Marky's neglect. He's over Talbot's neglect. He's getting on with his life. There are a whole lot of delicious cocks, out here in the big-wide world, like this one, which are waiting for him to come along and say hello.

Jason's cock expands within Jeffrey's hugging mouth and throat. "Take it! Take it!" Jason says. He feeds Jeffrey's eagerly sucking face with gallons . . . and gallons . . . and gallons of squirted boy-cream.

Jeffrey takes it all down. Happily. Giddily. Suckingly. He refuses to surrender a drop, no matter the force of Jason's exploding dick that jerks the cum-spewing pecker, this way and that, like a fire hose with water turned on full-force.

CHAPTER TWENTY-NINE

Marky is amazed!

Sex in the restroom of an airplane, mid-air, mid-Pacific. His big cock jammed to mating with another erect dick. Both cocks whipped near creaming.

Final exams, even graduation, chucked like yesterday's garbage.

Fate deals the hand that has Drake Stone of the *SandBox* cast, and Marky's favorite actor in the series, with an ankle broken in three places. The actor isn't one of the stars, but his injury, and resulting incapacitation, causes major shooting-schedule inconvenience and a mad-scramble shuffle of cast.

"If you want this chance-in-a-million, you're on the very next plane here," Marky was told. "An expansion of your character's part on the series means no longer shooting around you."

So, here Marky is. Everything else put on back burner while he runs off to Hawaii to jump-start, even farther, his chances for success in the acting business.

He argued, successfully, to his parents that such an opportunity comes but once. They only asked and received his promise that he'd complete his GED at the very first opportunity.

Oddly, Marky finds putting high school behind him not nearly the big deal he would have thought it would be only a few short weeks before. Before Marky found most of his spare time monopolized with learning lines. Before Jeffrey became suddenly so involved with modeling even before his yet-to-happen summer-shoot in Seattle. Before Talbot became sexually obsessed with a security guard, began having non-stop sexual fantasies of an architect who worked for his father, and shifted loyalties from Marky and Jeffrey to Gerald McTalen whose father has connections at Princeton.

Marky tried to call both his old buddies, pals, fuck-mates, before he rushed to make his plane. Neither had been home.

Fate, likewise, put Marky in the seat next to Jason Summer. Jason en route to Hawaii for an interview with none other than Ronnie Williamstaad, the *SandBox* producer. Jason commented as much upon seeing Marky so engrossed in a *SandBox* script.

Jason gay. Marky gay. Intuition told them the pleasure of their shared plane ride could be enhanced by a mutual squeeze into one of the small restrooms, by a mutual dropping of their drawers, by a mutual belly-to-belly mating of their dicks, by a mutual pump . . . pump . . . pump . . . while . . .

"Love the way our balls roll against one another," Jason says.

Marky doesn't know which feels better: the massage of their balls, or the constant petting of their stiff joined-at-the-neck dicks.

Marky's cock, with its slight taper and clean-cut lines, offers sexy contrast to Jason's truly unique cock, with its bulbous cockhead, its indented cockneck at the base of its coronal flare, its quick expansion to thick-thick cockroots. Jason's dick provides a bumpier ride for flogging fists, over united cocks, than had Marky jerked his own dick solo.

Speaking of bumpy rides, the plane has experienced a lot of rough. Marky and Jason fear the next slight dip of the airplane, them inside, will have a "Please Be Seated" announcements flash before they finish what their building passions insist be finished.

Their fists, one contributed by each participant, pump dicks all the harder, all the faster. Marky's free hand goes to Jason's naked, right asscheek ... Jason's free hand goes to Marky's right asscheek. Marky and Jason tug themselves and their cocks even closer together.

"I'm just about there," Jason says. He's less disappointed, now, in having left Dan-the-photographer's big cock. Even if Jason's masturbation for the viewing pleasure of this producer friend of Dan, in Hawaii, doesn't pan out, mile-high sex with Marky, in this plane's latrine, makes the trip worth it.

"A few more pumps," Marky says. "Please . . . please . . . just . . . a . . . few . . . more . . . pumps."

Their fists oblige. The outside weather obliges.

For the next couple of minutes, it's clear sailing for whipping stiff dicks, for kneading cum-bulged nuts, for flying the skies over the blue Pacific, for conjuring pleasure . . . from cocks . . . from balls.

"Jesus, pump!" Jason says.

"Whip, flog, pound, whack." Marky's voice is a sexy whisper. His buttcheeks taut.

"Cream on the rise," Jason says.

"Magma on the move," Marky says. His fingertips slide into the crease of Jason's sweaty asscrack and swiftly locate the small pucker.

"Uggghhh, yes!" Jason wiggles his ass so his pucker opens over the tip of one suddenly butt-poking finger.

"Oh . . . shit, shit!" Marky says to Jason's equally exploratory fingertip that finds Marky's asshole and pokes on through.

Jason's cock creams first, although neither boy tells from just looking or feeling. For all intents and purposes, both cocks erupt at one and the same time. Jason's thick streamers of creamy cum are flash-flood joined by the soupy explosions that whip free of Marky's dick and spiral like pinwheels before wet set-downs on the dual-head, dual-shaft, phallic up-jut between them.

There's the added pleasure of pumping fingers gone silkily slick with the rain of gooey spunk not just from one cock but from two

The experience leaves them exhaustedly giggly and looking forward, even more, to the rest of their air miles to the islands.

CHAPTER THIRTY

Hawaii.

Balmy breeze. Exotic, perfume-exuding night-blooming hibiscus. Sexy sweat on super-tan flesh. Naked Jason. Lotus-position. On the bed. Cock-in-hand.

Ronnie watching. In a chair.

"No one knows my cock, like I know my cock," Jason says. "No one, hard as he may try . . ." (except, maybe, quite by intuitive accident, Marky-from-the-plane and from-the-*SandBox*-cast). " . . . knows just how to pump my pecker just right. See how my fist, on the up and on the down stroke, twists? This way. That way. All around the pole? You probably can't see it, but the loop of my thumb and forefinger squeezes extra hard whenever it comes up and over, or slides down and off, my bulbous cockhead.

"Notice how far my dick shoots up through my fist. Like it's a nuclear-head missile on its way out of its silo. Then, as if a false alarm — 'Abort! Abort! Abort!' — back the rocket goes inside my silo-like fingers. Only for another red-alert screech of sirens, hammer blows of clangors, and . . . yet again . . . another appearance of rocket-tip, of rocket-shaft: a launch in progress! Up . . . up . . . up . . . but, not yet, away.

"Don't I feel good, my pecker fucking my hand! Don't I feel good, having already fucked my fist for so long! Just for you. Nothing more exciting, even whipping my dick on the sly, than having only you for an audience. A special audience. You know what good dick-whipping is all about, because you've seen more than your share. Hell, you've probably seen more than any man's share.

"You want me to do something different, by way of polishing my dolphin? You just tell me what you want. I know what's best for my dick, or pretty much figure I do, but I don't mind experimenting.

"Maybe you'd prefer I pump slower. Like this? Except, this slow a hand-job is damn hard to maintain, since I'm so far along. Although, I will try my best to keep it slow if you ask me to beat slow. All you have to do . . . is ask.

"Or, maybe, say, 'Speed it up a bit, kid.' I can do that, too. Can do it even more easily, considering my present state of boner-rubbed turn-on. See how fast? My fingers a blur.

"Oh, I can tell you enjoy watching me beat my meat like sixty. No need for you to tell me. I've this gut-feeling. ESP. Intuition. Sixth-sense. Besides, we've done this before, haven't we?

"Know what else? You're ready to see a show of my cum. Right?

"See these big nuts of mine? See me fondle them? See how tightly they've become attached, in their hairy bag, to the base of my dick? They're as big as they are, because they're as chock full of sex-juice as they are. They're stuffed with my heavy cream. They're ballooned with my gooey goodness. They're bullet-filled machine-gun clips. And, we're talking big machine-gun.

Machine-gun with specially designed barrel; big-tip; slender-neck, for just a bit, before a quick expansion to some real thickness. Ready to blast.

"You know my gut is set and ready for automatic firing? You see that? You feel that?

"Can't miss, can you, my skin going all pink, even through my tan? Even I see it. Coloring my cock, my belly, my chest. Warming my cheeks.

"Oh, I'm ready to blast away, yes, sir. My gun-cock is cocked and ready to fire. My balls are ready to shoot their load.

"You want me to try and hold off, you just say so. And, I'll try. Although, I just . . . might . . . already have come too far to stop the cum from coming. You know, I might already have reached the point of no return. Nowhere left to go but onward . . . forward . . . cum-blast upward.

"Ohhhhh . . . ohhhhhh . . . yes . . . I do think it's show time. Ahhhh . . . ahhhh . . . yes . . . I do believe you're in for . . . a . . . yes . . . yes ... yes . . . ready . . . ready . . . yes . . . aim . . . yes . . . aim . . . yes . . ."

10:38pm HST, 20 June: Summer comes!

THE END